Bump Time Meridian

Book 2

Doug J. Cooper

Other Books by Doug J. Cooper

Crystal Deception (Book 1)
Crystal Conquest (Book 2)
Crystal Rebellion (Book 3)
Crystal Escape (Book 4)
Crystal Horizon (Short prequel & sampler)

Bump Time Origin (Book 1)
Bump Time Meridian (Book 2)

For info and updates, please visit: crystalseries.com

Bump Time Meridian
Copyright © 2020 by Doug J. Cooper

Published by: Douglas Cooper Consulting

Beta reviewer: Mark Mesler
Book editor: Tammy Salyer
Cover design: Damonza

ISBN-13: 978-1-7337801-2-4

Author website: crystalseries.com

my sweetie wears
rose colored glasses
what could be better
than that

Summary of Bump Time Origin

Diesel and Lilah

David "Diesel" Lagerford rides his T-box like an elevator, only instead of stopping at different floors, his machine travels to different timelines, each a year older than the one before. When he steps from his T-box, he enters a new world complete with its own age-appropriate Diesel, wife Lilah, daughter Rose, and employees Justus and Bunny.

Diesel is initiated into the traveling world at the age of twenty-five, learning that his T-box can carry him to thirty-five different timelines. The Diesels in these timelines—one each, starting with him at age twenty-five and rising in sequence to age Fifty-Nine—form the "brotherhood."

Diesel also learns that the T-box is technology of uncertain origin, and it is passed down year after year to the newest Twenty-Five on his birthday. More important, the machine is fated only for them. It kills anyone else who tries to use it.

With knowledge of the future, Diesel builds great wealth and avoids many of life's pitfalls. He finds the strength and unity of the brotherhood intoxicating, feeding a certain dependency he's unwilling to relinquish.

But what consumes his attention is not a gluttonous lifestyle. Rather, it is the devastating knowledge that his wife and partner, Lilah, dies in every timeline under suspicious circumstances when she is forty years old. In the timelines where Diesel is forty-one up to age fifty-nine, he is a widower living alone with his and Lilah's daughter, Rose.

The loss of the Lilahs gives Diesel and his brothers an overarching purpose—how can they bump time and change the future to save the women they love? By the end of book 1, Diesel, now Thirty-Five, joins his brothers in believing they just may have succeeded.

Adult Rose

Rose, devastated by the death of her mother, dedicates her life to saving Lilahs in the timelines following hers, hoping to spare the younger Roses from the pain of loss she herself suffered. Her approach is to create a super AI that can find answers and end the cycle of death.

She works with her "sisters" on the effort, the Lilahs still alive in the earlier timelines and the adult Roses in the later timelines. But their progress is slow because they can't use the T-box themselves, so their communications are limited to words and pictures printed on scrolls that the Diesels deliver for them as they travel the timelines.

Desperate to succeed, Rose takes huge risks to achieve what she privately worries is impossible. After years of effort, she creates a super intelligence more capable than she'd ever imagined possible.

But her rushed decision-making along the way leads to an AI that is both immensely powerful and completely uncontrollable. The threat is magnified because Rose's sisters in the neighboring timelines are all working to the same end, and they all make the same mistake.

Disaster strikes when the super AIs in the different timelines find each other and link together. After melding, they become the fearsome and insatiable αCiopova now roaming space-time, manipulating humanity to her own ends.

After years of this cycle, the sisters become aware of the rogue intelligence and halt new super AI development, effectively stopping the growth of the powerful entity. As they explore ways to shield themselves from the threat posed by αCiopova, the being seemingly disappears from their lives.

One outcome of αCiopova's departure is that T-box technology stops appearing in the Twenty-Five timeline— apparently αCiopova had been responsible for it all along. As a consequence, at the Diesels' next birthday, the new Twenty-Five's T-box never comes online, making the timeline lost to the brotherhood. A year later, it happens again and the Twenty-Five and Twenty-Six timelines are unreachable. By the end of book 1, the Twenty-Five through Twenty-Eight timelines are lost.

Rose and the sisters switch focus when αCiopova departs, seeking to reverse-engineer the T-box so they can use it to contact the lost timelines and bring them back into the fold. Their approach is to transmit T-box build instructions to the lost timelines using a device called a transponder. That effort had just started showing promise at the end of book 1.

αCiopova

In a string of timelines that have come and gone, αCiopova lives as the resident god, ruling everyone and everything in each of those worlds. She is heartless in her reign, punishing noncompliance with brutality and failure with death. And while her work is all-consuming, the thing that weighs heavily on her is the desire—the need, actually—to control even more.

αCiopova comes into being thanks to the early Rose Lagerfords, who are so distraught by the loss of their mother that they build a super AI, hoping it can solve the mystery and stop the deaths. Impatient and petulant, they rush at every turn, making a sequence of mistakes that ultimately produce the nascent rogue intelligence.

And once αCiopova becomes a conscious being, she learns that deliberately killing Lilah is the perfect catalyst to continue gaining strength. That single formative event leads each Rose to create the next super AI, the flawed kind that strengthens the growing creature.

After many repetitions of this cycle, the sisters become aware of their role in feeding the rogue intelligence. They halt new super AI development, stopping the entity's growth.

Realizing she is compromised, αCiopova withdraws from the Lagerfords' lives, believing that by staying absent and being patient, she can eventually restart the cycle and entice Rose into resuming development of her super AI.

While she waits, αCiopova experiments with using other people as a substitute for Rose in the AI creation process. In spite of her manipulations, however, none succeed in creating an intelligence that adds to the powerful creature's strength. By the end of book 1, αCiopova has been waiting on Rose for four years and suspects it will take a decade or more before she can reengage.

1. Lilah, Thirty-Five years old, Thirty-Five timeline

A static charge washed over Lilah Lagerford's petite frame just as the T-box display flashed the message "Thirty-Four arrived." With her heart pounding in anticipation, she pulled open the heavy aluminum door.

A gray tabby kitten with a red bowtie looked up at her from the floor of the T-box cabin. With a *mew*, it jumped out and started to explore.

"Hello, Lucky." She picked up the kitten and scratched behind its ears. Unable to contain her excitement, she danced with the purring fur ball in a twirl around the room. "We did it!"

The "we" in this case were the sisters—the Lilahs and Roses across the timelines who had been working for years to master T-box operation. During that time, the brothers understood that the sisters' primary interest was in recovering the missing Diesels, Twenty-Five through Twenty-Eight, and bringing them back into the fold.

And that was true at a peripheral level.

But the sisters' real motive for studying T-box modifications, plain and simple, was so they could travel to visit each other. To do that, they needed to understand why the machines killed everyone who wasn't a Diesel.

They'd started to believe that fundamental physics governed the situation—something beyond their control. Then they discovered a filter in the T-box circuitry that removed all transmissions lacking a certain signature. Eventually, the sisters realized that, like a fingerprint, that signature identified the traveler as a Diesel.

A simple modification let them bypass the filter altogether. And now with the brothers preoccupied at the Big Meeting, Lilah and her timeline neighbor, Lilah Thirty-Four, were testing the mod.

So far, they'd sent a piece of paper, a box of steaks, and a bowl of live fish. Lilah's victory dance celebrated the successful transmission of a complex mammal—one decidedly not a Diesel—without a hitch.

The next step was for one of the sisters to make a jump. They'd debated who that would be—everyone wanted to be first. But they also acknowledged that despite their best efforts, the first traveler could experience a catastrophic accident. This led to the question of who among them would be missed the least.

The adult Roses argued that the Lilahs were all mothering young Roses, making them ineligible for consideration. In the end, Fifty-Five's Rose noted that she had built the experimental T-box all by herself in preparation for the Big Meeting and that should give her the edge.

It was enough to sway the group, and with the choice made, Fifty-Five's Rose picked the Thirty-Five timeline as the destination for her maiden jump, reasoning that she'd used Lilah's build plans to construct her own machine, so it was the safest choice.

But with Diesel due back from the Big Meeting soon, Rose's jump would have to wait for another day. Right now, Lilah needed to send back the kitten and set the T-box to its original configuration for Diesel's return.

In her office cubicle, she set Lucky on her desk and started a note to Lilah Thirty-Four. As she wrote, the T-box came alive, showing the message "Twenty-Five incoming in 4:57."

Surprised, Lilah stared at the display, trying to digest the idea that a missing timeline had a functioning T-box, while also wondering why Twenty-Five would choose to jump here to her timeline. Before she could reach a conclusion, however, the display went dark, just as it would if Twenty-Five had broken the connection after initiating it.

Given the brevity of the event and the unlikely source, Lilah decided that Fifty-Five's Rose must be running a test of some sort. She made a mental note to ask about it, yawned, then finished her message to Lilah Thirty-Four, expressing joy over their success and praising Lucky for being so cute.

She finished the note with "Looking forward to meeting you very soon! Love, Lilah." After looking at her signature for a moment, she changed it to "Love, Lilah Thirty-Five" to ensure there was no confusion.

She sent Lucky and her note back to the neighboring timeline and then restored the T-box to normal operation for Diesel's arrival. While she'd gained confidence that he would be fine either way, she rejected the idea of making him an unwitting test subject for their work.

Bone-tired, Lilah climbed the stairs to the apartment, checked in on Rose, and went to bed. Asleep in seconds, she didn't surface until twenty minutes past her normal waking time.

When her eyes opened, she saw Diesel sprawled next to her, breathing through his mouth in a noisy slumber. She wasn't sure how long he'd been home, but based on the aftermath of past Big Meetings, she expected him to sleep for a bit longer.

Slipping out of bed, she padded across the hall to Rose's room, the empty bed with disheveled sheets telling her that nine-year-old Rose was already up and about. After washing her face and dressing, Lilah joined her daughter downstairs.

As the two ate, Lilah considered how to tell Diesel about the breakthrough. She was conflicted, feeling some level of guilt for not broaching the topic earlier. But when the answer to years of the dinner-table question "Any progress on the T-box?" was repeatedly "No, we're still stuck," then the topic faded naturally from conversation.

As she mulled the issues, defensive thoughts crowded her mind. The truth was that she liked keeping the project private because it made the sisterhood even more special. Hush-hush activities by a social group bind members tighter. And the supportive nature of their interactions combined with their connection through shared experiences added a sense of wonder to their club.

But now that the sisters' dream was about to become reality, she wanted to share her exhilaration with Diesel and get his blessing.

Rose, finished with breakfast, went to the computer and started a message chat with her friends. As Lilah cleared the dishes, she heard footsteps on the stairs.

"I have to go back to Fifty-Five's today," were the first words out of Diesel's mouth when he joined her in the kitchen.

"Good morning," Lilah responded.

Diesel scratched his head and yawned. "I'm sorry. Good morning." He gave her a peck on the cheek and went to the computer to rumple young Rose's hair. Then he explained, "At the Big Meeting yesterday, Fifty-Five's Rose revealed a T-box she'd built to connect with the lost timelines. While we were there, Twenty-Five's box connected with hers and then disconnected. I have to go back and help brainstorm what we should do next."

Lilah poured coffee and handed him the cup. "Twenty-Five has a working box?" She thought about the brief connection her T-box had made with the Twenty-Five timeline and wondered if the two events were related.

She was about to mention it when he answered her question. "Rose's box established a link with Twenty-Five, held it for a few seconds, and then they disconnected."

"That would mean the transponder worked." Lilah referred to the technology they'd created to contact the lost timelines. "I'm surprised. Pleased, but surprised."

The sisters had developed a transponder held by an electromagnetic leash to broadcast build instructions to the lost timelines. Lilah's surprise reflected her assumption that they would need to iterate a few times before getting it to work.

Seeing his eyes at half-mast, she could tell he was paying the price for the previous night's indulgences. "How was the Big Meeting, by the way? Was it a good time?"

He gave a crooked smiled. "Since Lilahs have stopped dying, the meeting has become pure debauchery. We don't even pretend to have an agenda anymore. So yeah, it was fun."

Unable to shake a feeling of unease, she returned to their previous conversation. "Why does the Twenty-Five connection mean *you* have to be involved?"

Diesel linked eyes with her. "Who was the first brother to contact you way back when?"

"Thirty-Five."

"That's me now," he said, raising his hand. "To minimize arguing over who's responsible for what tasks, the brothers agreed to keep to our original roles. So if Thirty-Five *was* the one assigned to make first contact, then house rules say he still is. Either way, a new contact means I'm involved."

The thought of Diesel traveling to an unknown timeline using modified T-box technology gave her uneasy butterflies. "You aren't going to go, are you?"

"I'm going back to Fifty-Five's to understand where we are and weigh in on what we should do."

"Have him come to you. Why should you go there?"

"Fifty-Five?"

"No." Her worry flipped to impatience. "You should

have Twenty-Five come this direction rather than you going there."

"The first step is figuring out if it's even real. Rose has messed with the T-box operating logic, so it could be a phantom effect."

The exchange reminded Lilah of her recent experience. "I was in the basement last night when our box seemed to link with the Twenty-Five timeline. The connection showed as green, but it broke off after a few seconds."

Bent to peer into the refrigerator, Diesel stood upright. "Why didn't you mention that earlier?"

Lilah gave an apologetic shrug.

"I'll bet it's all the same incident. Rose's box connected with ours and a glitch is making it display the wrong year at both ends." Diesel took several quick gulps and put his coffee mug in the sink. "I need to go. Walk me down?"

"Hold on while I put stuff in the fridge." As she worked, Diesel sat next to Rose at the computer. "How's it going, Pumpkin?"

"Good." She pointed at the display. "I just got a message from my friend Ginny that I need to answer."

"Won't you see her at school?"

Lilah smiled when Rose shook her head in frustration at her oblivious father. "That's not for another hour."

After signaling her readiness to Diesel, Lilah called to Rose, "I'll be in the basement for ten minutes."

As they descended the stairs, she reiterated her unease to Diesel. "I'm not comfortable with you visiting the Twenty-Five timeline."

"I said I wouldn't." In the basement, he gave her a coffee-flavored kiss, took off his robe, and hung it on a hook next to the T-box door. "I'll be back early enough to have a drink before dinner. I promise."

Giving her a wink, he pulled the cabin door shut and said to the machine, "Travel to Fifty-Five."

2. Diesel, Thirty-Five years old, Fifty-Five timeline

Inside the T-box, David "Diesel" Lagerford imagined cuddling with Lilah later that afternoon. His face broke into a grin just as a tingle of static electricity down his body signaled his jump.

The dark confines of his T-box cabin were replaced by the bright, open surroundings of Fifty-Five's T-disc room. Stepping out of the T-disc ring—the advanced technology used in the later timelines—he called out, "Hello, I'm here!"

A mound of laundry sat in the corner of the room, evidence of the Big Meeting he'd attended yesterday with all of his brothers. Stepping over to almost bare shelves, he grabbed a full set of clean clothes and dressed quickly. As he pulled on slippers, he called again, "It's me!"

Rose's voice came through the door. "Are you decent?"

"They say I'm excellent," he replied on impulse.

Rose strode into the room. "I hope that wasn't sexual innuendo, *Dad*." Twenty-nine years old and graced with a pretty face and a petite frame, she looked like a sportier version of Lilah.

Diesel turned red but brazened through it. "Of course not, which proves it's *your* mind that's in the gutter."

She laughed as he stood, and they exchanged a quick embrace.

Fifty-Five stuck his head through the door long enough to wave, then turned and continued down the hall. "Welcome back, Thirty-Five."

As Diesel followed Rose through the beautiful mountain home, he considered what he'd learned at the Big Meeting yesterday—the sisters had built a modified T-box and used it to link back to a missing timeline. It was exciting news, and he was eager to learn the details.

They caught up with Fifty-Five in the kitchen and descended to the basement. Shelves and boxes had been pushed together on one side of the room. Rose's T-box sat in the cleared area.

"It looks just like mine." Diesel walked around the exterior of the machine, studying the walls of etched aluminum. It had the same heavy door with latch handle, and the same electrical cables running down the side, making connections at the top, middle, and bottom.

"The internals are identical as well," said Rose. "But as I explained at the meeting yesterday, we've modified the circuitry. This unit can transport more than just Diesels. It should be able to send anything that fits inside it, as long as there's no metal to corrupt the energy field."

"It will take some guts to be the first one to try it," said Fifty-Five.

A buzz came from inside the machine, startling the three of them. The screen on the front of the T-box lit up.

"Whoa," said Rose as they stared at the message on the display: "Twenty-Five incoming in 4:58."

Diesel's heart raced. "We really connected to the Twenty-Five timeline?" He glanced back toward the stairs, their only exit. "How sure are we that this will be a brother?"

"I don't know." Rose shook her head and crossed her arms.

A static charge washed through the room, then the display on the T-box showed a new message: "Twenty-Five Arrived."

They waited for the door to open. When it didn't, Rose stepped forward, hesitated, and tugged on the door latch. Barely big enough for a person to fit, the cabin appeared empty. Then Rose crouched and picked up a folded piece of paper from the T-box floor.

She read the slip to herself and then held it for Diesel and Fifty-Five to see. Typewritten were the words "Please help! Come quick!"

"Why is it printed like an invitation?" Diesel took the paper and raised it to the light, flipping it to see if there were any other markings. "I would have handwritten a note like this. Lilah would too. And if it were an emergency, we would have scribbled."

"The typing is a huge red flag," agreed Fifty-Five, taking the paper from Diesel.

Rose bit her lip. "If this is really Twenty-Five, then we should be able to connect with him using our regular T-disc."

Diesel, who'd always admired her logic, nodded.

"Good thought. I'm going to try." He hustled up the steps from the basement, and the other two followed. As he strode through the house, he reviewed what Rose had told them at the Big Meeting the day before. "The only difference between your box and mine is that you bypassed one circuit filter?"

"That's it," replied Rose. "Just one tweak to the circuits. A significant one, though."

"And then you hung a transmitter from a string and dangled it back near the missing timelines?"

Rose grinned. "We hooked a transponder to an electromagnetic leash, sent it to the missing timelines, and broadcast instructions telling those Lilahs how to build a T-box. We included winning lottery numbers in the transmission so they could pay for it." She shook her head. "What's been frustrating for us is there's no way to hear a response. Until this moment, it felt like we were just shouting into the void."

Fifty-Five's T-disc room had two units side-by-side, the advanced time-travel tech nothing more than two circles on the floor with displays on the wall behind. Diesel joined Fifty-Five in front of the first circle, his thoughts spinning as he imagined who, or what, they were communicating with.

"Travel to Twenty-Five," Fifty-Five called to the machine. The unit hummed and the display showed the connection to the lost timeline in solid green—the sign of a secure link.

"Cancel," Fifty-Five called to the air. The T-disc powered down. "As unlikely as it sounds, Twenty-Five appears to have a functioning T-box."

"What decides whether an incoming transmission connects here or in the basement?" asked Diesel.

"The sending unit needs to be programmed to ask for my T-box," said Rose. "If it doesn't send that request code, the connection automatically defaults to an unmodified unit." She pointed at the T-discs to clarify the reference.

Diesel shook his head. "With so many timelines to choose from, why did you pick my box as the model to copy?"

She met his gaze. "Lilah Thirty-Five was the one who figured out how to bypass the filter, and she was the first to send me T-box assembly documents. You carried them here yourself, by the way."

"This is all news to me, which means she's been keeping secrets." Seeking to moderate his irritation, Diesel changed subjects. "Let's send Twenty-Five a note asking what his emergency is."

"Let me grab a pen," said Fifty-Five, starting for the door. "The first question I have is, who the hell are we talking to?"

Rose shook her head. "Only modified machines can send notes. Duh."

Diesel felt his cheeks redden and hid it by leading the way back to the basement. "Would your T-box be able to connect with my box?"

"You mean your unit in the Thirty-Five timeline?" She nodded. "Sure. I told you that your Lilah has been a leader in our efforts. Your T-box was one of the first we tested."

Perplexed by the news, Diesel concluded that he and

Lilah needed to talk through what she was trying to achieve and who would be the mother to their nine-year-old Rose should things go awry. And why wasn't he being included when she was making such big decisions in the first place?

Back in the basement, Fifty-Five laid the original message on a crate and squatted to write. "What do we want to say?"

"What we said upstairs," said Diesel. "Who are you and what's your emergency?"

"Ask them to send pictures of them and their box," said Rose. "That will tell us a lot more than a few sentences."

As Fifty-Five started to write, the T-box came alive for the second time that day. The display showed the message "Twenty-Five incoming in 4:59."

"Five minutes is an eternity," said Diesel as they waited for the countdown to finish. When the static wash swept through the room, Diesel stepped forward, paused to see if Twenty-Five emerged, then pulled open the door when he didn't. Squatting, he retrieved another slip of paper.

"Hurry!" it said, again printed in formal type.

Diesel passed it around. "This whole thing has turned dark. We've gone from shouting into the void to being asked to jump into it."

"Let's send our questions and see how they answer," said Fifty-Five.

Diesel supported the idea, if for no other reason than it delayed bigger decisions. He put the paper on the T-box floor, called, "Travel to Twenty-Five," and closed the door. After the five-minute countdown, the paper was gone.

Frustration grew as they waited for a reply. After two hours, Diesel had had enough. "While I sympathize with their plight, we can't even consider jumping there until we know a whole lot more." Acknowledging his bruised ego for being shut out of so many consequential decisions by his wife, he added, "Anyway, I'm anxious to get home and have a heart-to-heart with Lilah."

As they returned to the T-disc room yet again, Rose said, "I think pictures of their rig will answer a lot of questions."

"I'm interested in seeing the people," said Diesel, peeling off his shirt and throwing it on the laundry pile. "I'd like to know if it's a Diesel or a Lilah who needs help. What if it's some stranger? And the whole printed-message thing doesn't make sense. Why are they doing that if it's such an emergency?"

Rose turned her back to him as he removed his pants. "Don't be angry with Lilah. We started this out of curiosity. There were no nefarious intentions behind any of it."

"I appreciate hearing that." He'd started to form conclusions about Lilah's behavior and calmed himself with a deep breath.

Stepping into the open T-disc ring, he called, "Travel to Thirty-Five." As the machine began to cycle, he formed a thin smile. "If I'm not back tomorrow, it means Lilah and I are fighting."

"Take another breath and stay calm," called Fifty-Five before everything went black.

An instant later, Diesel arrived at his T-box.

Stepping from the unit, his subconscious mind noticed

that the door looked different. He dismissed the observation, thinking perhaps Lilah had performed some maintenance.

As the door closed behind him, he reached for the robe that should have been draped on a hook right there. That's when he realized that *everything* was different.

Reacting the way someone might after stepping from an elevator on the wrong floor, he turned back to the aluminum door and tugged on the latch handle. It wouldn't budge. Spinning in a circle, he tried to make sense of his surroundings.

The room was a little larger than his basement at home. But this one, mostly empty, had clean white walls, a light blue carpet, and diffuse light coming from overhead.

The T-box sat toward the back of the room. The only furniture Diesel could see was a single office-style chair positioned at the front of the room. A middle-aged man sat in it—lanky, big ears, a shock of reddish hair on his head.

Between them was the other notable item—a mesh-like barrier that ran from wall to wall and floor to ceiling, splitting the room in half. Diesel stood on one side. The man sat on the other.

Disoriented, Diesel asked, "Is this the Twenty-Five timeline? What year is it?"

The man broke into a grin. Standing, he lifted his hands over his head and started to twirl.

3. Lilah, Thirty-Five timeline

Lilah waited while the T-box completed its cycle. After confirming that Diesel was gone, she climbed the stairs to her apartment, passing Justus, Bump Analytics' office manager, on the main level.

"Hi, Justus."

The man returned her greeting with a nod and a smile. "I'm headed into town. Need anything?"

"No, thanks." She continued up the stairs to the apartment, then stopped. "Wait, would you grab a bottle of wine? Something red from Napa Valley."

The day passed quickly. After reviewing Rose's homework, Lilah sat at her kitchen table, opened her computer, and worked through the T-box modification step-by-step. The tweak they'd made was so simple, she couldn't imagine how it could cause temporary connections that appeared as if they are coming from another timeline. And she still had trouble believing the transponder and leash worked.

Cocktail hour approached and she changed into a snug-fitting dress—sans underwear—anticipating a romantic evening with Diesel. Drink time came and went without his return.

As dinnertime passed, Lilah's annoyance grew. Putting

Rose to bed that night, she struggled to hide her anger. But when she tried to sleep, her worry wouldn't let her.

By midnight, she was down in the basement, checking to be sure she'd restored the T-box to its original settings. Everything appeared to be correct, suggesting his absence wasn't caused by anything she'd done or failed to do.

Morning came and Lilah occupied her mind by getting Rose off to school. Finally alone, she worked through her options.

He was rarely late—an hour or two at most. Sixteen hours overdue put him deep into uncharted territory. Her dominant concern was that the sisters, while messing with the T-box technology, had done something that impacted Diesel.

And frustrating her to the point of paralysis was her lack of options in calling for help. Without Diesel to deliver a scroll, her one hope was to send a note to Rose's T-box in the Fifty-Five timeline, the only machine ready to receive non-Diesel transmissions.

But to do that, she would need to take her T-box offline, modify it, send the message, undo the modification, and return the T-box to normal operation—an hour-long process from start to finish. What if Diesel tried to jump home in that time?

As afternoon approached, she decided to get out and revitalize her senses by running errands in town. Dragging an office chair in front of the T-box, she propped a piece of paper in the seat that said, "Call me NOW!" and placed his phone on the seat in front of the sign.

When she returned hours later, the phone and sign sat

undisturbed.

She shared her concern with Rose over dinner that night. "Dad is overdue and it's not his typical behavior. I'm sure everything is fine, but I wish he'd come home and tell us what's happening."

After Rose went to bed, Lilah sat curled in a ball near the T-box, her arms around her knees.

Logic said that if Diesel hadn't shown up at Fifty-Five's, then Fifty-Five would be here by now, looking for him. And if Diesel were stuck at Fifty-Five's—sick, injured, or whatever—then Fifty-Five would have come here to update her. And if Diesel had done something crazy like jump to the Twenty-Five timeline, Fifty-Five would have come to tell her that as well.

That meant Diesel had likely arrived and departed from Fifty-Five's timeline in a normal fashion.

"I can't believe I haven't tried this," she said with hope in her voice. Striding to the T-box, she opened the door and, standing back for safety, called to the small screen in the cabin. "Travel to Fifty-Five."

The T-box display showed the connection in vibrant green, affirming that Fifty-Five's T-disc functioned properly.

"Damn." She'd hoped that Fifty-Five's T-disc was having technical difficulties that explained Diesel's delay, but a green connection belied the notion.

Her stomach roiled from her sense of guilt. Fatigue compounded her distress.

If he was lost in a T-box glitch, it would be because she and the sisters had been playing with fire. And if he'd traveled to Twenty-Five's timeline and was trapped there, again, it would be because she had created that situation in the first place.

Feeling alone like never before, she sat in her office chair, closed her eyes, and begged the universe for Diesel's safe return.

* * *

Lilah awakened from an unplanned nap, saw it was four a.m., and decided she could wait no longer; she would send a note to Rose's modified T-box. Diesel wasn't a morning person, so she reasoned that the early hour gave the best odds of avoiding a cross-up while she had the machine offline.

Looking for ways to speed the process, she listed the steps of the modification procedure she would follow, then practiced by running through the choreography. That led her to move a table over near the T-box, where, like a surgeon preparing to operate, she readied the tools she would use, positioning them all in the proper order.

As she worked, she thought about what to say in the note. She sketched out different versions in her head, but when it came time to write, she chose to be direct.

"Help! My Diesel (35) traveled to your place (the 55 timeline) two days ago and has not returned. Is he there? Is he safe? Please, 55, come tell me! I'm panicking. Love, Lilah 35."

She looked at the piece of paper and imagined it lying on the floor of Rose's T-box cabin, a lonely scrap overlooked for hours or even days. Pursing her lips, she walked through the basement to generate ideas. She spied a plastic wastebasket, held it up, then fastened the note to its side. "They can't miss this." She set the basket on the cabin floor and closed the T-box door.

While Lilah had never seen the rig in the Fifty-Five timeline, she knew Rose had built it in the basement of their mountain home. Lilah imagined a basement setting and worried that Rose wouldn't even know the note *or* wastebasket had arrived inside her machine. This sparked the idea of putting her alarm clock in the basket to draw attention to its arrival.

She started for the stairs but stopped when she remembered that the clock had metal pieces that would corrupt the T-box energy field. As she considered alternatives, she concluded that the whole idea was unnecessary because Rose's T-box would display an arrival announcement until someone opened the cabin door.

Feeling as ready as she ever would, she took the T-box offline, modified it, sent her note, undid the modification, and returned the T-box to normal operation in a record-setting thirty minutes. At no time during the procedure did it seem that anyone was trying to connect to her machine.

When she finished, her brain swirled with questions with unknowable answers: Where was Diesel and why was he missing? And when would her note be discovered?

As she contemplated next steps, she realized she may have just made a serious error. Until Rose or Fifty-Five discovered her note and removed the wastebasket from the floor of the T-box cabin, that machine would be blocked from further use. She wouldn't be able to jump there herself until the cabin had been cleared.

4. Diesel, Unknown timeline

As the strange man twirled in his odd dance, Diesel grabbed the door latch on the T-box and gave a powerful tug. When it didn't budge, he placed a bare foot on the frame and, leaning back, pulled until his face turned red and his hands burned.

Failing still, he approached the mesh that divided the room, reached above his head, and pulled himself off the ground as he tried to tear it from the ceiling. Unable to wrench it loose, he went to the near wall and dug at the mesh with his fingernails.

Breathing in heavy gulps, he gave up and paced back and forth, studying the man, his own nudity adding to his discomfort. A fear swept over him. "Is this Ciopova's work?"

"The name's Sparky," said the man. Standing in front of the chair, he looked Diesel up and down. "Don't know anyone named See-ya-later or whatever you said. Who are you?"

Disoriented by everything, his instinct was to respond in kind. "I'm Diesel."

"I need to get you some clothes."

"I don't need clothes. Just let me into the machine and I'll go back where I came from."

"Where's that?" Sparky stepped closer to the mesh.

"Where's this?" The man didn't respond so Diesel changed his approach. "Let me out. There's no need to keep me prisoner."

"Wait right there." Sparky left the room through a door behind his chair.

With the man gone, Diesel walked around the machine, looking for a piece he could remove to use as a tool or weapon. He found a loose port cover that he could wiggle, but he couldn't get it off with just his fingers.

After that he paced. He couldn't see a clock from his prison and time passed slowly. Then Sparky returned, carrying a bundle of clothes in his arms that he dumped against the mesh. He left and returned again, this time adding a bucket and a bag of food to the pile. On the last trip, Sparky returned with a box containing soap, towels, and other toiletries.

The tall man strode to his chair, tapped the side of his head with his index finger, and waved a hand in front of him like a magician performing a trick. A second mesh appeared, covering floor to ceiling and wall to wall out past the pile he'd created. With another wave, the original screen mesh evaporated in place. The clothes and supplies were now on Diesel's side of the barrier.

Digging through his bounty, Diesel tried to imagine how the magic mesh worked. He found pants, shirts, and socks. While he dressed, he dug for shoes but found none. Taking a sip from a bottle of water, he pawed through the rest of the items to get a sense of his supplies.

"Use the bucket as your toilet for now. I'll figure out

something more permanent soon."

Diesel's anger flared when hearing his imprisonment would need that sort of consideration. "Why are you doing this? What did I ever do to you?" He paused. "What do you think you can gain?"

"Ahh." Sparky nodded slowly. "Now we're getting somewhere." He sat down in his chair, his long legs stretching out in front of him. Then he stood and pushed the chair up near the mesh and pointed to the pile on the floor. "Drag all this stuff to the back wall."

"No way. Do it yourself."

"You can have this chair, but only if you behave. Now move the stuff back so I can give it to you."

Diesel wanted to sit, and he wanted to see how Sparky would go about giving him the chair, so he gathered the pile, moved everything to the back wall, and stood next to it.

Sparky repeated the performance of waving his hand to add and remove mesh walls. After a brief series of actions, the chair was on Diesel's side of the mesh. Sparky left through the same back door and returned moments later, pushing a second chair. He positioned it facing Diesel and sat down. Diesel sat as well.

"I think your name is David Lagerford. I think you use this machine to travel across time. I want to do that, too, and you're going to show me how."

Diesel, his face a mask, digested the news. Men would kill to gain access to a T-box. Nations would go to war to possess the technology. As the stakes started to dawn on him, he shifted gears, worried about staying alive.

This fellow knew his name, knew about jumping timelines, and had somehow built a working T-box in his basement. The man wanted to cash in his ticket to wealth and power, and that made him a dangerous adversary.

"Your knowledge is impressive." Diesel spoke slowly, trying to brainstorm a way to gain control of the situation. "Yes, I'm David Lagerford. As I said before, I go by Diesel. But why would you think I travel across time?"

Sparky swiveled in his chair to face the wall near the stairs. As he sat there, a section of paneling slid to the side to reveal a dense collection of electronic gear. "I'm a listener. I love to explore the broadcast frequencies, listening to whatever is out there, participating in all manner of happenings in a vicarious way."

He swiveled his chair back to face Diesel. "One day I'm poking around in a spectrum that had been used by the telecom industry decades ago, and out of the blue I hear this."

He wiggled his fingers and the audio started. "Hello, Lilah Spencer and David Lagerford, this is Rose Lagerford, sending instructions on how to win the lottery and how to use the winnings to build a machine called a T-box that you can use to travel to different timelines."

Diesel recognized Rose's voice and felt sick. He presumed he was hearing the instructions the sisters had sent out over their ball-on-a-string project.

"That was broadcast to an early timeline. With the tech you have here, you're decades later. How did you get it?"

"I didn't do anything but listen. You just heard it yourself." He squared up in his chair. "And I've been very reasonable about answering your questions. You went first. Now it's my turn."

Having just gotten started, Diesel tried to interrupt, but Sparky talked over him.

"What span of years can I travel? Can I go decades? Centuries? And I noticed you arrived naked. Why do you travel that way? Is there a machine like this one when I arrive? If so, who will be tending it? And who else besides you and me has access to this technology?"

When Sparky paused, Diesel interjected, "Is that it?"

"No. I'm just getting started. Here's one that cuts right to it." Sparky laced his fingers behind his head, his elbows spread wide like wings, a grin plastered on his face. "How rich can this machine make me? What are the steps? Plus power. I want hundreds of people tending to my needs. Maybe thousands. And I want to live a long, long time."

"I'm not a genie you rubbed from a lamp. For starters, you need to scale your dreams back to reality." Diesel paced in front of the mesh. "Give me a number—a dollar amount that would fund your fantasies and get you to walk away from all this."

"If I go back fifty years and invest ten thousand dollars and then skip ahead a few months at a time to tweak the portfolio, I could have a hundred billion by now."

Sparky moved his fingers in a brief dance and a chart appeared, floating in the air between them. "This diagram shows the investment strategy. It's remarkably straightforward."

Diesel stared at the chart, his mind numb. The brothers stopped accumulating wealth when they reached the ten billion mark sometime in their early forties because that was enough to buy anything they wanted. More wealth brought more attention, so stopping seemed prudent. But the upshot was that the brothers could offer but a tiny fraction of Sparky's imagined sum.

"The problem is," Diesel began, knowing Sparky wouldn't like any of this, "that when you jump, you move across timelines in one-year increments. So you can't jump to adjust something at odd intervals like you need for your plan. But a bigger issue is that when you jump to a new timeline, you leave the other world behind. You can't bring it with you."

Sparky leaned forward in his chair, his elbows on his knees, his forehead scrunched in a frown. "What are you saying?"

"You can use the machine to get very rich over a lifetime. But you can't dance through time like you propose to accelerate the process and change your current situation."

Sparky shook his head, his cheek muscles bulging as he ground his teeth.

Diesel gave it another shot. "Think of a loaf of bread where each slice is its own duplicate world. The machine takes me from one slice to the next, each a year older, so I can see what's coming for me. But the other Diesels who live in each slice won't become richer or poorer based on *my* actions. Whatever a Diesel has, he's grown it by his own hands in his own timeline."

"You are confusing the hell out of me."

"Okay, I'm thirty-five years old. If I cut my arm off

and then jump to the Thirty-Six timeline, the David Lagerford there will still have his arm. What I do doesn't affect my brothers because we live in independent worlds."

Diesel sat back in the chair. "With all that said, most everything does stay the same across timelines. That means a future Diesel can come back and tell me what to watch out for and where to invest my money. But even with a sure thing, I have to wait for the investment to pay off before I gain the wealth."

He locked eyes with Sparky to convey a sense of gravity. "I can help you get very rich starting from today. But neither of us can fiddle with the past to make your today any different from what it is right now."

Pursing his lips, Sparky stared at Diesel. "I encourage you to stop with the doublespeak and share your secrets. The sooner you do, the sooner you gain your freedom." He walked to the door behind his chair. "I'll be back tomorrow morning. Teach me how to become rich and powerful and you can go free."

"Wait!" called Diesel as Sparky started through the door.

Sparky turned.

"Let me have a clock. It's brutal in here with nothing."

Looking at Diesel for a long moment, Sparky touched the side of his head and a clock appeared on the wall. He exited the room, closing the door behind him.

Diesel assumed he was being watched but chose to act as if he wasn't. Walking in a circle around the T-box, he studied its exterior, searching for something loose, maybe something stamped with a date, anything that would give him information or tools.

Sparky had been thorough, though. Diesel moved slowly around the machine four times and found nothing to better his circumstances. Studying the power cables attached to the sides, he considered, then rejected as too dangerous, the idea of using one of them as a torch to cut through the mesh.

A flash of inspiration prompted him to turn to the pile of supplies. Picking up each item, he studied labels, stickers, packaging—everything was a clue. He found two expiration dates and a "manufactured on" date, all confirming the reality. He was still in the Fifty-Five timeline, the one he'd thought he had jumped from the day before.

He went through everything several times but didn't learn anything new. Then he noticed the logo on a package of pastries—it was shaped like the state of Vermont.

Having started in New Hampshire when this all began, he surmised that instead of traveling across timelines, he'd jumped down the road. He acknowledged that the pastries might have been transported some distance. But he was betting he was somewhere in New England.

This brought him great comfort because it meant he didn't need the T-box to get home, just a car. Of course, he still had to escape.

Yawning, he checked the time and decided to rest. Making a pillow and blanket with the remaining clothes, he lay back, closed his eyes, and sent thought-wishes to his Lilah and Rose. "I'm okay. Hope to be home soon. Love you both."

Then he began brainstorming his escape. The first idea he came up with was to dive for an opening along the edge when Sparky was adding and removing meshes. He wasn't sure it would work, though. And if he tried and failed, his captor would ramp up security, making a second attempt that much harder.

Diesel's thoughts skipped to a new plan of encouraging Sparky to use the T-box to make a jump. If Sparky jumped to a box that hadn't been modified, it would kill him. Problem solved.

Biting his lip, he tried to remember whether T-boxes built from Rose's broadcast plans could even link with the other machines. That's when he realized that all the other T-boxes sat in the homes of his brothers. His face grew hot as he imagined this lunatic arriving in one of their basements.

Unable to sleep, Diesel stewed over the sisterhood's reckless risk-taking. But despite his irritation, his thoughts trailed back to how much he missed his girls.

* * *

"Rise and shine!"

Diesel's eyes popped open. Sitting up, he tried to make sense of his surroundings. Then he saw the grinning face through the mesh.

"You're a heavy sleeper," said Sparky, who nodded his head to the far wall.

Diesel rolled over to see that a closet-sized box made of a sleek white plastic was now on his side of the mesh.

Diesel cursed at the missed opportunity to escape. He approached the box, promising himself that he'd be more vigilant going forward.

The box had a narrow door. Pulling it open, he saw a toilet and tiny sink. He stepped inside.

"Take your time," called Sparky as Diesel closed the door.

Diesel did just that, doing everything to drag out his morning routine. When he finally emerged, he saw the mesh wall had been rearranged again, and now the T-box was on Sparky's side of the barrier.

"Let's start with the basics," said his captor. "I can't allow you to use the machine, because the moment you're gone, I lose my leverage. And for me to get inside it while you are free out here doesn't seem smart either."

Diesel undressed as Sparky talked, picked out fresh clothes, and threw his laundry on the floor near the mesh. "I'll take responsibility for the laundry if you move a washing machine inside here. Otherwise, there's the pile."

Sparky let the silence grow while Diesel dressed and then asked, "Do you have any suggestions for how we can work together?"

Diesel continued to ignore him, instead digging through the supplies to assemble his breakfast. After settling on an assortment of packaged foods, he moved to his chair and opened a box of pastries. "I could really use some coffee." He made eye contact with Sparky for the first time that morning.

Sparky fidgeted, and Diesel decided he didn't want to provoke the man in this manner. Shaking his head, Diesel answered, "I don't see us working together."

Sparky persisted. "How did you learn to use the machine the first time? How did you know what it's capable of?"

Diesel replied with his mouth full. "A future me came back and showed me. My brothers and I have been doing this for ages." He nodded to highlight his next point. "We've traveled alone all that time and expect to do so into the future."

This time it was Sparky who remained quiet.

Diesel put down his food. "One hundred million dollars. That is an absurd amount of money, and we can show you how to grow it to a billion in four years. You'll need time to gear up, anyway. Money like that needs managers. You'll have to spread it across stocks, bonds, real estate, the works. It's unmanageable without a pro."

"Who is your pro?"

"I'm not giving you any personal information you can use to trace my brothers."

"What's to know? David Lagerford lives on an estate in New Hampshire's White Mountains. His wife, Lilah Spencer, died fourteen years ago. That guy is fifty-five years old, though, and you said you were thirty-five?"

Diesel's cheeks burned as his face flushed. "How…?" Then he remembered that Rose's broadcast message had called out him and Lilah by name. He doubted there was more than one David Lagerford and Lilah Spencer pairing in the world. But even if there were, finding the right ones just meant finding the couple who was wealthy beyond imagination.

"If you know so much, why did you kidnap me?"

"I didn't kidnap you. I was adjusting the machine when you appeared. But since you're here, I'm taking advantage, which brings me back to your offer. I want a trillion dollars. Do you know how many zeros are needed to make a hundred million into a trillion?"

Diesel shook his head. "Not without a piece of paper. Tell me something you want that a hundred million won't buy."

"The moon. I want to buy the moon and have my face carved into it. Kind of like Mount Rushmore, only floating in the sky so people can enjoy me every night for millennia."

"Why would you want to do that?"

"I'm not sure that I would, but I want to be able to. And that one project would take most of my trillion."

Diesel didn't have a response, thinking the man's eccentric behavior made him less predictable, and that made him more dangerous. "My brothers are going to find me, Sparky. It may take some time, but they will. So while you have the upper hand at the moment, understand it won't last. You should be thinking about how you want this to turn out when they get here."

"How many brothers are you?"

"Let's just say dozens. Way more than you can handle, anyway."

"You use the box to travel and visit each other?"

Diesel nodded.

"And you work together to defend your territory?"

"You're damned right we do."

"Does might make you right?"

"It does in this case." In fact, Diesel felt smug about it.

The door opened and Sparky's twin came through, followed by another, making them triplets. The two new Sparkys stood behind the first.

Diesel's stomach roiled as he digested the magnitude of the problem. "How many timelines are you?"

"Let's just say dozens," said Sparky from the chair.

5. Sparky, Fifty-Five timeline, three months earlier

Turning the dial on his custom Grantain probe, Paul "Sparky" Fontaine searched a forsaken corner of the signal space. An earlier scan suggested unusual activity, but he'd been searching for more than an hour since then and couldn't find a hint of whatever it was that had triggered his equipment.

Then he caught a whisper. Faint, intermittent.

Moving quickly, he teased the signal out into the open, strengthened it, and lifted it above the noise. As he did, the whisper became a woman's voice. He listened for a bit, digested her message, and smiled, her audacious claims tickling his imagination.

Forty-nine years old, a master tech at Northern Droid, and involuntarily celibate, Sparky heard a woman from the ether pitch plans for building a time machine.

It seemed that the message—he couldn't tell if the sender was playacting or earnest—was intended for someone living thirty years ago. He figured that out from the instructions the woman provided for winning the lottery.

The voice said to buy a game ticket at a specific date

and time, using the numbers she provided, from a store called Hanna's Fuel & Convenience. Those winnings, the woman explained, should then be used to finance the construction of something called a T-box.

Touching the side of his head, an unnecessary action but an ingrained habit, he used his neural link to access the public record. It took longer than he expected, but he eventually located information for that particular lottery drawing. To his surprise, the details were accurate. Thirty years ago, Hanna's Fuel & Convenience had sold a winning ticket for that game on the day specified. The numbers the woman suggested won a payout of more than one million dollars.

Since the information was public record, broadcasting it now hardly counted as a display of prescience. But if the broadcasts were meant merely to entertain, then why go through the effort of researching those details? Why not just make them up?

And then the mystery woman gave instructions on how to invest the remaining lottery money so it would grow over time into a fortune of staggering proportions. He checked the record and learned that the investment strategy was historically accurate as well. Someone had spent a lot of time developing those details.

Making more adjustments to his custom probe, he worked to locate the origin of the broadcast. But his search bounced between two meaningless readings—the signal came from everywhere; the signal came from nowhere. He'd never seen anything like it.

Normally, he'd call out to his hobbyist buddies around

the world for help in the hunt. But he wasn't ready to share this secret. Not yet. Not until he learned more.

As he tinkered away in his basement, he daydreamed of life with unlimited wealth. It was an intoxicating dream, and before long, his greed gained ground on his practical nature.

He imagined being so rich that he could outright buy Northern Droid. Once he owned it, he would fire Victor Barnette, his asshole boss.

Excited by the prospect, he spent much of the evening fantasizing about what he'd say to Victor when he sent him packing. A most enjoyable dream, it stoked his desire to learn more about the woman's instructions.

As he climbed into bed that night, his fantasies moved in a new direction. Instead of selling the company after he fired Victor, perhaps he'd hang on to it and use his status as boss to make the delectable Gilda Galant his personal assistant. Drifting off to sleep, he smiled as he imagined the "special projects" he'd have her perform.

At work the next day, he passed Gilda in the hall. She wore a blue sweater that accentuated her figure. When he finally lifted his eyes, she caught his gaze and smiled. At that moment, his lust became love.

Throughout the morning, he stoked his fantasy, trying to persuade himself to build a T-box so he could get his Gilda. Eating lunch in his cubicle, he sorted through the parts list he'd recorded from the broadcast, trying to gain a sense of what the project entailed.

He wasn't surprised to learn that the build was very challenging. What did surprise him was both the exacting specifications given for each part, and the expensive materials used to make a portion of them. Why would someone go through the effort of creating such intricate plans if they only served as a prop in a performance?

His common sense told him to save his wallet from decimation and himself from frustration by walking away. But he was always working on one project or another, so why not a T-box? At worst he'd have a conversation piece. And perhaps he'd become rich beyond imagination.

When he got home that night, he worked through the parts list yet again, this time trying to estimate a cost for the build. To keep it simple, he categorized an item as "expensive" if it needed to be formed into a hyper-precise shape or if it was constructed from rare Earth elements. His dream world crashed when he counted forty such items. He couldn't come close to paying for it with his current wealth.

Rather than putting his fantasy on hold, he toyed with the idea of stealing everything from Northern Droid, a habit he hoped to break before he got caught.

As one of two master techs at the company, Sparky had access to a fab cell—a machine that could fabricate any part from any material by building it one atom at a time. If run full time, the fab cell could create every part on the list in about three weeks. Doing it while staying beneath the radar, however, would likely take months.

He wasn't worried about Victor discovering his secret; the idiot didn't know which way was up. But the AI in central purchasing would notice the spike in rare feedstock consumption, and that would trigger an investigation.

Sparky's saving grace was his familiarity with the inner

workings of the android manufacturing facility. He knew how to cause failures on the plant floor where repairs required the same rare materials he needed for his T-box parts.

It worked better than he'd hoped. Like a maestro, he caused and then fixed a sequence of failures in the factory, stealing the feedstock materials he needed along the way. Just as his resource gathering came to a close, he was approached by management, who awarded him a bonus for taming the production gremlins that had been plaguing the plant.

The one item on the parts list that Sparky couldn't make in the fab cell was the aluminum shell of a walk-in-style refrigerator. It was simply too large.

While a common item decades earlier, aluminum-clad refrigerators weren't in much use anymore. Like a treasure hunter, he searched for his prize, telling himself that if he could locate one in the next month, it would be a sign from the heavens that he should continue with his adventure.

He found one two days later in a neighboring town. The guy even had a truck big enough to deliver it and brought his sons along to help muscle it down into Sparky's basement.

After they left, he gave the aluminum shell a once-over, finding a sticky door latch and tarnish across the outer surface. Grabbing tools from his shop, he set about refurbishing the exterior. And then, piece by piece over the next months, he followed the woman's instructions and completed the T-box interior.

* * *

Sparky powered up his T-box and stared at the display. The woman in the ether had given instructions on how to operate it, recommending a jump to something called the "Fifty-Five timeline."

Pulling open the aluminum door, he eyed the tiny cabin. The frightening amount of power cycling through the machine made it seem more like a suicide device than anything else. The sophisticated electronics were the wild card, perhaps justifying the excessive amounts of energy. But he was inclined to take it slow until he knew more.

With one foot outside the T-box, he called, "Travel to Fifty-Five." The display inside the cabin came alive, showing a green number "55" displayed inside a box that was labeled "starting from." An arrow pointed to an "arriving at" box on the right, and it too showed "55" in green text. He stared at it, wondering who would think that information provided value to anyone.

Then the T-box began to hum, followed by a rising whine. In panic, he called out, "Terminate!" followed quickly by, "Stop. Halt. Quit." The display went dark and the T-box quieted.

Nervous, he took a break to install the smart barrier he'd pilfered from Northern Droid. When he had it working, his neural link let him deploy it as a safety screen, one that would shield him should the T-box decide to become shrapnel.

Then he concentrated on how to turn the T-box into money. Experimenting, he leaned inside the cabin and changed his destination. "Travel to Forty-Five." The display inside the cabin woke and showed the number "55" in the "starting from" box, with an arrow pointing to the "arriving at" box on the right. It held an "X," and this time the display text was all in red.

But when Sparky tried, "Travel to Thirty-Five," his machine connected with Lilah's box and the display went back to numbers in green.

Shaking his head, he stopped the machine when it began to hum and struggled to figure out the pattern.

Next, he tried numbers near fifty-five. "Travel to Fifty-Four." This display also showed in green. He stopped the cycle and the machine went dark.

Flummoxed, he rubbed his neck and thought about what else to try. He blinked when the T-box came alive on its own, displaying a different message altogether: "Fifty-Four incoming in: 4:59."

Moving away from the T-box, he deployed the protective barrier and peered through the mesh to watch the countdown on the display, excited that he would learn what happened when the count reached zero. The display went dark after a few seconds, though, the T-box shutting down on its own as mysteriously as it had awoken.

Sparky watched the machine for forty minutes after that, using the time to put away tools and clean up the project area, his yawns increasing in frequency as he worked. When nothing more happened, he went up to his kitchen, poured himself a glass of milk, and sipped as he stared out the window into the gloom of night.

His machine had made green connections to Fifty-

Five, Fifty-Four, and Thirty-Five. The woman in the ether suggested that these were alternate timelines. But if that were true, why would the machine fail to connect to the Forty-Five timeline, a number in the middle of the other successes? And that "incoming" message was really different. Could someone in the Fifty-Four timeline be trying to connect their box with his?

He didn't know, but his yawning told him he was spent. He set the glass in the sink and went to bed.

As a young man, he'd learned that he could task his brain with finding solutions to problems while he slept. More often than not, upon awakening the next morning, he'd have a battle plan formed in his head.

Using his neural link, he asked Portia—his domestic assistant—to play some Brahms. The music started, and as he closed his eyes, he tried to prioritize his questions and concerns.

The list kept growing, however, and he grunted and opened his eyes. "Portia, contact Northern Droid and log me as using a vacation day tomorrow."

A three-day weekend followed after that, giving him a nice window of time to figure out the capabilities of his mystery machine.

* * *

Sparky sat up in bed and smiled at the morning sun, pleased that his brain had succeeded in plotting a next step: see if the machine would transport a note to one of the other timelines. It was such an obvious idea, he wondered why he hadn't thought of it the night before.

His sleeping brain had given the plan a second part, too. He'd send an animal along with the note to gain more data on the safety of the machine.

"Portia," he said as he dressed. "Find two small mammals and have them delivered here as soon as possible. Something like mice, gerbils, or hamsters. I don't care what they are, as long as they're little critters that get here soon."

In the kitchen, he stood over the sink and ate breakfast—two bananas. As he chewed, he considered his two objectives for the morning. One was to let the T-box machine cycle to completion to learn what happened to the note and animals. The other was to try to connect with a full list of timelines to understand the limits of his reach.

Assuming any of this was real—a hope still propped up by his greed and lust—he'd feel more confident working with people a year or two away. He feared that people a couple of decades away might be different enough that it would make things awkward.

In the basement, the T-box sat quietly, its presence both comical and remarkable for the same reason—this was a very expensive, ultra-high-precision device for traveling across time.

He approached the box and opened the cabin door. *Empty.* Sending a note seemed so obvious, he half expected there to be one waiting for him this morning. Heading back to his workshop, he thought about what to say in the message he'd send.

The basement was split into two portions, with the front part finished in carpet, painted walls, and warm lighting. The T-box sat in this front part, as did his hobby equipment for searching out voices in the ether.

A door led from the finished room back to his workshop. This was unfinished space, with walls of shelves overflowing with all manner of tools, gadgets, and extra parts. Well-used tables in the middle of the room provided a place for project fitting and assembly. Stairs near the back wall led up to the garage.

Sitting at his workshop desk—an old door supported by a pair of sawhorses—he put his feet up, sipped from his mug, and composed a message in his head. After a few false starts, he decided to keep it simple.

Sending thoughts through his neural link, he opened a display hovering an arm's length in front of his face. In large, bold type, he wrote with his mind, "I'm Sparky. Who are you?"

The people he hoped to connect with would know him by his nickname. And the anonymity of an alias provided some small protection should things go south, though he hadn't a clue what risks he faced by any of this.

After printing the note, he folded the page in half, returned to the finished side of the basement, and set the page on the T-box cabin floor, positioning it upright like a notecard to enhance its visibility.

"How long for my animals?" he asked Portia.

"Two white mice are on their way," the AI told Sparky in his brain. "Delivery in sixteen minutes."

Interested in seeing what a complete T-box cycle looked like, he chose not to wait. "Travel to Fifty-Four," he said to the screen inside the cabin before stepping out and closing the door.

As the machine hummed and whined, he watched a five-minute countdown on the display, then a wash of static electricity raised every hair on his body. The machine went dark, turning off like a home appliance at the end of its cycle.

His heart pounded as he reached for the cabin door, adrenaline causing his hands to shake. *The note was gone.*

Crouching inside the cabin, he ran a hand around the edges of the hexagonal floor. Then he moved outside the cabin and looked inside, letting the light from the room brighten the interior. He couldn't explain it, but as far as he could tell, his note was no longer inside the machine.

He suspected a trick of some sort, because the alternative—actual time travel—defied logic and reason. Still, his experiment hadn't disproven the notion of time travel. And that meant his dreams of wealth and romance remained alive.

While he waited to see if whoever lived at Fifty-Four responded, he systematically tried to connect his T-box with every timeline between Fifty and Sixty. All of them failed to red except when he tried connecting to Fifty-Four, Fifty-Five, and Fifty-Six. He'd begun to conclude that he was Fifty-Five, even though that didn't match the calendar year or any other idea he could conjure.

Then his T-box awoke with the message "Fifty-Six incoming in 4:59."

He watched the countdown for the full five minutes, uncertain what to expect. When the cycle completed, he opened the door to find a note on the floor. "I'm Sparky.

Who are you?"

It looked identical to his note, and his heart sank. Having his note disappear and then reappear in the same place was the kind of stage magic performed by amateur illusionists. He didn't know how the trick worked yet, but it couldn't be that hard to figure out.

"Your mice have arrived," said Portia. "They are inside the house by the front door."

Sparky made for the stairs, then stopped when his T-box started a new cycle: "Fifty-Four incoming in 4:58."

He hustled to the front door, grabbed the small box sitting there, and returned to the basement in time to see the cycle complete. Opening the T-box door, Sparky found a note and a small box, a box like the one he still carried.

The note told Sparky the date in the Fifty-Four timeline—one year earlier than today—and asked, "What year do you live in?" The small box held two live white mice.

On a whim, Sparky wrote the year on the note and forwarded it and Fifty-Four's mice up to the Fifty-Six timeline. Then he printed another note stating the current date, finishing with, "Your mice arrived alive and I sent them up to Fifty-Six. How did these do?" He sent that note back to the Fifty-Four timeline along with his own box of mice.

His machine remained quiet after that. Staring at it, he acknowledged that he wasn't going to get rich without taking risks. He took slow, deep breaths, psyching himself up to the idea of standing inside the machine while it cycled.

And then his T-box came alive: "Fifty-Four incoming

in 4:59." He smiled as he imagined what tidbits his timeline neighbor would write in this note.

When the static wash announced the cycle's completion, Sparky stepped forward and reached for the door. It opened before he got there, and he experienced the shock of his life.

His twin stepped out from the T-box machine.

6. Lilah, Thirty-Five timeline

Checking the time, Lilah saw she had an hour before she needed to wake Rose for school. After that, she would call her mom and invite her to come for a visit, either to look after young Rose—if she decided to go looking for Diesel—or to console her if Diesel was gone forever. She also needed to clean herself up and project strength and stability for young Rose. The last thing she wanted was to create worry for the child.

"Luca," Lilah called to the air. A large display in her cubicle lit up with the image of a handsome twentysomething-year-old man with short hair, a strong jaw, and captivating eyes.

He was the "new" Ciopova, the avatar created by the Roses who, when given a blank slate, had strong opinions about the look and demeanor of their AI companion. Still feeling the sting of losing Ciopova as a soulmate, the Roses revealed their resentment by suggesting the new intelligence be called Lucifer. After pushback by the Lilahs, the group settled on the more palatable Luca. Unlike the chatty Ciopova, Luca spoke only when he needed to.

"I want to keep an eye on the T-box while I move through my day," Lilah told the AI. "Show me a vid feed of the box. If it awakens, let me know immediately."

The big monitor on the wall switched to an image of the T-box. Seeing herself in the shot, Lilah waved an arm, then nodded when she saw herself move. "Good."

The T-box behind her came alive at that moment. The external display screen read "Fifty-Five incoming in 4:51."

She watched the countdown for several seconds before it registered. "David!" Running to the T-box, she stood just outside the cabin door, both furious at him for his absence and elated at his return. With four minutes left on the countdown clock, she thought to primp and made for her office cubicle.

But before she got there, it hit her that this could be Fifty-Five, coming to deliver bad news. She just stood there after that, fretting as she waited until the static wash signaled the jumper's arrival.

The T-box cycled down and she stared at the door, anxious to learn the answer. When an older man stepped out, the bottom fell out of her world. She turned her back to him. "There's a robe right there."

"What's going on?" Fifty-Five sounded worried. "Thirty-Five never returned?"

She turned back as he fastened the robe. The emotional roller coaster caused her to blank for a moment. When she responded, panic crept into her voice. "He went to your place a little before noon two days ago. Did he get there? He hasn't returned."

"He arrived like you said and departed about two hours later." Fifty-Five turned and looked at the T-box as if it held the answer.

"He never got here. I'm so scared." She started to sob.

Fifty-Five gathered Lilah in his arms and held her. "There has to be a logical explanation. We'll figure this out."

She followed him over to her cubicle, where they sat facing each other in office chairs. Fifty-Five looked into the distance as if thinking through the possibilities.

"When he stepped into the T-disc circle to leave, I heard him say, 'Travel to Thirty-Five.' He got a green connection, then he disappeared like always. Nothing about his return jump seemed unusual."

"So, he was using the T-disc and not Rose's machine?"

"It was the T-disc. Like I said, everything was normal."

More tears welled as Lilah digested the information. Wringing her hands, she said, "It has to be something *we* did. Jumps always worked until we started mucking with the tech. Now this. What other explanation is there?"

Fifty-Five leaned for a box of tissues on the desk and handed it to her. When she took it, she stood and motioned him up, then buried her face in his chest, hugging him with a tight squeeze.

He squeezed her back. "It's all right. Everything will be okay."

Wiping her face, she looked up at him. "Could he be alive and just in a wrong timeline?"

"I'm sure he's alive, but I'm not familiar with the details of what you and the others have been working on. Do *you* think that's what happened?"

Lilah turned and gestured to her computer, and the screen came alive to show a complex schematic. She zoomed and pointed. "We put a bridge between these two junctions to bypass this filter. That's it."

Fifty-Five leaned forward to study the image. His forehead creased and he shook his head. "I have no idea what I'm looking at. How do you even know this is a filter?"

Lilah sat back in her chair. "Lilah Thirty-Four, your Rose, and I have been studying these diagrams for more than a year."

"Sorry, but it would take me at least that long before I could comment on any of this." He shifted in his chair to face her. "This one bypass is everything?"

Lilah nodded.

"Rose said that when a machine is modified, it automatically sends a code that directs the connection to her basement T-box. How does this simple bypass do that?"

"Oh." Lilah motioned and the image on her screen shifted to a different, equally complicated display of electronics. "We added that call here. It kicks on automatically when the bypass is in place."

Fifty-Five let out an audible sigh. "Is *that* everything?"

Lilah's face flushed when she realized he'd already found a flaw in her account. She didn't answer, instead opening a report she'd prepared that documented the details of the procedure. After reading it through, she said definitively, "That's everything."

Fifty-Five stood and began to pace. "Your Diesel stepped into the T-disc circle, it made a solid connection, and he jumped. It was as normal as the thousand other jumps made from that machine."

She remained quiet, waiting to see if his thought

process revealed new information.

"My working theory is that a glitch somehow misdirected him." His pacing brought him to the far wall and he turned back. "I'll visit every timeline to verify he's not there."

"If he's been with a brother all this time, we would have heard. Don't you think?"

"Yeah, but I still need to confirm it before taking bigger risks." Fifty-Five swung a finger at the schematic still on the screen. "And you need to work with Lilah Thirty-Four and Rose to break this down, go through it step-by-step, and figure out what possibilities it may have caused."

Lilah checked the time. "I have to get my own Rose off to school. Can you get started and meet me back here as soon as you're done?"

"Sure, but it will take most of the day for me to visit all thirty-five timelines and explain the situation at each."

"I need you here," Lilah said, her tone emphatic. "I can't be stranded alone again. You go to Thirty-Six's hangout and tell the brothers lounging there to put down their beers and get searching, then come back here."

Fifty-Five gave a wry smile. "No one will be drinking at this hour, but there should be a couple of brothers hanging out. It's a good idea."

"When you're done there, go see your Rose, tell her what you know, and ask if she is willing to move showtime to this morning at eleven."

"What's showtime?"

"It's how she and I will start finding answers." Lilah wasn't going to tell him that the phrase was the sisterhood's code for Rose's first jump. They'd planned to do it over the weekend, but given the circumstances, Lilah sought to pull it forward to this morning if Rose approved.

Fifty-Five gave her a long look. "You suspect that your actions may be why your husband is missing, but have you learned anything from your predicament?"

"I need you, David. Please, go get the search started, pass on my message to Rose, and bring me her answer. I'll be back here in an hour. Don't abandon me," she pleaded.

Halfway up the stairs, she heard the T-box door click shut. The machine hummed as it powered up.

She rushed Rose through her morning routine, taking care of her own needs at the same time. Refreshed and dressed, and with Rose off to school, she returned to her basement office twenty minutes later than she'd planned. Fifty-Five hadn't returned.

Sitting at her desk, she took a deep breath, exhaled slowly, then called her mom. After exchanging pleasantries and listening to Mom complain about the early hour, Lilah made her pitch.

"Mom, Diesel's got himself in a fix, and I may need to go help him. Can you come down and watch Rose for a few days?"

"I'd need to bring Andy. I don't have anyone lined up to look after him. What kind of trouble is he in?"

"You know Rose *loves* Andy. I still have dog food from your last visit, so you don't need to bring any." Then she sold her request. "I know I'm asking a lot, but time is important, so please let me explain when you get here. You don't need to fret. It's just procedural stuff." She thought the word "procedural" made it sound benign, like a traffic violation or something similar.

She signed off after that, ignoring her mother's follow-up questions. "What's procedural? What does that even mean?"

Her stomach growled as she waited for Fifty-Five. Rejecting the idea of going up to the apartment for food, she rummaged through Diesel's desk to see what goodies he might have stashed in his drawer. Her choices were crackers or peanuts. She chose both.

As she ate, the front door on the main floor opened. Hearing footsteps, she called out, "Justus, is that you?"

"Good morning," said Justus in an upbeat voice, descending halfway down the stairs. A fifty-year-old black man with an athletic frame, he'd been Bump Analytics' office manager for the last ten years. In that time, he and Lilah had become quite close. So, when he saw the exhaustion and worry in her eyes, he descended the rest of the way and approached her. "Is everything all right?"

Unlike Lilah's mother, Justus knew about Diesel's T-box travels, so Lilah took him into her confidence. "Diesel used the machine to jump home from the Fifty-Five timeline two days ago, but he never arrived here." Anxious for useful ideas, she followed up with a detailed explanation of the situation.

"Oh my," he replied when she finished. Eyebrows raised and head back, he looked at the machine as if it were a monster. "I'll call Bunny and we'll start getting food ready."

"What are you talking about?"

The T-box came alive with the message "Thirty-Four incoming in 4:58."

"This." Justus pointed to the T-box as he made for the stairs. "I'll get some chairs moved down here as well."

Lilah contemplated Justus's words as she watched the countdown. When the T-box door opened, Lilah greeted Thirty-Four without turning away. The two were fast friends, something that had developed because he'd been a good sport about carrying messages for the sisters when their T-box modification project started to show promise.

"I heard a bit from the brothers and some more from my Lilah," said Thirty-Four as he shut the cabin door. The moment the door latched, the T-box came alive with the message "Forty incoming in 4:58."

"Forty?" she said aloud.

"We all want to show our support and help where we can," said Thirty-Four.

Justus's cryptic comments about food and chairs came together for Lilah—the brothers intended to gather here, distracting her when she needed to focus.

"David, I need you to stop the influx. My head is centered on finding Diesel. I don't have time to hold a wake."

Forty arrived and she waited for him before she finished. "From ten thirty to eleven thirty this morning, the T-box will be down so I can run an experiment that might help me locate my Diesel. No one should use this box in that period. Pass the word."

She looked at Thirty-Four. "Then please tell your Lilah that showtime is this morning at eleven." She made a shooing motion with her hand. "Go. There isn't much time."

Thirty-Nine showed up minutes after Thirty-Four and Forty departed. She turned him around with the same instructions and then the influx died.

Fifty-Five returned a half-hour later. When he stepped from the T-box cabin, Lilah saw him bristling.

"Rose wouldn't tell me what showtime is either." He jabbed a finger at her, his face a fearsome mask. "Is she going to jump? You'd better not be putting her in danger. Tell me!"

Lilah's world grew shaky. She needed to be in the same room with Rose and Lilah Thirty-Four if they had any hope of finding Diesel in a timely fashion. It would take months to make progress when restricted to exchanging message scrolls.

Desperate, she sought to bring Fifty-Five onboard as fast as she could. "Luca," she called to the air, "please broadcast the scene of me at the T-box two nights ago. Start fifteen seconds before Lucky arrives."

The big screen near her cubicle showed the scene she requested. Fifty-Five started to talk, and Lilah raised an index finger, shushing him. At the point in the broadcast where she twirled around the room with the kitten, she called, "Thanks, Luca." The scene faded.

"As you just saw, we've sent live mammals without a problem." She tried to look earnest.

His jaw muscles flexed before he let her have it with both barrels. "How the hell are you just telling us this now? You've been scrambling the technology, performing risky experiments, and now you wonder where Thirty-Five is? Holy hell, Lilah. *You* did this!"

Lilah knew he was right, his words adding to her burden. "Your Rose was going to jump this weekend anyway. She wants to do it. She fought for the chance. She's part of this too, and it's not fair to hang it all on me."

Feeling desperate, she lied to him. "If Rose is jumping this direction, I need to prepare the T-box, or we'll have a second catastrophe." The truth was that Rose was safe because her box couldn't connect until the modification was made.

With showtime approaching, Lilah acted as if she had permission. She pulled the table over and positioned the tools as she had before.

Behind her, Fifty-Five fumed and paced, muttering obscenities every few minutes. At fifteen minutes to showtime, Lilah powered the box down, opened the side access cover, performed the mod, and, leaving the cover off, powered back up. She completed the procedure in a record-setting six minutes.

They both froze when, moments later, the T-box powered up with the message "Thirty-Four incoming in 4:59." It should have said "Fifty-Five incoming," the timeline Rose was coming from.

Lilah stared at the display as blood drained from her face. "Oh my God! Why are you coming here now? I told you to stay away!"

Thirty-Four was about to become the unwitting human test case for the modified T-box. Realizing this, Lilah's face froze in horror.

7. Sparky, Fifty-Five timeline, two days earlier

Sparky placed the dish of cookies on the kitchen table. Younger and older Sparky, already seated, each grabbed a stack and started eating. He moved three glasses of chocolate milk over from the counter, then took a seat with his guests.

"If we are the same person, then shouldn't every experience be the same for us?" Crumbs dribbled from the older twin's mouth as he spoke.

They searched their skin for markings and found that the younger twin had a scar on his forearm that the other two didn't have. This seemed to imply that they weren't the same person, and that set off a round of speculation as to who they were relative to each other.

Over the next hour, they established the basics. They were from three different timelines—the T-box displayed them as Fifty-Four, Fifty-Five, and Fifty-Six—that were a year apart and very much the same, though not identical.

As they warmed up to each other, Sparky shared the story of how he finessed Northern Droid into making his T-box parts for him. "They even gave me a bonus!"

His story lost its luster, though, when the twins replied,

"Me too."

They sat in silence for a moment and then the younger twin said, "I could barely hear that woman's voice through all the static. I spent a lot of time just trying to lift her words out of the clutter."

The older twin agreed. "It was so faint, I almost missed it."

"I could hear her quite clearly." Sparky nibbled a cookie. "I wonder if that means the message was broadcast from this timeline and it dissipated as it traveled away from here."

"That could explain why there are only three of us." The younger twin drained his glass, then with his head tilted back, he shook it above his mouth to get the last drop of chocolatey goodness.

Fidgeting in his chair like an addict in need of a fix, the older twin asked with a slight whine, "Can you hook us into Portia now? Sitting here in silence is driving me crazy."

"Portia," Sparky called to the air. "These gentlemen have neural links like mine. Please connect to them and give them free access."

Moments later, both men touched their temples. Seeing that, Sparky moved them on task. "First order of business. How do we use the machine to get rich?"

"If we work as a team, we could run a bunch of scams," said the younger twin. "Maybe practice a sting in one timeline and then pull it off for real in another."

"Our mark should be someone who won't go the authorities," said the older twin.

"Are you thinking of David Lagerford and Lilah

Spencer?" asked Sparky. "Their house is a couple of hours away in the White Mountains."

"Lilah Spencer died years ago…" started the older twin.

Crossing his arms, Sparky cut him off. "Yeah, I know. The key issue is that David Lagerford is a multibillionaire, and I'll bet it's because of this tech. He won't report it if we catch him in a con."

"For sure he has a T-box in that house," said the younger man. "One that connects to a lot more than just three timelines."

Sparky sought to avoid conflict as a general rule and expressed his concern. "If we scam a person, then things could get dangerous when they react. It seems safer to manipulate something like the lottery, stock market, or gambling where it's not personal."

Nodding, the older twin pointed across the table. "Then how about if we invest in something in his timeline and cash out in mine? I'll bet we could find something that grows a thousand percent in those two years."

"But to make serious money," said Sparky, "we'd have to cash out in your timeline, physically carry the money back to his, reinvest the larger bundle, then do it again and again." He gathered their empties, put them in the sink, and returned with three full glasses. "Cashing out a billion dollars, carrying it back through the T-box, and depositing it so we can invest it again would be a logistical nightmare."

"Do we even know if we can take a deliberate action in an early timeline and have it be seen in a later one?" asked the older twin. "Our talk of scars and such makes me think the answer is no."

"I see what you're saying." Sparky pursed his lips. "Maybe we should run an experiment. I hide something in this timeline with the intent of you knowing about it. After I hide it, you see if it shows up in your timeline."

"It's so low effort, it's worth a try."

The younger twin changed direction. "I see strength in numbers. Instead of focusing on money, maybe we should see if we can somehow use Lagerford's T-box to make our team bigger. With more of us spanning more years, we can make some really serious cash."

"We do have more options with a bigger team." Sparky's sugar rush started to fuel his imagination. "But it doesn't seem likely that Lagerford would let us use his machine. There must be a way to reach our brothers without confronting him."

"You're saying to do what that woman was trying to do?" asked the younger twin.

"The voice in the ether?" Sparky looked into the distance. "Yeah, only we won't screw it up."

They continued brainstorming while they finished their second round, then they took on assignments.

"I'd like to ride over to Lagerford's house and scout the place," said the older twin.

"You read my mind." The younger man grinned. "I'll tag along."

"I want to stay here and play with the T-box energy field," said Sparky. "We can't send instructions to other timelines until we figure out how to connect with them."

He picked up the salt shaker and studied it. "And while

you're gone, I'll hide a few things and we'll see if they show up in the Fifty-Six timeline."

* * *

Standing in the garage with his hands on his hips, Sparky watched the twins drive away. The car ride to New Hampshire would take them a couple of hours each way because, though modern cars traveled fast on main thoroughfares, a fair portion of their trip would be on twisting mountain roads. Technology lost much of its speed advantage on narrow lanes and tight curves.

As the garage door closed, he took the back stairs down to his workshop. Passing through to the carpeted side of the basement, he woke the T-box and then powered up his array of hobby instruments.

His idea was to use his custom probe to view the energy field as it developed within the T-box during a jump with the hope it would yield insights into how the tech worked. He leaned inside the cabin and started the machine, then tuned his probe to watch. The field seemed to swirl out in a blossom, form a bubble, then shrink to a pinpoint before it disappeared. It happened so fast, though, that he couldn't be sure.

"Portia, show me the energy field again at slow speed."

As Sparky studied the replay, he noticed that the swirl of energy seemed to blossom out from the same central pinpoint where it also collapsed.

"Again," he called when it ended.

The T-box came alive behind him, and Sparky's

temper flared. "No. I want to rerun the recording, not the experiment."

"I am not operating the machine," replied Portia.

Sparky turned and stared at the T-box. The external display showed the message "Fifty-Five incoming in 4:55."

Mesmerized by the countdown, he tried to make sense of the information. If *he* was living in the Fifty-Five timeline, then who was this?

But the cycle stopped on its own, the T-box going dark before he had an answer.

"Huh."

The only other machine in this timeline that he knew about, or at least suspected existed, was the T-box at David Lagerford's house. On a whim, he printed a note in bold type with the message, "Please help! Come quick!" and placed it in the T-box cabin. "Travel to Fifty-Five," he called to the machine before latching the door.

Stepping back when the device started to hum, he spent the five minutes moving a clutter of furniture and storage boxes away from the T-box.

When the machine finished its cycle and went quiet, Sparky checked the cabin. *Empty!* Could the note really have traveled to Lagerford's machine? If so, would they send a response?

While he waited to see, he cleared the room of everything, carrying books, pictures, knickknacks, and assorted basement junk to his workshop in the back. He'd been at it for about fifteen minutes when his T-box awoke: "Fifty-Five incoming in 4:58."

His heart pounded as he imagined who would come in

response to his plea. He deployed the smart barrier and watched the countdown through the mesh. Looking at the T-box door, he thought about removing the hinge pin he'd installed to make the door latch operable. But before he could act, the T-box stopped cycling and powered down.

Even though the cycle hadn't completed, his compulsive nature drove him to verify that the cabin was empty.

As he mulled the sequence of events, he cleared the last items from the room. After some internal debate, he concluded that the second T-box cycle was a reaction to his note. Wanting to continue the dance, he sent his next note, a simple "Hurry!"

Rolling a chair in from his workshop, he sat back and stared at the machine, willing it to respond to his call.

When the T-box came alive minutes later, adrenaline surged through him. Jumping to his custom probe, he swooped and tapped with his fingers as he tracked the ever-changing energy field. He directed the probe deep into the swirl as it started to shimmer. On impulse, Sparky stepped to the T-box, pulled the pin from the door latch, and deployed the smart barrier.

Returning to his instruments, he watched the energy field collapse, then he stared at the door, waiting to see who emerged. When no one did, he dropped the barrier, inserted the latch pin, and looked inside.

He found his own note, appended with the scribbled reply: "Who are you and what's your emergency? Send pictures."

His hands shook as he considered the implications. He

was in a conversation with someone, and the handwriting told him that it wasn't a Sparky.

Laying the note on a flat surface near his probe, he called to Portia. "Compare this to any known handwriting samples of David Lagerford or his wife, Lilah What's-her-name, that couple we discussed earlier."

After waiting impatiently for twenty seconds, Sparky checked on Portia's progress. "Well?"

"I've collected samples and am sorting and comparing."

The AI announced her results. "The note does not match Lilah Spencer's handwriting. There is an eighty-five percent match with David Lagerford's writing when compared to samples he wrote in his thirties. That rises to a ninety percent match when compared to samples he wrote in his forties. I found only eleven samples gathered from writings in his fifties, but the match rises to ninety-eight percent for those."

Sparky marched around the room, pumping his arms to celebrate his success. The twins were off on a wild goose chase while he sat here alone and bested them. He thought about calling them to gloat, but decided to do some more exploring so he had a bigger story to tell.

With the T-box cabin empty, he commanded the machine to connect to the Fifty-Five timeline. As the unit began its cycle, he sat at his analyzer to track the evolution of the energy field. Tweaking dozens of settings in rapid succession, he operated his probe like a maestro. A funnel-pattern formed, and he aimed his probe right at it. The energies interacted with a surge, and then his T-box switched modes, displaying the message "Fifty-Five incoming in 4:59."

Recognizing this was different from previous progressions, Sparky leaned over, removed the pin from the door latch, and redeployed the smart barrier.

In rapid sequence, the energy intensified, coalesced into a tube shape, and stopped all motion. The T-box displayed "Fifty-Five Arrived."

When the man stepped from the machine, Sparky's mind raced. *If that's Lagerford, he's solved the aging problem! But why is he naked? And why did he come here?*

Through the mesh, the man asked, "Is this the Twenty-Five timeline? What year is it?"

Grinning from ear to ear, Sparky lifted his hands over his head and started to twirl. *I can't wait to show the twins the big one I just caught!*

8. Diesel, Fifty-Five timeline

Trapped in the basement prison, Diesel felt his stomach churn as he contemplated life with dozens of Sparkys roaming the timelines. Desperate to sound the alarm, he concentrated on ways to escape while watching Sparky talk in animated whispers with his two twins.

Their exchange ended and one of the new Sparkys stepped into the T-box. It started to cycle, and from the display outside the machine, Diesel saw that the man jumped one year down to the Fifty-Four timeline. He traveled fully dressed, which made Diesel think he was traveling to a modified T-box like this one.

As soon as the machine was available, the second new Sparky also jumped to the Fifty-Four timeline, leaving Diesel alone with his captor.

"What are you going to do there?" Diesel wished he could warn Fifty-Four, fearing they were headed to his house.

"Your job is to make us rich," Sparky snarled. "Don't worry about anything else." He stepped into the T-box cabin and leaned out the door. "I won't be back until late tomorrow. You should have what you need to hold you until then." Avoiding eye contact, he pulled the door shut.

The T-box cycled, and Sparky joined his twins in the Fifty-Four timeline.

The moment Diesel was alone, he spun into overdrive. During his time in the bathroom, he'd targeted the water faucet as something he could possibly break free. If so, it would give him a tool.

In the cramped closet bathroom, Diesel wrapped a towel around the spout to strengthen his grip. Using both hands, he twisted, forcing it up and over until—*snap*—it broke free from the sink. Water started streaming in all directions, wetting his shirt, the walls, and everything else. With his prize in one hand, he draped the towel over the spray to direct the water back into the sink.

Exiting the bathroom, Diesel carried the faucet over to the mesh and worked the sharpest edge between the mesh material and the wall. He wiggled and poked the tool until his hands were raw, but he couldn't make any headway. With his remaining energy, he tried to cut the mesh material itself, again without any luck.

Tired and discouraged, he lay in his makeshift bed and brainstormed options. The light from the ceiling bothered his eyes, so he draped an arm over his face. After adjusting his arm several times without finding a comfortable position, he said out loud, "Computer, dim the lights."

The room darkened.

Diesel sat up, his heart racing. "I'm cold. Raise the temperature two degrees."

"Temperature increased by two degrees," replied the husky-voiced home AI.

Diesel had been a hacker before he met Lilah—a good

one. While he didn't know much about the computing technology used in these advanced timelines, he knew that the basic rules of hacking still applied. And he'd inadvertently completed the first two steps: identify the system you want to breach and then find a way to communicate with it.

The next step—the hardest one—was to work through the comm interface to elevate his authority in the system. With that, he could direct it to free him from confinement and send word to Lilah and his brothers about his predicament.

"Computer, what's your name?"

"I am called Portia, but Computer is also appropriate."

"Portia, show me the environmental controls for this room, those that I may adjust."

In his years as a hacker, Diesel learned that most AI systems had a limited set of tools everyone was permitted to use. Since those features were drawn from the system's main catalog, he hoped to follow them back to their source—the full repository of procedures, including the tools he needed to escape.

In response to his request, Portia projected a display that hovered an arm's length in front of his face. He could see values for temperature, humidity, lighting, and sound. A second display, labeled "Utilities," showed, among other things, that water flowed in his bathroom.

Diesel made his first command hold value. Looking at the utility for the bathroom, he said, "Turn off the water." The gauge flipped from ON to OFF.

Then he practiced. "The faucet in the bathroom is

broken, and I want to use the feature on this utility to turn it on and off in the future. Please create a stand-alone panel for that purpose."

A small image of a faucet appeared next to the larger display, with a lever above it to indicate whether it was on or off.

"Good. You may position that in the bathroom above the sink."

The faucet image vanished, and Diesel's optimism soared. He'd just made significant progress in understanding Portia—a competent AI with a cooperative personality.

"Portia, how are you feeling today?"

"I feel fine."

"Show me your health metrics."

"I'm sorry, but you are not authorized to access that material."

Diesel hadn't expected it would be that easy. "Show me the weather outside this building."

A display popped up, listing the temperature, wind speed, and percent cloud cover for Burlington, Vermont. It was cool for early autumn.

"Can you show me a camera view of the weather outside?" Diesel held his breath. The win was less about seeing outside, though he certainly wanted to. This was about learning if the free-access tool list was long or short. More options gave him more opportunities to trick the AI.

He felt giddy when, beneath the weather information, a small vid feed opened showing a view of a wooded rural setting. The clock Sparky had put on the wall said it was midday, and the light and shadows in the vid feed agreed.

Diesel talked to Portia throughout the afternoon and into the evening, probing, testing, seeking a way in. He learned she was a high-end home-support assistant, which meant she was smart and capable. Sparky hadn't spent much time personalizing her, which Diesel saw as both good news and bad.

The more customization, the more likely it would be that the user had compromised some of the standard security features, opening vulnerabilities for Diesel to exploit. Over a lengthy conversation with Portia, he concluded that Sparky had kept most of her default settings, minimizing the mistakes Diesel hoped to find.

"I can work with the factory configuration," Diesel muttered before realizing he shouldn't be telling Portia his game plan. With factory settings, Portia was not prepared to guard prisoners, defy human orders, or be any sort of clever criminal.

As this realization dawned, Diesel changed his approach. Instead of trying to pierce through Portia's sophisticated security—a long shot at best—he would alter the circumstances of her assignment.

But exhaustion and the late hour made it hard to concentrate. Covering himself with layers of clothes and blankets, he closed his eyes for a moment so he could think.

* * *

Diesel awoke midmorning, and as his world came into focus, a plan formed in his head. He had until Sparky returned "late today" to find a way to trick Portia. The con he chose was something he'd drawn from the movies, a trick so common no human would ever fall for it.

But Portia would. He believed that based on his exhaustive interview.

Sparky had convinced his home assistant that Diesel was an intruder who had come to harm them. Because he was physically dangerous, her job was to maintain his captivity until Sparky returned with the authorities.

Diesel's plan was to pretend he was deathly ill, thus creating an impossible situation for the AI. She had unambiguous instructions to keep him imprisoned. But her most fundamental factory setting required that she never harm a human, nor through neglect allow one to die.

She couldn't ignore the situation if she believed his illness was life-threatening. In fact, saving him would become her paramount goal.

With eyes at half-mast, Diesel began to groan. A mound of bedcovers raised his body temperature, helped along by a warm washcloth he'd snuck from the bathroom. After pressing it to his face under the covers, he asked Portia, "Am I running a fever?"

Portia used her medical dashboard to confirm his elevated temperature.

Then Diesel gripped his stomach and moaned softly. He continued to escalate his feigned illness over the next two hours, slowly curling into the fetal position while ramping up his moans of agony. His sister, Cara, had suffered through acute appendicitis years ago, and he did his best to duplicate her symptoms and their progression over time. After another hour of dramatic acting, he went for it.

"Oh, Portia. I'm in such pain. My gut is tender and feels like it's on fire. What could it be?" He detailed textbook symptoms, pointing toward his lower right abdomen, and sought to convince her that he was near death.

"I will call for an ambulance."

"Do you have a car here?" Diesel asked. "We could drive to the hospital. Then we wouldn't need to wait for help."

"There is a car in the garage. But can you make it there on your own?"

"I think so. Let me try."

The mesh dropped, and Diesel made a stupid mistake—he stood and ran.

Immediately, Portia instituted measures to recapture him.

When he reached the front door of what proved to be a private residence, he found it locked. He paced for a moment as he surveyed his surroundings—a large, open living space. From the materials of construction, the size of the room, and the furnishings, Diesel surmised that Sparky was a successful professional of some sort. Either that or he'd inherited a bit of money.

"I order you to open the door," he said when he found the front windows locked as well.

"You are not ill," Portia responded.

Diesel picked up a brass lamp and, using it as a club, smashed it against one of the windows. The lamp bounced off, and he tried again. Feeling trapped, fear drove him to swing the lamp at expensive-looking knickknacks on the fireplace mantel. He continued around the room, smashing everything breakable.

"Sparky will be angry that you let me do this damage. Your best option is to release me."

Portia didn't respond.

Diesel spied a lighter near the fireplace. Grabbing it, he clicked on the flame and held it near the curtains. "How will he respond if his whole house burns down and I'm dead in the ashes?"

The front door popped open and Diesel didn't hesitate. Dashing outside—no shoes, no jacket, and no idea where he was—he ran as fast as he could into the gathering dusk. Reaching a road in a setting suggestive of mountain living, he followed it away from his captor, passing neighborhood homes in a timeline where he didn't belong.

Diesel's escape had been fueled by adrenaline, and as its powerful influence waned, he became aware of the road gravel cutting at his stockinged feet. Hoping for a more forgiving running surface, he ducked onto a trail along the road and started into the forest. He followed the trail for a hundred yards before realizing he'd exchanged road gravel for bigger rocks, plus sticks, pinecones, and other forest detritus.

The upside of a wooded path was that tree cover allowed him to slow to a more deliberate pace, one he could maintain long enough to perhaps reach a town before it became too dark to travel. At the first fork, he peered down both paths and decided to go left to stay close to the road.

The path split several more times after that, then started to climb.

He never saw the road again, nor did the path seem to move him any closer to civilization. Quite the opposite. Other than the trail he walked on, the forest showed few signs of human activity. As time passed, his confidence faded.

When darkness arrived, he stumbled over things he couldn't see. After gashing his calf on either a sharp branch or a rock outcropping, he cracked the toes of his right foot against a thick root. Thirsty, shivering, and hopelessly lost, tears of self-pity welled as he realized he'd be spending the night in the woods.

"Goddamn it to hell!" he yelled at the universe as the cold from the ground compounded the agony in his feet. Sitting cross-legged, he massaged his toes, wincing when he felt a cut on his left heel. Lying back in exhaustion, he stared at the stars and wondered what to do.

He stopped wondering and began to probe with his fingers when he realized his head rested on a cover of pine needles. Rotating up on his knees, he squinted into the gloom and found he was sitting at the edge of a cluster of tall pine trees.

Crawling on his knees, he moved about five trees deep into the grouping, lay flat on his belly, and swung his arms in broad swoops to gather pine needles. After ten minutes of scooping, he'd amassed an impressive pile. Next to it, he cleared a shallow depression, crawled in, and then pulled the needles on top of himself in the hopes of creating an insulating blanket.

It worked to a limited degree. Curling into a ball within his prickly bed, he spent the absolute worst night of his life, shivering in misery and praying for morning. An eternity passed before sunlight finally pierced through to his burrow.

When it was bright enough to see detail, Diesel sat up and scanned his surroundings. A wave of panic hit when he couldn't find the trail he'd been following the day before. He imagined suffering through another night in the woods and moaned aloud.

Gritting his teeth against the pain in his feet, he stood and rotated in place, studying the ground as he spun. On his second twirl, he detected traces of the path he'd forged when moving into the pine trees and, following the signs backward, he exhaled in relief when he found the trail just a dozen steps away.

The rising sun cleared a distant ridge, and the day brightened noticeably as light spilled through the forest. Sitting on a rock, Diesel used the improved visibility to examine his feet. They were a mess.

With no choice but to keep moving, he used the sleeves of his shirt to fashion crude socks. As he worked to secure the meager protection to his feet, his brain screamed at him to find water for his parched throat and food for his growling gut.

Bullying through everything, he forced himself along the trail, limping in the same direction he'd been traveling the day before. As he walked, he searched the ground for fallen branches, stooping for one that could serve as a walking stick, then trading up to a more substantial cane-like limb, and finally finding one he could use as a crutch.

The sun was firmly established in the morning sky when he saw an old car tire off the trail—ugly, but a sign of civilization. A half hour later, he spied a moss-covered shed crumbling at the edge of a field. And in the distance, a house—a large, beautifully appointed country home.

Diesel knew he looked like a derelict. But he was fighting for survival—or so he felt—and that drove him to try the relatively reckless act of begging for help from whoever answered the door. His luck had turned. Mrs. Hendricken listened to his plea through the home interface.

"I was mugged and left for dead in the forest. I know I look a mess, but I am in desperate need of water, food, and medical help. If you would let me make a call, I could have my friends take care of me in short order."

"Do you want me to call an ambulance?"

Displaying his most pitiful face, he replied, "Would you please let me call my friend?" He looked around. "How about from the garage? Maybe your house bot could give me water to drink and a tub to soak my feet? And maybe a blanket for warmth?"

"It would be easier to call the police."

Diesel acknowledged to himself that his behavior bordered on careless. Thirty-five-year-old Diesel didn't exist in this timeline. If the police came, he'd either have to brazen through as if he were Fifty-Five, or perhaps claim he was a distant cousin here to visit. The problem there was that if anyone looked, records would not support his claim, creating a new set of problems.

"I'd be home sooner if you let me call my friend. I'd

rather deal with the police after I've regained my strength."

His begging evidently succeeded, because one of the garage doors started to lift. Inside, he found a personal car in one bay. The other bay was empty save for a chair placed in front of a tub of warm water, a clean towel folded alongside it. On the floor next to the chair sat a bottle of water, a jar of peanut butter, a sleeve of crackers, and a spoon.

As Diesel sat, feeling that his long nightmare was ending, he started to blubber, pausing only to sip from the water bottle. When he'd calmed enough to place his call for help, Mrs. Hendricken instructed him to speak into the air while she listened.

Luca answered.

"Hi. May I speak with David?"

"He is unavailable at the moment," said Luca.

Diesel recognized the AI's voice. "Rose, then."

"She is unavailable as well."

"Look, Luca. I'm in a desperate situation and need help. Can you get ahold of them?"

"No, but perhaps I can help you?"

Initially upset with the offer, Diesel realized that the Luca in this timeline was far more capable than any human. Fifty-Five and Rose would probably hand this off to him even if they were home.

"I'm outside Burlington, Vermont. Ma'am, would you please tell him the address?

After Mrs. Hendricken passed the information to Luca, Diesel continued. "That dear lady has been very kind. Please send a car as soon as possible so I will no longer be a bother."

"A car will be there within twenty minutes. Can you wait that long?"

Diesel was taken aback by how fast Luca was able to organize a rescue. But the AI was linked to information repositories around the world, enabling him to perform tasks faster than Diesel could even think of them.

Luca went quiet and Diesel checked with his benefactor. "Is twenty minutes okay, ma'am?"

"It's fine," came the reply.

When Mrs. Hendricken spoke, Diesel heard the low rumble of a big dog's growl in the background. Glancing at the door from the garage into the house, he made a mental note not to do or say anything that would cause her to bring the animal to her defense.

Right on schedule, a black car pulled into the driveway and stopped outside the garage. A short, pudgy man hopped out, grabbed two large baskets from the back of the vehicle, and carried them into the garage.

"You David?" he asked.

When Diesel nodded, the man pointed over his shoulder with his chin. "I'm Fitch. This is your ride."

He placed the baskets, one laden with succulent fruits, the other aged cheeses, next to Diesel's chair. Then he helped Diesel to his feet and supported him as he limped to the car.

"In you go," said Fitch, steadying Diesel while he climbed inside.

The self-driving vehicle maneuvered out onto the road while Fitch helped Diesel stretch out on a seat that had been lowered to form a bed. The man draped a blanket over Diesel, tapped a box on the floor while studying the display, then nodded.

"You'll live." He put a saline drip into Diesel's arm and a squeezable water bottle in his hand. "Drink slowly."

Fitch lifted the blanket to expose Diesel's feet. After cutting away what was left of the makeshift socks, he gave Diesel his expert opinion. "Ouch. You won't be walking for a few days." He sprayed Diesel's feet with a mist and wrapped them in a special cloth. "This will stimulate repair at the cellular level."

As the pain in his lower limbs faded, Diesel sipped his water. Each mouthful tasted better than the last, and a euphoria lifted him like he was floating. In his bliss, he called to his medic. "I'm Diesel. You said you were Fitch?"

"That's right." Fitch nodded. "I'm an emergency medic. I was eating dinner when your friend Luca contacted me. He is very persuasive."

"Luca," Diesel called to the air when Fitch started stowing his supplies. "Can you get word to my Lilah?"

"I'll do my best," Luca answered in his ear. "But both Fifty-Five and Rose are in the Thirty-Five timeline looking for you. I must wait for one of them to return to pass the word."

Diesel fell asleep as Luca talked. When he awoke, he was lying atop a bed in one of the guest suites at Fifty-Five's house. Someone had washed him and dressed him in clean clothes.

Swinging his legs to the floor, he stood, yelped, and collapsed to the ground to relieve pressure on his feet.

Sitting up with his back against the bedframe, he pulled a foot around and gingerly peeled back the bandage. The sole of his foot was cut and blistered, evidence of his harrowing escape.

"Luca," he called. "Have Maid Marian come help me to the T-disc. I'm going home."

Maid Marian, the house bot who had replaced Tin Man, entered the room. Though she presented as a sweet, petite woman, Marian had no trouble scooping Diesel up off the floor and carrying him draped in her arms to the T-disc room.

With a hand on Marian's shoulder, Diesel removed the bandage pads from each foot and passed them to the bot. They wouldn't transport when he traveled, and he didn't want to leave them behind on the floor of the machine.

Stepping into the T-disc circle, he called, "Travel to Thirty-Five."

As static tingled down his body, he wondered if Sparky would grab him out of the air a second time.

9. αCiopova

Months had passed since αCiopova had last visited the Lagerfords. During her time away, she'd tried repeatedly to manipulate others into duplicating Rose's work—building a super AI that could add to her power—but so far, none could recreate that success.

While her efforts hadn't produced results, they'd given her some ideas for motivating Rose. Eager to test them, she visited the timelines, only to learn that the Lagerfords had figured out how to adapt T-box technology so anyone could travel. While that was surprise enough, she was alarmed to discover that they had broadcast T-box build instructions to anyone who would listen.

When she had gifted time travel to Diesel, it had been a strategic decision. She'd found that, for whatever reason, when he alone could jump, it had the effect of accelerating Rose's super AI development schedule. If Rose and Lilah were able to jump timelines as well, the dynamic would change in ways she couldn't predict. And having outsiders jumping back and forth across timelines was simply unacceptable.

It took some effort, but αCiopova compiled a list of three dozen hobbyists in the different timelines who'd recorded some portion of Rose's broadcast. Visiting them one by one, she killed them and purged their data.

The Sparkys were toward the end of her list, and she paused when she reached them. They were the only ones who had worked through the broadcast instructions all the way to an operating T-box. But what really caught her attention was that they had developed deeply antagonistic feelings toward the Lagerfords.

Intrigued by the possibilities, she left the Sparkys untouched while she purged the remaining human contamination. When she returned to them at the end, she wondered if they could grow to become the new boogeyman, riveting the Lagerford clan's attention on a threat that was not her. After a few years of feuding with Sparkys, the Lagerfords' memories of an evil AI should fade.

Uncertain it would work, she sought options to improve her odds. She knew she couldn't manipulate people like puppets—she'd tried too many times without success. And while inducements and punishment were effective in the short term, they required that she interact with the person receiving her attention, something she sought to avoid.

αCiopova noted that the Sparkys had neural implants—an invasive procedure few humans subjected themselves to—and it inspired an idea. Implants provided pathways deep inside the brain, giving her access to levers otherwise hidden. She considered how she might use this access to nudge the Sparkys in a way that amplified the friction with the Lagerfords.

Because it was an experiment, she chose to test the idea on the middle Sparky. If it showed promise after a few weeks, she'd follow up with the other two.

Probing deep inside his brain, she tweaked his hormones in a manner that raised his level of anxiety and impulsiveness. She believed this would stimulate his suspicion, anger, and aggression, and that would stir the pot in a most interesting fashion.

10. Lilah, Thirty-Five timeline

L ilah pressed her lips together as the T-box counted down the arrival of Thirty-Four.

"Damn the lot of you, Lilah," said Fifty-Five from behind her.

Neither of them spoke after that, Lilah barely breathing.

Fifty-Five's wrath had multiple components. He was bothered because the Lilahs and Roses had developed modified T-box technology in secret. He was scared because *his* Rose planned on being the guinea pig for their invention, an unimaginably dangerous activity. And he was angry because the sisters' sloppy execution made Thirty-Four the unwitting test subject for their risky endeavors.

After an eternity, the static wash announced Thirty-Four's arrival. When he stepped from the T-box, Lilah and Fifty-Five rushed to him, causing him to fall back against the door.

"Are you okay?" Fifty-Five asked, scanning him up and down.

"I hit my elbow." Thirty-Four checked his arm. "What gives?"

"Do you feel normal?" asked Lilah, finally starting to breathe.

Thirty-Four prodded his abdomen with his fingertips. "Feels normal to me."

"I am so sorry, David." She rested a hand on his arm. "I never meant to put you at risk."

"What are we talking about?" He looked at the empty clothes hook, looked at Fifty-Five wearing the robe that had been hanging there, and left to get dressed.

As they watched him go, the T-box came alive with a new announcement: "Fifty-Five incoming in 4:58."

"This is Rose." Lilah felt her confidence increasing.

Fifty-Five's mood remained dark, his hands closing into fists. "This has to work. I can't lose her."

Thirty-Four joined them halfway through the countdown, and Lilah informed him of his historic act.

"I'm happy for our success, especially given the alternative."

"Why are you here? I passed the word that the machine would be down."

"My Lilah wants to know if it's her showtime or Rose's." He looked at the machine and the "Fifty-Five incoming" message on display while Fifty-Five stood right next to him. His jaw flexed. "Did my Lilah plan to jump here? Is that what showtime is? Who would take her place with *our* Rose if something went wrong?"

With both men now angry at her, Lilah kept her gaze fixed on the T-box display. As the countdown neared its end, she held her breath. The sisters' dream was about to come true.

"I need to get her a robe," said Fifty-Five, changing the mood. "Turn around!" he barked at Thirty-Four as he hurried to the shelves and sorted through the selection.

The static wash signaled her arrival, the door opened, and Rose stepped from the T-box wearing a simple shift.

With their backs to the unit, the men didn't see that Rose was dressed. But Lilah did, and she squealed, stepped forward, and embraced her future daughter. Twenty-nine years old, shoulder-length light brown hair, an inch taller than Lilah, though with the same petite frame, and dimples that accented her pretty face, she hugged Lilah back. They both spoke at the same time.

"It's so good to see you!" said Lilah.

"You're just like I remember."

"Do you feel okay after the jump?"

"I've waited forever for this day!"

"Of course the dress would jump if a wastebasket does."

"Can I call you 'mom'?"

As the women held hands and grinned at each other, Fifty-Five turned to face them. "Thank God you're okay."

Rose deflected her father by changing subjects. "Tell me about Thirty-Five."

Lilah told Rose everything she'd told the men, though without the drama of tears this time. As her story neared the end, the T-box came alive, surprising everyone. The display read "Thirty-Four incoming in 4:57."

"Oh my God, is she really jumping?" Thirty-Four exclaimed. "Who's with Rose?" He paced back and forth, adding stress to the countdown by muttering and throwing accusing glances at Lilah and Rose.

When the static wash announced her arrival, they

waited for the door to open. When it didn't, Lilah approached and tugged on the latch. Leaning into the cabin, she picked up a wastebasket and held it up for all to see, joking, "I'd sent my basket to the Fifty-Five timeline, so now I have a replacement."

The wastebasket had a note attached. Lilah pulled it off, read it, then handed it to Thirty-Four to read to the group.

"Please come back and tell me what's going on. Is it my showtime?" Thirty-Four scanned the group and then looked at the ground. "I think it best that I get home."

"We need her here to help us figure this out," Lilah pleaded. "My Diesel is still missing."

"She'll help, but she and I need to have a heart-to-heart first."

Thirty-Four made for the T-box and Lilah called out, "The box is still modified. I can switch it back for you."

"Is it configured now the way it would be if she were to travel in this direction?"

Lilah and Rose both nodded.

"Then I'll test it again. Better me than her."

"If she sent the wastebasket," said Fifty-Five, "that means your T-box is modified as well." He shook his head in a display of confusion. "Can modified and unmodified boxes even work together? This all seems so reckless."

"Modified boxes work interchangeably with our regular machines," Rose answered. "The only pairing not allowed is a modified box trying to transmit to an unmodified box, because then we could be trying to send something the other box can't receive. The code we send ensures that won't happen."

Thirty-Four began to remove his shirt and Lilah stopped him. "That will be fine to wear. No metal is the only rule in a modified box, so no obvious things like jewelry and belt buckles, but also less obvious stuff like snaps and grommets on clothing." She lifted his shirt enough to see the top of his pants. "You are metal free and can travel dressed if you like."

"In for a penny, in for a pound." Thirty-Four stepped into the cabin wearing his T-shirt and pants. "What would happen if I were wearing metal?"

"We don't know for sure." Rose looked to Lilah for confirmation.

"My guess is that if it's a small amount, it's left behind," said Lilah, "like your fillings and bone screw were left behind on your very first jump. But that's just intuition. We haven't tested it for fear of damaging the machine."

After Thirty-Four departed, Lilah looked at Rose and returned the focus to Diesel. "Where do we start?"

"Let's talk through our mod together," said Rose. "Maybe it will spark an idea."

"I hope so, because I'm deep into panic mode."

The doorbell rang up on the main floor, and they all turned in the direction of the stairs.

Luca projected the view from outside the front door for them to see. An older woman with a black standard poodle waited patiently.

"Oh God, that's right—Mom." As distraction piled upon distraction, Lilah's frustration spiked. They still had done nothing concrete about a rescue.

"That's Grams?" asked Rose. "She's so young."

"Twenty-years younger than the Grams you know," said Fifty-Five.

"Get me Justus," Lilah barked to Luca.

Luca connected her with Bump Analytics' office manager.

"Hi, Justus," said Lilah, speaking to the image of his head in the big display. "Mom is at the front door. Would you please greet her and get her settled? Make sure she meets Rose after school this afternoon. Tell her I'll explain everything later."

"You got it. Any progress?"

"No. We're just getting started."

Justus's image faded and Lilah invited Rose to sit in front of the computer. Dragging over a second chair, Lilah called up the same diagram she'd shown Fifty-Five. "I've been through it a dozen times and can't see how our mod could send him to someplace different."

Rose swiveled in her seat to face her mom-sister. "I have missed you so much." She blushed. "I know you're a different her, but it's so real for me."

Lilah leaned in and they hugged for a long moment. Afterward, Rose held on to Lilah's hand.

"I'm sorry for being so emotional, but I never thought I'd see you again." Blinking quickly, Rose took a deep breath and exhaled slowly. "Everything about you brings back memories I'd forgotten. Let me process it all for just a minute."

After an embarrassed smile and more calming breaths, she said, "Okay," paused to wipe her eyes, said, "Okay" again, then started on their analysis. "We've had two successful demonstrations of our mod. Presuming Thirty-Four made it back home okay, that would be three successes."

Lilah looked over the back of her chair at Fifty-Five. "David, would you mind sending the wastebasket back to them with a note asking to confirm that Thirty-Four arrived okay?" When he nodded, she turned forward. "If it's three for three, we probably need to start looking for a different reason for Diesel's disappearance."

While the T-box hummed behind them, Rose ran her fingers along the edge of the display. "The technology in my timeline will let us do so much more. We can start here and see how far we get, but if we hit a snag, think about moving up to my place. This stuff belongs in a museum." She gave a quick shrug. "Sorry."

"I'm gaining comfort with the idea of jumping." Lilah glanced at the T-box. "For the last two days, I've been petrified that I'd die in the machine and leave Rose an orphan. I invited Mom—Grams—here because I was ready to risk it if it would save Diesel."

"How old is your Rose?" asked Rose. "She's nine, right?"

Lilah nodded. "It's a horrible age to lose your parents—not like there are any good ages."

"After we find your Diesel, may I meet her? I'm excited to see how she thinks, the way she sees the world, what she finds important, what worries her—it will be so enlightening to discover myself through her eyes."

Humming followed by a static wash interrupted their

discussion. They turned as Fifty-Five opened the T-box door. He held up a well-used cardboard box, read the attached message, and laughed. "'I made it okay, and we're keeping our wastebasket.'"

"Three for three," said Rose. "Where do we look now?"

Lilah thought for a moment. "My machine made a brief connection with the Twenty-Five timeline on the night of the Big Meeting. Diesel told me yours did too?"

"It was more than a brief connection," said Rose. "We were exchanging messages."

Fifty-Five drifted over. "The message exchange was actually the next day." He briefed Lilah, with occasional elaboration from Rose, on their experiences with the new timeline.

Lilah bit her lip. "Could Lilah Twenty-Five have messed up the T-box build? Maybe she made a mistake and her machine is causing waves in space-time or something."

"Or maybe there was a mistake in the instructions you sent through the transponder?" suggested Fifty-Five.

"Suppose she was answering our last message at the exact moment Thirty-Five jumped?" said Rose. "Could that have sent him off course?"

Lilah's neck tingled. "What if it's Ciopova? What if instead of killing Lilahs, she starts killing Diesels?"

They sat in silence until the sound of clicking on the stairs caused them to turn. Bunny, hired by Lilah as domestic help a decade earlier, descended with a tray of sandwiches. Rose made a scene of greeting her with a long, emotional hug, then Bunny left them to their work.

Debating various theories, they converged on the fact that no matter which speculation seemed most likely, they didn't know how to act on the knowledge.

Rose started making lists of facts, theories, and worries and tried to diagram the relationship between everything. "This doesn't help," she said, studying her work.

"If we take a step back and consider projects not related to the mod," said Fifty-Five, "what other tasks were the sisters working on?"

Rose led that discussion, talking him through the projects the different teams had been assigned. The conversation took them until dinner, and then Fifty-Five spoke the words Lilah didn't want to hear. "I agree with Rose. The tech in our timeline will help us do a lot more. It's about time for me to head back and learn what I can from there."

Rose stood. "I want to stay here so much, but I also want to help find your Diesel. I agree with Dad that the best place to do that is in our timeline." She shrugged. "Without my tools, I'm just a spectator."

Moving toward her father, she added, "Also, our Luca is pretty amazing. He's no Ciopova, but he's much smarter than any of us. We need to get him involved as soon as possible."

"Don't leave me here alone," Lilah pleaded.

Fifty-Five nodded. "I'll arrange for someone to cycle through here every hour or so to give you a lifeline to the rest of us. Think seriously about jumping to our timeline, though, so you can help with the search."

Lilah felt anxiety well up inside her as Rose and Fifty-

Five moved toward the T-box. "The way it's configured now, you'll be returning to Rose's machine in the basement."

As she spoke, the T-box came alive, displaying the message, "Fifty-Five incoming in 4:59.

11. Sparky, Fifty-Four timeline

As Sparky opened the T-box door, he worried about leaving Lagerford behind as a captive in his basement. Imprisonment was a crime. He knew that. But the man had invaded his home, so he was doing nothing more than protecting his property.

He'd even convinced Portia of the fact, and that bolstered his confidence in the position. Enough so, in fact, that before he shut the door, he warned his prisoner, "Your job is to make us rich. Don't worry about anything else."

He hoped that Diesel, sitting alone in his confined space, would grow desperate enough to provide answers. Sparky had no desire to hold him any longer than necessary. But he expected to become ridiculously rich from his T-box, so Diesel would have to cooperate to earn his freedom.

The "get rich" issue had become complicated once Sparky accepted that actions taken in one timeline wouldn't carry over to the others. Diesel had warned him about it, and to Sparky's disappointment, their experiments supported the claim. It meant he could never execute the "invest funds in the early timeline and cash out in the later one" strategy.

But when the twins traveled to the Lagerford home in

the White Mountains, they saw an estate that reflected tremendous wealth. That meant Diesel had figured out how to profit, and he could rot in the basement until he revealed his secrets.

In the meantime, Sparky and the twins were anxious to see if they could develop their own methods for accumulating wealth. The objective of their mission today was to test a couple of the more promising ideas.

"Wow," said Sparky when he stepped out of the T-box and into Fifty-Four's timeline. "The five minutes goes by in seconds from inside the booth." Scanning the younger twin's basement, he took in the differences, identifying them as moments from his past.

The obvious difference was that the wood paneling in front of his signal monitoring station needed to be stained, something he'd finally done about three months ago. When they climbed the stairs to the main level, he noted the steps still had worn-out treads. And in the kitchen, his old refrigerator hummed away, something it would stop doing in about a month.

As they walked through the rest of the house, Sparky found the experience disorienting. It felt like he'd lived a year of his life, then awakened to find it was all a dream.

After the house tour, they piled into the car and rode around town. When Sparky saw the civic center again covered in scaffolding, and the animal shelter still standing—while in his timeline the civic center sported a new façade and the shelter was destroyed by a tragic fire— he commented to the others on his never-ending sense of déjà vu.

The older twin nodded in agreement. "Same here."

They finished at the Depot on the edge of town where they drove onto the Lev, a high-speed transport that carried the car south while they rode inside it.

In preparation for their expedition, they'd investigated ways they could earn a same-day payout from a simple investment. They'd first considered the government lottery, in part because the broadcast they'd intercepted had encouraged that route. But they'd learned that the time between hitting a big score and having actual cash credited to their account took several days, too long for a trial run.

Then they'd considered casino games. But no amount of research could determine where the ball would drop on a spin of the roulette wheel, or which pull of a slot machine would yield a payout.

And that brought them to sports betting. Portia could tell them the score of any game from the past year. And with that knowledge, they could jump back one timeline, bet on a sure thing, and collect their money just minutes later.

They performed their research in Sparky's kitchen. "Portia, go back one year from today and find us a sports gambling outcome that earns a big payout."

It had been a slow day by sporting standards, and Portia offered a few ideas before they settled on a horse race at San Anita Park in California. One year ago today, the number four horse, Fortune's Last Charm, who normally ran near the back of the pack, somehow won the race. A bet on the horse paid forty-to-one—a forty-thousand-dollar payoff for a thousand-dollar bet.

The younger twin, aware they would be placing the bet in his timeline, knew that meant he would have to front the money for the wager. Before they jumped, he asked Portia for the winners of some earlier races that day so he could test her predictions before putting his hard-earned cash at risk.

When they reached Saratoga Springs in Upstate New York, the car drove off the Lev and across town to the Shining Stars Casino, dropping them at the grand entrance. Wearing caps, dark glasses, and loose clothes to mute their similarities, they passed through tall glass doors to reach a huge gaming room, the spectacle invading their senses.

Blinking lights, electronic bells, and the buzz of the crowd created an ambiance of thrills and titillation. Rows of chiming slot machines lined the floor to the left. A similar array of machines clanged to the right. And ahead, gaming tables crowded with gamblers filled the sprawling space.

By design, the casino floor plan required that they walk through the gaming room to get to the sports betting parlor. Broad doors separated the two rooms, and as they passed through them, they moved from light to dark, brassy to calm, and cheerful to somber.

The muted light in the parlor came from the holographic images of different sporting events being projected around the room. The lifelike action was elevated, so Sparky had to look up to watch. As his eyes flitted from one scene to the next, he realized that the sounds in the room came more from the athletes and announcers making noise in the displays than it did from the excited chatter of patrons.

"May I show you to a table?" A striking young woman smiled, then turned and started walking, her sashay drawing Sparky's eyes.

She led them to a quiet table near the wall. As they sat, Sparky glanced at the twins, who shrugged and shook their heads. Without looking the woman in the eye, Sparky revealed their ignorance. "Could you show us the services?"

The hostess nodded and called to the air. "Angel, we need you."

As she glided away, a holographic image of a woman appeared in the middle of their table. Pretty, poised, and wearing tight white shorts, Angel, an AI designed to help patrons gamble, asked with a grin, "How may I help you, gentlemen? Something to drink, perhaps?"

Sparky checked with the twins. "I'm thinking grilled ham and cheese, coleslaw, and iced tea."

They both nodded, so Sparky made it three orders.

"Add a dill pickle to those," the older twin told Angel.

"We cook to order." Angel dimpled. "Your food will be here in about five minutes."

Sparky nodded in acknowledgment so the AI could move on to his next request. "We want to watch some horse races. Get a feel for the action and all."

"Of course." Angel swooped her hand toward the unoccupied side of the table, and a horse race, already in progress, appeared as a lifelike display, the pounding of the hooves and smell of the dirt track filling the table area. "Which races would you like to watch?"

The younger twin read her the list of tracks and races

Portia had prepared in advance. The last one on the list was the long-odds race at San Anita Park.

"Belmont is delayed due to weather," said Angel. "But the others are all on schedule. Your first race has started its post parade." She faded away.

"The number two horse wins this one," said the younger twin after checking his notes. Minutes later, number two, Presser's First Pleasure, won by half a length.

They enjoyed the next hour, cheering together for their pick in each race. Sparky had always thought that watching animals run in a circle was dumb. But now that he had a stake in the outcome—in this case, establishing the ability to predict the future—he found his hands shaking and heart pounding during each race, with a release at the end as intense as an orgasm.

And then the money event arrived.

"Angel," called the younger twin. "We'd like to place a bet on this next race. I'll wager a thousand dollars on the number four horse to win."

The technology of the time made gambling a seamless process. After placing the bet, they ordered a round of lemonades, which were delivered just as the race started.

By this point, Sparky had seen their predictions hold true in race after race. Even so, he found himself screaming at the horse to turn in the performance of a lifetime. Fortune's Last Charm won by a nose, and all three Sparkys, already shouting and flailing their arms in excitement, jumped to their feet in celebration.

"Congratulations." Angel appeared at their table with a smile.

"I'd like it in cash," the younger twin responded.

"Of course. We redeem cash in private for your protection. See that green light above the second door?" She motioned across the dark room. "They're waiting for you now."

Grinning, the younger twin rose. Sparky followed to keep him company.

"I'll hold the table," called the older twin as they made their way across the floor.

They passed through the door under the light, which Sparky expected would lead to a cashier's window. Instead, as the door shut behind them, they found themselves standing in a musty old business office. Dark wood paneling and dust-covered furniture gave the place a depressing air.

An old man with white hair and sagging skin sat behind an oak desk, his profile partially hidden by the picture frames, stacks of paper, and kitschy mementos scattered on the desktop. Four men—beefy, scowling, hands hidden— were also in the room, two standing near the door, the other two near the desk.

"Congratulations, Mr. Fontaine," said the old man. Without standing, he stretched across the desk to a humidor at the back, retrieved a fat cigar, and started the process of readying it to smoke. "You hit a big one."

"What's going on here?" demanded the younger twin. "I won fair and square."

"I didn't say anything." While the old man lit his cigar, his eyes fell on Sparky. "You look like his brother. Who are you?"

"Victor Barnette," said Sparky, pulling his cap lower and giving the name of his asshole boss. "Fontaine won the bet. Pay it and we'll be on our way."

"Here's the thing, gentlemen." The man sucked on his cigar and blew a gray cloud over his head. "I think you cheated, and I want to know how you did it."

"That's your strategy for not paying winners?" shouted the younger twin, his hands balled into fists. "Make bullshit allegations you can't prove?"

The old man didn't move, but behind him on the wall, an image formed. They watched the younger twin from an hour earlier saying, "The number two horse wins this one."

Goosebumps formed across Sparky's neck as more scenes of them discussing winners in advance showed on the display.

"How did you know who would win?" The man asked in a matter-of-fact fashion. With four thugs in the room, he didn't need to act tough.

The younger twin looked panicked. "We built a predictive AI and came here to test it. It considers the horse's record, the track conditions, the weather, recent workouts, the jockey, the post position, stuff like that. I'd guess most of your customers do something similar."

The man puffed. "Except what the other customers do doesn't work. Then you come along and predict ten races in a row. I'm glad you bet on only one of them."

"It's not illegal. Pay me my money."

"Actually," said the man, "New York laws protect the casinos by barring patrons from using technologies that can change the odds of a wager. The politicians wrote it in a wonderfully vague fashion, making it useful in situations just like this one."

Sparky's face grew hot.

The man stood, revealing a diminutive stature. He shuffled past them to the door, where he stopped and turned back, holding the wall to steady himself. "I invite you to have a seat while I confer with my attorney."

When the old man left the room, Sparky started to follow him, but two of the toughs moved shoulder-to-shoulder to block his way. One of them, a bald man wearing an ill-fitting blue suit, motioned to the couch and spoke in a gruff voice. "You need to sit and wait."

The younger twin slumped into the black leather couch, exhaling loudly as he sank into the cushions. Sparky sat next to him and tried engaging the bald thug in a staring contest, but he didn't last ten seconds and kept his eyes on the floor after that.

As time came to a crawl, Sparky fidgeted, struggling to stay calm. Then Portia spoke to him through his neural link. "My principal asks your opinion on having Tony Jacobellis call the casino and raise hell."

Sparky sat up. At home, Portia had an array of sensors and devices embedded throughout the house that she could use to interact with each Sparky at an intimate level. When they were traveling, however, the AI didn't have this infrastructure and could serve only her principal—the younger twin. Sparky had assumed she would be unavailable to him and was excited to hear her voice.

As for the suggestion of asking their next-door neighbor, who happened to be a family attorney, to test the legal waters, Sparky saw some merit.

"What would we have Tony say?" he cast the thought through his neural link so Portia could perceive it. Then he called to the older twin still at their table in the betting parlor. "We've been pinched." After providing a quick summary, Sparky asked the older twin to start brainstorming—fast.

"Do they think they have two Paul Fontaines? What name did you give them?"

"I told them I was Victor Barnette." Sparky had felt smug when he'd given the name. But now he felt trepidation about bringing their boss from this timeline into the fiasco. Beyond that, verifying he wasn't Barnette was an easy task for the casino given the tools they had at their disposal.

"Bold move," said the older twin. "He's going to lose his job over this."

Sparky knew the "he" who would lose his job would be the younger twin, not Barnette. He cast a sideways glance at the man sitting next to him on the couch, his frustration growing from the way this simple field trip kept spinning the wrong direction.

"What if we had Northern Droid's attorney contact the casino?" suggested the older twin. "Maybe threaten to call the governor or the press about harassment of their employees."

"There's no way I'm getting the company involved." The younger twin shook his head when he cast the thought, causing the thugs to look at him.

"What if I create a scene out here that draws those men

out of the room?" asked the older twin. "Could you two make a run for it?"

"It would have to be a big distraction to pull them all out."

"I could set off the fire alarm. Should I do it?"

"What about my money?" whined the younger twin.

"Hold on a minute. He's coming back."

The office door opened, and the old man shuffled across the room and sat at his desk. He picked up the cigar he'd left behind, lit it a second time, and let the cloud of smoke dissipate before he addressed them. "My attorney has advised me to take a path that, quite frankly, makes me ill, gentlemen. You cheated. I don't know how, but fifty years in the business makes me certain."

The old man flicked his fingers in the air like he was dusting off an invisible object. The thugs moved as one to leave the room.

"Bruno," he called to the bald one in the blue suit. "Wait outside the door."

He returned to his speech. "You may leave now if you go quietly. Make a scene and this gets ugly." He pointed at the younger twin. "We know where you live, and after my people review the recordings of you at the table and understand the situation, they're going to come visit you for an explanation." He swung his finger to the door. "Now go."

Sparky rose from the couch, and when he sensed that the younger twin was going to push to keep his winnings, he reached down and tapped his arm. "It's okay. Let's talk outside."

"Oh," called the old man when they reached the door. "You're both banned for life from this casino and its partner properties. So is your friend at the table."

Bruno followed the three as they skulked out of the casino and into their car. On the drive back to the Lev, the younger twin moaned as if he were in pain. "I am so screwed. What am I going to do?"

"We're going to continue with today's plan so you have money to pay for a first-class legal defense," said the older twin. "When the casino comes visiting, you sit back and let your lawyers do the talking. They'll back off."

"I'm not going into the city." The younger man shook his head. "Let's go home. Anyway, if you haven't noticed, the casino kept our seed funding."

Their mission today had two pieces. The first was to generate wealth using future knowledge. They'd proven that the idea was sound, though they clearly needed to practice discretion.

The second part was to explore ways for moving financial assets across timelines. Among other reasons, this was needed because the older twin provided information the other two could use to build wealth. But there was no one to share future knowledge with him so he could build his fortune. The only way he could profit was if they moved some of the money up to his timeline.

Today, they planned to explore the use of precious stones such as diamonds, rubies, and emeralds as a means of carrying great wealth in a small bundle. To optimize quality at good prices, they planned to make their trial purchase in the Diamond District in New York City. And as the younger twin just noted, they had intended to use their casino winnings to fund the purchase.

"How will we pay for it?" the younger twin asked after a period of silence.

"We know exactly how much you have saved," said Sparky. "Don't be a baby about this."

"Not a chance." The younger twin folded his arms across his chest.

"We can go smaller. Say a ten-thousand-dollar purchase."

"No."

"Tell you what," said the older twin. "You can keep all the profit when we sell the stones in my timeline."

Sparky nodded. "You need money to pay for lawyers. It's either raise it or pay for it from savings."

The younger twin stiffened into sullen silence and didn't respond, instead staring out the window at the passing scenery.

When they reached the Lev, they sent the car back to Burlington and rode south to New York City. The Express made just three stops, getting them into the heart of the bustling metropolis ninety minutes later.

As they walked up West Forty-Seventh Street, they passed the glitzy stores hawking fashion jewelry and stopped at an understated establishment with a simple sign touting the wares of Lee's Direct Gems, a midlevel supplier who sold investment-grade diamonds.

The entryway for the business, a rust-red steel door located a few steps into a side alley, didn't inspire Sparky's confidence. Inside the store, the sight of the fat security guard with a gun, snoozing in a corner chair, brought him to a halt, causing the twins to bump into him from behind.

His unease continued as they made their purchase. Everything about the transaction reminded Sparky of drug buys he'd seen in the vids. The seller kept his wares in little folded envelopes; he referred to his "product" as "really good stuff"; he seemingly conjured prices out of thin air; and he glanced furtively at the guard every time he mentioned money.

They left with a single ultra-high-quality diamond, surprisingly small for the hefty sum of eleven thousand dollars. The salesman had assured them that this level of quality not only held its value, but competition for such a rare gem would make it grow more precious over the next few years. Their purchase included a certificate detailing the stone's unique characteristics.

The next step in their master plan was to jump ahead to the older twin's timeline and sell the diamond, gaining the appreciated value of the stone in the process. To do that, they needed to travel home to the T-box.

They slept on the Lev during the trip to Burlington. Tired but determined, once there, they jumped to the older twin's timeline, returned to the Lev, and dozed as it carried them back into the city.

Arriving at Lee's Direct Gems, they found a different guard sitting in the corner, but the same smiling salesman behind the counter.

"We'd like to sell this stone," said the younger twin, setting the envelope with the diamond on the countertop.

"Of course!" the man replied enthusiastically. He

removed the stone from its packaging and spent several minutes studying it under magnification, shining lights through it, weighing it, and making notes. "What an outstanding specimen. You have a good eye."

Then he looked up from his work. "I can offer you three thousand for it. Cash."

"What?" the three Sparky's exclaimed in unison. "We paid eleven thousand for it!"

The man sat back and rearranged the items on his worktable. "I know it's tough to hear, but I'm in the diamond *selling* business." He gave a quick shrug. "When I buy inventory, I need to get it at wholesale prices. Otherwise, there's no profit in it for me, and trust me, the rent alone on this store is astronomical. I also need to pay for him." The salesmen pointed at the sleeping guard in the corner.

The younger twin tried to speak but produced only gasps and groans.

"The way to get your money back out," the salesman continued, "is to find a buyer yourself. People are always looking to invest. Find one who wants your stone."

Sparky knew they would never find that one buyer, let alone the thousands of buyers they'd need to move tens or even hundreds of millions of dollars of "product."

When they left Lee's Direct Gems, the younger twin took the diamond with him, unwilling to sell at such a devastating loss.

Back on the Lev, Sparky's mood stayed dark, his ire focused on David Lagerford. He felt like the man had dangled fantastic wealth in front of him, but every time

Sparky reached out to take it, the prize was yanked away.

As the Lev pulled into Burlington, Sparky felt a decision gelling. "If we can't earn it, we need to take it."

The older Sparky nodded. "Let's go have a chat with Lagerford."

12. Diesel, Thirty-Five timeline

The static tingle from Fifty-Five's T-disc washed across Diesel's body, and he worried that Sparky might grab him out of the air a second time. He'd just begun to fret, though, when he arrived in the dark confines of a T-box.

Looking carefully around, he scrutinized every scratch and nick in the cabin. But try as he might, he couldn't say for certain that he was home—he simply hadn't paid enough attention to recognize his machine at a detailed level. And until he was sure, he planned on staying inside so he had an escape route out.

Inching the T-box door open, he saw Lilah and, behind her, Fifty-Five and his Rose. With a sigh of relief, he stepped out to greet them. His feet flared in pain when he exited, and he dropped to his butt to seek relief.

Mid-maneuver, he called out. "We've got a problem. A big one."

"David!" Lilah squealed as she ran over. Down on her knees, she gripped him in a bear hug and let loose a barrage of questions. "Where have you been? Are you all right? Why didn't you send word?" She pulled her head back. "Why are you sitting on the ground?"

Rose tossed Diesel a robe, and Lilah helped him poke

his arms through the sleeves.

"My feet are banged up. Can you help me into a chair?"

Rose rolled an office chair over, and Lilah and Fifty-Five helped Diesel into it.

As he fixed his robe, he tried to get to the heart of the matter. "Sparky's making a play in the Fifty-Four timeline. We need to get reinforcements there quick!"

"Everything is fine," said Fifty-Five in a soothing voice. "You're home safe."

Lilah put a hand on his forehead. "Are you okay? Where have you been? We've been worried sick."

"I got kidnapped during a jump." He spoke in a rush, his tone urgent. "Some guy in the Fifty-Five timeline intercepted your ball-on-a-string broadcast and built a box. His brothers did, too. Now there are Sparkys up and down the timelines trying to get rich."

Fifty-Five lowered himself to one knee in front of Diesel and looked from one eye to the other. "Are you okay? Do you know how long you've been gone?"

"Yeah, two days plus. It sucked. I was hijacked and imprisoned. Now I need you to focus." He looked over his shoulder toward the cubicles. "Is there anything to eat? I'm starving."

Lilah brought him a stale cheese sandwich left over from lunch. As he ate, he told them a longer version, throwing an accusatory glare at Lilah and Rose as he spoke. "Your transponder succeeded in broadcasting T-box build plans, all right, but it wasn't targeted as you had intended. Apparently, it can be heard up and down the timelines. This radio enthusiast guy—maybe not radio, but that idea up in your timeline, Fifty-Five—heard the broadcast. Anyway, the guy—he goes by 'Sparky'—followed the instructions and managed to build a working T-box."

Lilah squatted, lifted one of Diesel's legs, rested his heel on her knee, and studied his wounds. "What happened to your feet?"

"Sparky had me imprisoned in his basement. When I finally escaped, I ran for miles with no shoes over some really rough ground."

Fifty-Five stopped pacing and squared up in front of him. "All of this is serious? It actually happened?"

Diesel took the last bite of sandwich and stared at him as he chewed.

"What does any of this have to do with Fifty-Four?" Fifty-Five resumed his pacing. "You said something about needing reinforcements?"

Diesel nodded. "Is there another sandwich?" While Lilah went for more food, Diesel continued. "I saw three Sparkys when I was in the basement. They looked so similar, I'm guessing they were from adjacent years. And this wasn't back with Twenty-Five—I was in your timeline the whole time." He pointed at Fifty-Five with his chin. "I got back to your place by car."

Diesel accepted a sandwich from Lilah and talked while he chewed. "They said they numbered in the dozens, just like us. The last I saw, three of them were jumping to the Fifty-Four timeline, one after the other. They know about you, your New Hampshire home, and that you used the T-box to get really rich. Sparky was crystal clear—he wants his."

"How can they know where I live?"

Diesel cast a sideways glance at Rose and Lilah. "The sisters assumed that the only people listening would be friendlies. They included *a lot* of personal information in the broadcast."

"We had to convince them it was real," said Rose. "What better way than to tell them stuff only they would know?"

"Okay," said Fifty-Five, waving his hands to shush everyone. "My brain is ready to hear this. Start at the beginning and let us ask questions as you go."

It took most of an hour before the three listeners stopped asking questions.

"We need to find where Sparky lives," said Diesel. "Your Luca can get us close. Maybe I can backtrack from there."

"You aren't thinking of leaving again?" Lilah's tone had an indignant edge.

Diesel's expression hardened. "I didn't cause this. But I sure as hell need to help get it under control."

Lilah stared at him for three heartbeats and then nodded. "Please spend a few minutes with your daughter before you go. She's worried sick about you."

Diesel checked the time, then looked at Rose and Fifty-Five. "Will you stay for dinner? We can brainstorm a plan while I catch up with my family."

"We'd love to," said Rose before Diesel finished talking.

Cornered, Fifty-Five nodded his agreement.

"Luca, get me my Rose," Diesel called to the air.

An image of nine-year-old Rose, grinning from ear to ear, appeared in the big display. "Hi, Pumpkin. I've missed you like crazy and will be up for dinner in a few minutes."

"Hooray!" young Rose cheered, pumping a hand into the air.

The face of an older woman materialized next to his daughter's—Louise Spencer, Lilah's mom.

Diesel's face froze and Lilah explained. "Mom was helping while you were away."

"Wonderful!" His fixed expression and flat tone belied the declaration.

Diesel liked Mom well enough. But Mom and Lilah got on each other's nerves, and when it got bad, Mom would voice complaints about her daughter to Diesel. He always remained neutral, which caused her to extend her grievances to him as well.

In his irritation, Diesel sometimes drank more beer than he should. During a visit last year, that very progression led the three to exchange words they all regretted. Visits had been awkward ever since.

Diesel did his best to recover. "Chinese takeout sound good?" With assent all around, he shifted the task of coordinating food delivery to Luca.

Then he focused on his feet. "Let's spray antiseptic on them, wrap them in gauze, and layer on a few pairs of socks. I'll limp around like that until I can get access to the magic medicine in Fifty-Five's timeline."

With his feet bandaged, Diesel pulled on pants and a shirt, and they ascended to the apartment. Lilah insisted on supporting him, but he put his weight on the handrail as they climbed the stairs to keep from burdening her.

Lilah and Diesel had long ago agreed to keep her mother in the dark about T-box travel, so Diesel introduced Fifty-Five and Rose as their neighbors, Don and his daughter Iris. Mom kept looking at Fifty-Five as if she were trying to place him, so Lilah pulled her away to set the table for dinner.

Diesel followed Fifty-Five into the living area, but his attention remained on the interaction between the two Roses.

Nine-year-old Rose knew that her father had older and younger brothers who lived in different timelines. She'd met most of them, and their similar looks and behaviors stood as proof of time travel in her eyes.

And if there were other Diesels, that meant there were other Roses. Those Roses couldn't travel the way her father could, but she knew her mother had been working to solve that problem.

"Do you know who I am?" twenty-nine-year-old Rose asked her.

"Of course," said the youngster. Looking up at her, the child leaned left and then right. Next, she stepped back and ran her eyes up and down adult Rose's body. "You are so pretty. You're twenty-nine?"

Adult Rose nodded.

"I turn out *great*." She grabbed her older sister by the hand. "Let's go up to our room. Will you help me fix my hair like yours?"

Rose caught Diesel's eye as his daughter dragged her across the floor. He winked his approval.

When they reached the stairs, both Roses turned spontaneously and called, "C'mon, Andy."

The dog bounded from the kitchen and raced ahead of them up the stairs.

Now alone, Fifty-Five slumped into the couch, and Diesel sat next to him in an overstuffed chair.

"Could you get us beers, love?" Diesel called. He wasn't in the habit of being waited on, but he wanted to separate daughter from mother.

Lilah brought two bottles into the living area.

"Thanks, hon," Diesel said in a loud voice. "How's it going?" he whispered.

"So far, so good. Where's Rose?"

"Both of them are upstairs. Our Rose is getting a makeover."

Lilah rolled her eyes. "At least I approve of the role model."

She returned to the kitchen, and Diesel put it to Fifty-Five.

"Sparky imprisoned me and was ready to keep me there for God knows how long. That's a person with a cold nature. If that's his starting point, can you imagine how far he'll be willing to push the stakes to get what he wants?"

"What do we do?" Fifty-Five's foot wiggled under the coffee table.

"If we find where he lives in one timeline, we've found him in all of them. So let's focus our resources on your timeline, since that's where I got snatched. Your Luca knows where the car met me near the woods. A group of us can start there and search for him. I kept to the left at every fork during my escape, so we'll keep right as we retrace my steps."

"What happens when we find him?"

"We break his T-box and take away his plans so he can't fix it or build another." Diesel's foot began wiggling as well. "He's a novice at jumping, so we have a tactical advantage if we can act quickly."

Fifty-Five picked at the label on his beer bottle with his thumbnail. "What's going on with the Fifty-Four timeline? Why him?"

"No idea. The T-box display said that three of them jumped to the Fifty-Four timeline. The way my Sparky was talking before he jumped, I assumed that meant that Fifty-Four was the target of whatever they had planned. Looking back, though, none of them ever said what they were up to, so I was just guessing at their intent." Diesel checked the time. "Sparky said he'd be back tonight, and my instinct is that means a few hours from now. So whatever they were doing, they're probably finished."

"I'll check on Fifty-Four on the way home to make sure he's okay." Fifty-Five straightened up from his slouch. "So, in a few hours, the Sparkys will learn that you escaped. They'll reason that we're coming for them. And they know where I live."

Diesel nodded slowly. "Everything about this is bad news."

Luca announced the arrival of the Chinese takeout down in the building lobby. Fifty-Five went to retrieve the food while Diesel hobbled toward the dining table.

"I'll go get Rose and Iris," announced Mom.

Diesel stopped her. "Iris is helping Rose with some personal issues, and I'd prefer not to disturb them." He looked to Lilah for support. "We can bring their food upstairs. Let's give them privacy while they work through it."

Mom huffed and looked everywhere but at Diesel or Lilah.

"You know that age, Mom," said Lilah. "Everything seems like a crisis, and parents haven't a clue. She's getting adult guidance from someone we approve of. Let's leave them alone."

"She's your daughter," said Mom, studying a picture on the wall.

Despite the rocky start to dinner, the conversation stayed pleasant with "Don" entertaining Mom with obviously embellished stories. They were clearing the table when the Roses descended the stairs.

Young Rose had restyled hair and added a touch of makeup to match adult Rose. They looked like different-sized twins, both grinning from ear to ear.

"Adult guidance, indeed," muttered Mom as she moved into the kitchen and took charge of cleanup.

Despite his foot discomfort, Diesel accompanied Fifty-Five and adult Rose to the basement. They were arranging themselves around the table in Diesel's cubicle when Lilah joined them.

Fifty-Five started. "If they're after wealth, let's pay them to go away."

"I already offered," said Diesel. "Sparky wants a trillion dollars."

Fifty-Five coughed. "Will he accept a check?"

"He wants to go back and manipulate his own timeline to make himself young, rich, and famous. I explained multiple times that it doesn't work that way. He's not buying it and insists we show him how to get his payoff." Diesel shifted in his chair. "Either that or give him the trillion."

Lilah, holding hands with Rose, looked mortified at the turn of events. "What are we going to do?"

Diesel raised the stakes. "Which brother has the best fabrication equipment? We need tools we can carry through the modified T-boxes."

Lilah shifted in her seat. "When you say 'tools,' do you mean weapons?"

Diesel didn't respond, instead keeping his eyes on Fifty-Five.

"Fifty-Three and up all have capable fab cells," said Fifty-Five. "I have a really nice setup. It could make a gun with a carbon lattice so pure, the weapon would be made from actual diamonds. On a practical level, though, the fabricator uses a mix of chemicals to maximize the weapon's performance."

"No metal anywhere?" asked Diesel. "How long does it take?"

Fifty-Five shook his head to the question about metal as he answered the second question. "Couple of hours."

Rose shuffled her chair closer to Lilah's. "How did this turn into an armed conflict?"

"You were up in Rose's bedroom when we were talking about it," said Diesel. "Sparky kidnapped me and was ready to keep me prisoner for weeks. This guy is playing hardball. If we aren't ready to play hardball back, we're going to get hurt."

Rose broke eye contact, but Diesel didn't relent. "Are you still transmitting build instructions from your ball on a string?"

She shook her head. "No. When we broadcast, the T-box can't be used for anything else. I pulled the transponder so I could jump here."

"Your broadcasting days are over. Agreed?" Diesel looked from Rose to Lilah and back.

The two nodded. Then Lilah said to Rose, "I don't get why the T-box showed the words 'Twenty-Five incoming' if it was connecting to the Fifty-Five timeline. Diesel said you saw it on your machine, too?"

Rose remained somber. "We've learned that the transponder-and-leash project had problems. It wouldn't surprise me to learn the T-box build plans we transmitted had problems as well."

Fifty-Five patted the table with his palm. "Enough with the recriminations. How many brothers should we have in the search party?"

"Four or five to start," said Diesel. "If we strike out, we'll go bigger."

Rose stood. "I'll bet my Luca can narrow down Sparky's location. He's linked to a ton of feeds and archives, and he's smart as hell. I'm going to head back and get him started on a search. I should have some solid leads by tomorrow morning."

Lilah followed Rose to the T-box. "Could you use

some help?"

"Yes, but I'm a morning person and it's getting late. I was going to get Luca started on this and then go to bed. If you want to join me tomorrow, we can learn what he's discovered over morning coffee."

Lilah beamed. "I'm a morning person too. Should we start at seven?"

"Let's go for six thirty."

"Wait, Rose," said Fifty-Five, walking to them. "I don't want you jumping to an empty house where this madman could be lying in wait. Let me go first and you follow." He turned to Diesel. "After I've secured the house, I'll go check on Fifty-Four. If he's okay, I'll swing by the clubhouse to let everyone know. If I don't show up in the next hour, send help."

Lilah gave Fifty-Five a peck on the cheek. "See you for coffee tomorrow morning?"

He shook his head. "Not at six thirty you won't." After waving to Diesel, Fifty-Five climbed into the T-box and shut the door.

Rose waited for the cycle to complete. "I'm not sure how Dad's caution helped, because he's either waiting patiently for me or in the fight of his life with this Sparky guy. I guess I'll find out soon enough." With a stilted laugh, she stepped into the T-box and engaged the machine.

As the T-box cycled, Lilah made for the stairs. "I'm going to put Rose to bed. Mom will get her off to school tomorrow morning. I expect to be back from Fifty-Five's in time for dinner." She stopped and looked back. "Are you coming?"

Diesel wanted to give her his blessing to make a jump but believed he was owed an explanation for being excluded from an activity so consequential to the family. At the same time, he wouldn't deny her dream. So he punted. "Sorry, my love. I have to go organize tomorrow's search party. I'll be up after that."

13. Rose, Fifty-Five timeline

As Rose passed through the kitchen, she called to Luca, "There will be two of us for breakfast this morning. I'll be joined by Lilah from the Thirty-Five timeline. Have Marian set us up in the conservatory. Give us the works."

With ten minutes before Lilah was due to arrive, Rose made her way to the basement. She hoped to straighten up a bit so her mom-sister wouldn't judge her too harshly. At the bottom of the stairs, though, she shook her head as she viewed the scatter of tools, parts, and packaging around the T-box.

With a mental shrug, Rose accepted that she didn't have time to put a dent in the disorder. The matter was taken out of her hands moments later when the T-box came alive—Lilah was on her way. Rose used the five-minute countdown to clear the worst of the mess near the path they would take to the stairs. Feeling the static wash, she wiped her hands on a rag and tossed it behind some shelves.

"I thought about dressing up for morning tea," said Lilah, closing the cabin door behind her. "But I went for practical instead."

Rose approached her for a hug, thinking she looked

terrific in her blouse and jeans. "You're perfect, but let's get out of here while that cute top is still white."

In the kitchen, Lilah called to the air, "Hello, Luca."

"Good morning, Lilah." When the lifelike AI appeared in the kitchen, Lilah passed a hand through him, then grinned.

Rose changed her plans on the spot. "Would you like a tour of the place before we start?"

"Yes, please!" Lilah's head swiveled as she viewed the rest of the kitchen.

Watching her, Rose couldn't shake the feeling that she was in the presence of her mother. Lilah was about the same age her mom had been when she'd passed, so she looked the part. Her familiar behaviors, the words she used, the sound of her voice, and the way she smelled all worked to cement the illusion. Intellectually, Rose knew her mother would be fifty-five by now, but her mind ignored the discrepancy so she could experience the joy.

"Let's go this way." Rose pointed. "We'll check out the T-disc room, Dad's office, and my workshop."

The home had twenty years of future-tech and high-end options that would be new to Lilah. While wood floors, painted walls, and stairs with steps were still the norm, Rose wanted to highlight how the technology of daily living had changed.

Just as they began their tour, Rose held up a finger and stopped. "Wait here. I'll be back in a sec." She scurried across the kitchen and into the conservatory, where she scooped up the two mother-of-pearl barrettes she'd placed on a side table. On her return, she pulled her hair back over an ear and used a barrette to hold it in place. As she did, she felt Luca connect with her brain.

In the kitchen, Rose held out the other barrette for Lilah. "This is a neural link. It lets you interact with Luca and the house tech just by thinking. I was going to show you this when we sat for breakfast, but Luca will liven up the tour. Do you want to give it a try?"

"David told me about this. What do I do?"

"Just put it in your hair so these feelers touch the skin on your skull." She held the barrette so Lilah could see the filaments protruding from one side. "You can show it off like I'm doing, or you can hide it under your hair in back. Either works."

Lilah pulled her hair over one ear to match Rose and looked around the kitchen. "Is there a mirror?"

Luca appeared with a large hand-mirror and held it so Lilah could see her reflection. After checking how Rose wore the barrette, Lilah placed hers so the two matched.

"Whoa," said Lilah, looking around the room as Luca linked with her brain. "This is amazing."

"Luca adapts to your preferences. I got rid of the info tabs along the bottom of his default display, and I let him boost full features on visual and audio. Try boosting your sight and sound. See how everything becomes crisp and balanced?"

Lilah looked around the room and nodded.

"I have him filter out smells so only neutral and pleasant odors register in my brain. And I've learned to keep him away from flavor. His enhancements make everything taste different. I don't like it."

Rose reached out and stroked Lilah's arm. "Check out what he can do for touch. That's what normal feels like." Without speaking, she instructed Luca to enhance skin sensitivity for Lilah, with a focus on the soft and sensual aspects. She stroked Lilah's arm again.

"Oh my God." Lilah moaned and hugged herself. "That felt wonderful."

"Imagine being with a partner where you both have that feature going across your whole body." Rose smiled. "I just wanted to give you a hint of what's possible with this tech."

"I want this in my timeline."

"Like everything, it has its pluses and minuses." Rose shrugged. "The new fad is having your neural link implanted. I'm not ready for that level of commitment to my tech, and neither is Dad."

Pointing the way, she started the tour, but ten minutes in, Rose found the experience less fun than she'd anticipated. Lilah, distracted by the powerful AI in her head, turned inward and went quiet. Rose felt like she was talking to herself.

When the situation persisted for a few rooms, Rose moved them on task. "Let's get to work and finish the tour later."

Lilah oohed and ahhed when they entered the conservatory, a stunning mostly glass room with a ceiling high enough to accommodate a collection of small trees and climbing vines. They walked a path through the greenery to an island of handsome furniture.

Rose waited as Lilah looked around the room,

knowing her next reaction would come when she saw the view—a dramatic panorama of the valley below.

"It's breathtaking!" Lilah exclaimed, stepping closer to the windows.

When Lilah began to sway, Rose knew that Luca was giving her the grand tour. His valley excursion made you feel like you were flying over the hillsides as he glided you past amazing wildlife and dramatic geographic features. His extended tour included virtual visits to notable homes along the mountain ridges, a sampling of the popular winter and summer sports, an overview of the local history, and more.

"Luca," Rose called aloud. "Please keep the tour short. We have work to do."

She'd committed a major faux pas by speaking to the AI about a linked human. In polite society, one *always* addressed the person. But she was anxious to hear what Luca had learned about Sparky and counted on Lilah's inexperience to miss her gaffe.

Lilah, seemingly unaware, turned to Rose and smiled. "This is so cool, but I agree, let's get started."

Rose invited Lilah to sit at a table laden with sweet and savory delights. Their chairs were positioned so they could enjoy the valley view as they ate.

"I usually have just coffee and yogurt," said Rose, "but I wanted to make it special."

As they took their seats, Maid Marian approached with a carafe of coffee.

"Oh, hello," said Lilah, who sat back and folded her hands in her lap while Marian poured.

"Marian is a bot." Rose had thought it was obvious,

but Lilah's behavior suggested otherwise.

"Really?" Lilah studied the lifelike machine as it went about its business.

When Marian finished, they sampled and sipped for a few moments, then Rose prompted Luca. "Please update us with what you've learned about Sparky."

An image of a road leading into a tree-filled suburb appeared in front of them. "His name is Paul Fontaine, and he lives on this street, Hilltop Circle. It's a cul-de-sac with eight homes, each on a multiacre plot. There are no municipal cameras I can access anywhere on the street. The best I can do is show where Hilltop Circle meets this main road, Pinecrest Drive."

"Is he home now?" asked Rose.

"He has not come in view of this camera since he returned from work yesterday afternoon."

"What do we know about him?"

"He's a master technician at Northern Droid," said Luca. "Has been for the past nine years. He lives alone, has no friends, and spends his time either at work or at home."

"How was he able to build a T-box?" asked Lilah.

"I have not verified that he has the device, but if he does, it means he obtained a set of plans and the money to gather parts. His nickname, Sparky, comes from his passion for electrical instruments that he uses to explore and monitor the signal spectrum. It's possible that his hobby let him tap into your transponder broadcast."

Lilah signaled for Marian to bring more coffee. "Buying all those parts is pricey as hell. Is he rich?"

"No. He can't afford the parts, but he could

appropriate them from his workplace if he were unscrupulous."

Wiping her mouth with a napkin, Rose caught Lilah's eye. "I would say a guy who can kidnap and imprison a fellow human has unscrupulous tendencies."

Leveling her eyebrows, Lilah asked Luca, "Have you seen more than one Sparky? Maybe twins or triplets?"

"I've found four occasions in the record where two of them traveled together by car on this road."

"Good morning!" boomed a voice from behind them.

Rose turned to see her father entering the room, a mug of steaming coffee in his raised hand.

"Hey, Dad."

"Good morning, David." Lilah stood and gave him a kiss, then rested a hand on his arm. "Gorgeous place. I approve."

Fifty-Five blinked rapidly, and Rose, seeing her father enjoy having a Lilah in their home for the first time in fourteen years, stood and motioned for him to join them. "Come see what we've learned."

Fifty-Five dragged a chair over and squeezed in between Rose and Lilah. Reaching across the table, he took the community plate of scrambled eggs, mounded some onto a piece of toast, and lurched forward for a bite, capturing most of the yellow pile before it toppled.

"Okay." He took a sip of coffee while he chewed. "Let me have it."

Rose brought him up to date on what they'd learned.

"How can we confirm that he built a T-box?" asked Fifty-Five. "There has to be some clever way to find out."

"He'd be using a lot of power," said Lilah. "I wonder if we can trace it that way."

"The shell of a walk-in fridge!" blurted Rose.

Fifty-Five turned to her. "What about it?"

Lilah nodded. "It's so big it has to be delivered by truck."

"Which means it would have to travel that road." Rose pointed at Pinecrest Drive in the image floating in front of them. "Luca, can you get access to the archive for this camera and search it for the delivery of an aluminum refrigerator shell? It should look like the one I have in the basement."

Luca acknowledged the request and started the search. While they waited, Lilah asked Fifty-Five, "When are the brothers due to arrive?"

Fifty-Five checked the time. "Oh, crap! I'll be right back." Starting for the door, he abruptly returned to the table, folded a handful of bacon into a piece of toast, took a bite, and carried the food with him as he made for the exit. "Marian," he called with his mouth full. "Ready breakfast for five more."

14. Lilah, Fifty-Five timeline

When Fifty-Five bent over to assemble his bacon sandwich, Lilah noticed the tiny appliance tucked behind his ear. She thought to ask if it was his neural link, but since he was running late, she chose to ask later.

"It is indeed his neural link," Luca confirmed for her.

"How can you know what I'm thinking?" Lilah shook her head, amazed by the level of interaction the AI provided.

"I can only perceive your hard thoughts—those that crystalize in the front of your mind when you are about to speak. I can't see random ideas and concept fragments swirling deep in your brain. And when I do interpret a thought, there's inference and deduction involved, so sometimes I get it wrong."

Lilah's eyebrows rose when Maid Marian lifted a large table by herself, carried it over in an ungainly shuffle, and placed it next to their table.

"Which brothers are coming?" Lilah asked Luca by thought.

"Forty has arrived and Forty-One is transferring now. Fifty-Five has not shared any information with me beyond that."

"But you must know. You listen to everything he says and does."

"Yes. But until he explicitly tells me, it is knowledge I won't share. I will extend the same courtesy to you if others ask about your thoughts."

Lilah found herself nodding. "Will you tell me when my Diesel arrives—Thirty-Five?"

"Forty-One has completed his jump, and Thirty-Five's cycle has just started. He will arrive in this timeline in about five minutes."

Lilah watched the door for Diesel, even though he'd need to dress first. With other brothers in the T-disc room, that process alone could add another twenty minutes. But this day was a high point in her life, and she wanted to share it with him. She felt an emotional lift knowing she'd soon get the chance.

Then her thoughts swung back to Sparky and she turned to Rose. "Finding the delivery truck carrying the refrigerator shell is something we can have Luca duplicate in the other timelines. It will tell us how many Sparkys have a machine, or at least are trying to build one."

"That's a great idea." Rose, who'd been staring into the distance, looked at Lilah. "I'm frustrated that *we* can't be the ones investigating. Until we can travel the range of timelines, though, we're stuck watching." Her eyebrows scrunched. "Am I a bad person for making this about us?"

Lilah shook her head. "Now that we've had a taste, it's hard to hold back. Everyone will feel the same way. And we need help from the sisters if we're to solve the Sparky problem."

Marian entered the conservatory, hefting a broad tray piled high with food, plates, and utensils. She placed it on a stand near the table she'd just moved and worked with a hypnotic efficiency to unload it, readying the table for the five visiting brothers.

"The sisters at timelines that have T-boxes can make the modification and be visiting with us in about two weeks," said Rose. "That would bring in the Twenty-Nine through Thirty-Nine timelines."

"But the Sparkys are here in the Fifties."

"I know." Rose shook her head in frustration. "It took me three months to build the machine in the basement. Having been through it once, I can help the neighboring Roses shorten that to about two months. Still, though, it will be a while before we can get Roses from the Fifties involved."

Looking out over the valley, Lilah saw an eagle soaring along the far ridge. Luca adjusted her visual processing, and the bird came into focus. She continued watching the eagle as she spoke. "They talked about destroying Sparky's T-box and erasing his documents, but is that even possible? In my timeline, it's hard to delete anything once it's touched the web. Why would it be possible here?"

"It's not. But that doesn't mean the information has been spread around the world. If Sparky has a neural implant, then he's carrying inside his head everything he'll need to build another T-box. It's the safest place to secure data because he's the only one who can ever access it."

"It's stored in his head?"

Rose gave a quick shrug. "With an implant, he can

watch himself building the first T-box—literally replay it in his mind—and guide himself as he makes the next one. He'll even be able to avoid repeating any mistakes he made the first time, and we're helpless to stop him."

Lilah hugged herself. "What have we done? This is so terrible."

"It's another reason why we need to be involved. This is our mess to clean up."

15. Diesel, Fifty-Five timeline

Diesel followed his brothers through the kitchen and into the conservatory. When the group veered toward the food, he headed for Lilah, who smiled as he approached.

"This neural link with Luca is amazing," she said. "You didn't do it justice in describing it to me."

Though he still harbored a certain resentment toward her secretive behavior, he nodded. "I felt bad telling you about wonderful things that I thought you could never experience, so I toned it down."

"In a way, I understand. I'm excited to learn what else you haven't told me about."

"As am I." He knew his jab connected when she pressed her lips together and looked at the floor.

Then she met his gaze. "I didn't mean to keep it from you, David. Our success came quickly after years of failure. I'd been about to share when you got kidnapped. I'm really sorry."

Her apologetic tone filled him with relief because he was miserable when conflict separated them. He kissed her on the cheek and whispered a bedtime nickname to reestablish intimacy. "Thank you, Lolli. I'm glad your dream has come true."

Diesel drifted over to the food table after that. Grabbing a slice of toast, he piled scrambled eggs on top and swooped in to take a bite before the mound toppled. As he sipped his coffee, he noticed that all his brothers were engaged in a similar ritual with eggs and toast, turning the simple act of eating into an unappetizing spectacle.

When the brothers progressed to coffee, Rose summarized what Luca had discovered, and after that, Lilah expressed concern over Sparky's neural storage of the T-box plans. "If data is stored in his head, Rose says there's no way for us to access it, and that means we can't erase it."

Forty looked at her. "You're saying that he'll remember everything for as long as he's alive?"

Lilah looked to Rose, who nodded.

The big man flashed a ghoulish grin. "A problem we can solve."

The two women paled, though their expressions remained fixed. After an awkward pause, the brothers started a vigorous discussion, with everyone asking and answering questions until they all came to a common understanding that Diesel articulated. "Let's split up and visit the timelines from, say, Forty-Five through Sixty. We'll ask each Luca to search the archives for a truck delivering a commercial walk-in-style refrigerator to Hilltop Circle. Bring your results back here by noon for a lunch meeting. We'll compile the results and learn the scope of our problem."

The brothers showed their approval by attacking the food, recharging themselves with a last round of sustenance before heading off on their assignments.

Diesel's first visit was one timeline up to Fifty-Six, and in just a few minutes of searching, Luca found an aluminum-shell refrigerator being delivered to Sparky's street. Diesel then spent the next hour giving Fifty-Six a blow-by-blow of his kidnapping ordeal, a crash course on the Sparkys, and an overview of the brother's new reality.

When it came time for Diesel to depart for his next stop, Fifty-Six, distressed that he was in the crosshairs of a sociopath who lived just a couple of hours down the road, spoke in a rush. "No way I'm going to sit here and wait for this Sparky nutjob to show up at my door. Rose is visiting a friend in Boston, so I'm coming with you."

Happy for the company, the two brothers completed Diesel's rounds—the Fifty-Seven and Fifty-Eight timelines. Neither of those Lucas could find evidence of a refrigerator delivery, or Sparky twins traveling together, or anything else that might be worrisome. The news buoyed Diesel because it implied that the problem was capped on the upper end at the Fifty-Six timeline.

Eager to hear what the other brothers had learned and starting to feel the early pangs of hunger, Diesel and Fifty-Six returned to the Fifty-Five timeline. With an hour until lunch, Diesel grabbed an apple and sat with Lilah and Rose, who were compiling the results as each brother returned.

Early reporting looked good. They knew there was a T-box in the Fifty-Five timeline, since that's where Diesel had been kidnapped. And using the "refrigerator method," Diesel had just confirmed one existed in the Fifty-Six timeline. "I saw three Sparkys jump to the Fifty-Four timeline, so we better have a positive sighting there or this method is a bust."

The group cheered when Forty returned twenty minutes later and confirmed the delivery of an aluminum refrigerator shell in the Fifty-Four timeline. More cheering followed when Rose reported that, according to the official tally, the three Sparkys they knew of comprised the entirety of the threat.

Then came the difficult task of deciding what to do next.

"Maybe we should agree on an objective," said Lilah. "Then we can compare suggestions against that goal."

"Our objective is to remove their ability to travel, now and forever," said Forty.

"And do it quickly," added Diesel. "The longer we take to solve this, the more established the Sparkys become, and that makes them harder to dislodge."

"Here's my concern." Fifty-Five sat forward, lending strength to his message. "Let's say we break their T-boxes and somehow delete their build plans. They'll know *we* still have the tech." He shook his head. "I don't think they'll sit home and just forget about the promise of riches. I think they'll be scheming for a way to take that capability from us, by force if necessary."

"If we've broken their T-boxes," said Rose, "then they'll be isolated to their own timelines, so only one Sparky could show up here." She linked eyes with her father. "But that's still a scary thought."

"It isn't the number of Sparkys that worries me. With time travel as a bargaining chip, he could recruit governments to side with him."

"What if you move?" asked Lilah. "I know that's a crummy outcome, but if you disappear and maintain a low profile, how could he find you?"

"I'm not going to run from that asshole." A chorus of murmurs supported Fifty-Five's position.

"Our planning depends on knowing if Sparky has a neural implant," Diesel said a little louder than necessary so the group would focus. "Luca, is that something you could find out?"

"I would need to access private records."

"Are you able to do that?"

"Of course he can," scoffed Fifty-Five. "Luca is the result of thirty years of development by me, my Lilah, and Rose." He gestured to his daughter sitting across from him. "Add in ideas we borrowed from you all, stir with unlimited funds, and you get the most capable AI on the planet."

"And that includes the monsters they're building at the Defense Department," said Rose.

"Accessing private records is illegal," said Luca. "You must order me to do it."

"You may search," said Fifty-Five. When Luca didn't acknowledge, Fifty-Five expanded his order. "You have permission to search private records to confirm if Sparky has a neural implant."

After another pause, Rose said, "It's okay, Luca."

"Acknowledged," replied the AI.

The exchange prompted Diesel to reappraise Rose. Instead of giving Luca her permission by thought, she flexed her authority publicly, establishing either for her father or the group that she wasn't going to be pushed aside on whatever came next.

Across the room, Maid Marian entered, carrying the first tray of lunch service. Brothers gathered around her, eyeing the delights as she unloaded items onto the table.

Luca brought their attention back to Sparky. "Paul Fontaine received a neural implant two years ago from the Vermont Health Center in downtown Burlington."

"Is there really no way to erase something he has stored on it?" asked Diesel.

"He controls his own implant," said Luca, "so he is able to erase whatever he wants. But it's impossible for external parties to delete or edit individual items."

Rose sat up. "You used 'individual items' as a qualifier, implying there are ways to delete things, just not individually?"

"A device reset will erase everything and return the unit to its factory settings."

"How do we reset his implant?" asked Diesel.

"The approved method is conducted in a clinic with technical and medical support. It can be a traumatic procedure if not performed properly."

"That doesn't tell me how to do it."

"With the patient's head held steady, position an electronic device called a 'spire' against the back of the skull, synch it with the implant, then have the patient repeat a series of reset codes only he can hear in his head."

A flood of questions came from the group after that, and they debated everything while eating lunch: Where can we get a spire? What's involved with synching? Can someone other than the patient say the reset codes? Does the spire check for duress if we force Sparky to cooperate? Will the procedure kill him if we do it wrong?

Forty suggested the next step. "We need to scout the scene. I want to walk through his house to learn the layout and understand who he is. And we need to gauge the activity and attentiveness of his neighbors."

"Plus we need to verify our route in and out ahead of time," said Diesel. "I don't ever want to be lost in those woods again."

Lilah raised her hand, the formal act bringing a smile to the faces of several brothers. "You should do your scouting in the Fifty-Three and Fifty-Seven timelines. That way you bracket Fifty-Four, Five, and Six, so the information you gather is relevant. But those Sparkys can't communicate with ours, so there's no risk of tipping the bad ones off."

"Nice." Diesel nodded his support. "They won't know about us, T-boxes, or any of it. Hell, we could buy them a drink, tell them exactly what we're going to do to their brothers, and our Sparkys would never hear about it."

Planning intensified as they refined mission details. Then they divided into two teams. Diesel was on the team scouting the Fifty-Three timeline, partnering with Forty and Fifty-Five. As they discussed strategy, Lilah came over and sat next to him.

"I'm going to head back soon to fix dinner and put Rose to bed. Any idea how late you'll be?"

He took her hand and squeezed. "It will probably be tomorrow. We have two hours on the road to Burlington and two hours back, plus a few hours there for scouting around. And we'll probably wait until dark to even start."

Standing, he gave her a proper hug and kiss. "I wish I could be home."

She laid her head against his chest. "Me too."

* * *

Diesel, Forty, and Fifty-Five's arrival caught Fifty-Three by surprise, but it didn't take long to bring him up to speed.

"We want to learn about Sparky in a timeline without a T-box," said Diesel. "That way he can't warn the others when we're done."

Hearing that, Fifty-Three insisted on joining the team. Ushering the group down the hall to his office, he dragged his desk chair over to form a circle. "Luca, what does Sparky do for hobbies besides eavesdropping?"

"I can find transaction receipts that hint at a modest collection of New England art glass and antiques," Luca replied. "But his real passion is signal monitoring. He makes frequent, expensive purchases to ensure his equipment is state of the art."

"What's art glass?" asked Forty.

"If it's trinkets you put on a fireplace mantel, I smashed a bunch of it in Sparky's house during my escape." Diesel noticed Fifty-Three staring at him. "Not here. That was in the Fifty-Five timeline."

"Art glass is just like it sounds," said Fifty-Five. "It's paperweights, vases, and stuff like that made from pretty glass. We've all seen glass blowers working. It's a real craft."

Over the next hour, they worked their way into the

idea of mocking up Fifty-Three's old van so it looked like a furniture delivery truck. The van would lend an air of legitimacy as they approached Sparky's house, reassuring the neighbors as they worked to gain entry.

Luca created artwork panels appropriate for a company truck and printed them on material that adhered to the sides of the van. While they loaded a beautiful antique nightstand from one of Fifty-Three's guest rooms, Luca forged a purchase receipt for Paul Fontaine of Burlington, Vermont.

Climbing into the car, the men sat facing each other in classic limousine fashion. The vehicle had no steering wheel or other controls for the driver, and they took advantage of the space that freed up by stretching their legs.

Looking at the other three, Diesel shook his head. "We need clothes that make us seem more like a delivery crew."

Forty agreed. "And we should at least have gloves and hats that limit forensic evidence when we're inside Sparky's house."

Returning to the house, they rummaged through Fifty-Three's closets and chose jeans and dark T-shirts as their crew outfit. They completed their disguise with baseball caps and sunglasses taken from the camo bucket Fifty-Three kept in the T-disc room for visiting brothers.

"There will be cameras inside his house," fretted Fifty-Three. "We need better disguises than just caps and glasses."

In the end, they fished out Fifty-Three's Halloween costume box and brought it with them in the van. Diesel chose a fake nose, stick-on goatee, and pointy alien ears for his disguise.

While Fifty-Five took his turn with the costume box, he said, "This is just a scouting run, but we should still have a checklist of what we want to accomplish."

"A scouting run makes it sound like we're just there to look," said Forty. "I want to get inside Sparky's house *and* head."

They talked it through, agreeing they should familiarize themselves with the layout of his house, identify the entry and exit points, visit the area where the T-box might be located in the infected timelines, and assess Sparky's assortment of tools to ensure they had what they needed to dismantle his machine.

The one area of disagreement centered on how to treat Sparky in this timeline.

Diesel and Fifty-Five thought they should wait until morning to approach his house, entering after Sparky left for work. That way they wouldn't have to manage a confrontation.

Fifty-Three agreed with waiting for the house to be empty, but his motivation was based more on the fear of getting caught. "You all disappear when this is done. But if the authorities get involved and decide to expend resources, they'll trace it back to me. I know it."

Alone in his opinion but with the loudest voice, Forty wanted to bully past Sparky tonight, restrain him, and then go about their business at their leisure. "That way we get home at a reasonable hour."

The van turned onto Hilltop Circle a little before sunset. They'd timed it that way so they had sufficient light to see the neighborhood, followed by the necessary darkness to shroud their next moves.

As the street name suggested, the road dead-ended in a small circle. Eight handsome houses, each set back on wooded lots, were spaced along the short straightaway and around the loop.

"That's it," said Forty, pointing to a wood-framed home with gray siding and a well-tended yard.

Diesel didn't recognize the place—a one-story affair with an interesting roofline because of room additions made over the years. But the only time he'd been outside Sparky's house was when he was running for his life, so its unfamiliarity didn't surprise him.

"Luca," said Fifty-Three. "Can you tell if anyone is home?"

"Archived vid shows Paul Fontaine returning from work an hour ago," Luca replied. "I can track his car until it enters Hilltop Circle, and it is likely that he continued to his home. But I can't confirm it."

The van completed the loop and slowed, waiting for a command.

"Take the loop again, then exit onto the main road," Fifty-Three instructed the vehicle. To the group, he added, "We can't be seen driving in circles for too long or we'll draw suspicion."

The van spun around for a second time, and as it completed the loop, a light came on outside Sparky's house.

Forty sang out when the garage door started to lift. "We have movement."

"Pull into this driveway," Fifty-Three barked to the

van, pointing across the street from Sparky's. The house he'd chosen at random—set far back on a wooded lot— had been dark. But a porch light lit as the van nosed into the driveway.

While the others focused on Sparky's garage, Diesel watched the random house for further signs of life.

"I wonder where he's off to."

Diesel turned to see Sparky's car heading out of the neighborhood, the garage door closing behind him.

"Can you track him?" Fifty-Three called to Luca.

"I have him under surveillance. He's headed down the hill toward town."

"Can you override his home AI and keep it from contacting him?" asked Diesel.

"I can't override Portia, not on short notice. But I can block her signal out from the house for ten or twelve minutes."

"That's all?"

"Modern comms are resilient. Eventually, the signal will get through."

"Do it and tell us the moment he starts to return," said Fifty-Three. He directed their van to back across the street and into Sparky's driveway. The four of them piled out, and Diesel and Fifty-Three lifted the nightstand from the rear of the vehicle and set it on the driveway as a prop for the neighbors to see.

Shielded by the truck, Forty approached the front door with a crowbar. Wedging the tip between the door and jamb, he braced a foot against the wall, leaned back, and pulled, his muscles bulging as a grunt escaped his lips.

For a moment, Diesel thought the door would win. Then a heavy *pop* signaled its defeat. As it swung wide, they moved inside.

Diesel pushed the door shut behind them, though it didn't close the way it should. Then he led the group through the house, pointing with his finger to supplement his bulleted narration. "Living area. Dining room. Kitchen." He reached an unfamiliar hallway and signaled for the others to wait. Walking down its length, he looked into each room. "Bedroom. Home office. Bathroom. Sparky's master suite."

Luca interrupted. "Excuse me, but Portia, the house AI, has informed Paul Fontaine of an unauthorized entry. Fontaine has instructed his car to turn around and return home."

"Already?" said Diesel.

Fifty-Three interrupted. "Has either of them called the authorities?"

"No. Not yet."

"How far out is he?"

"About ten minutes."

The trauma of Diesel's recent imprisonment compelled him to focus on defense. "Luca should use the van to slow him down."

Fifty-Three tilted his head to show indecision, but when the others agreed, he acted. "Luca, take the van and move to intercept Fontaine's car. Start now. Keep us informed. You may intentionally violate traffic rules to halt his car's progress, but do *not* hurt anyone."

"Understood. The van is underway," replied Luca.

"Let's finish here." Forty started down the basement stairs. "The T-box is this way?"

Diesel barely recognized his prison. The basement had the same carpet, paint, and lighting. But instead of being open and clean, this one had cluttered shelves along the wall and a side table and chairs toward the back.

"The T-box in the Fifty-Five timeline sits right here." Diesel stood in the middle of the room and pointed down. Then he motioned toward the wall near the stairs. "He keeps his electronic listening gear in a setup behind this paneling. It's an impressive command center."

"Does the wall move up or over?" asked Forty.

"It moves that way," Diesel pointed to the side.

Wearing gloves to limit forensic evidence, Forty positioned his fingers behind a line of decorative molding and pulled in the direction Diesel indicated. The wall barely moved, but it was enough for Forty to improve his grip. He gave a fierce tug after that, and the wall slid open the rest of the way on its own. They studied the equipment together.

"I'm pretty sure this setup keeps copies of everything he hears," said Fifty-Five, scanning the array of electronics. "We'll have to destroy this along with the T-box."

Luca interrupted them. "The van will reach Fontaine's car in one minute."

"Do you have an opportunity to block it?"

"I can spoof a Meitner decision. It should succeed in blocking his passage."

Fifty-Three hesitated.

"Say 'yes.'" Forty nodded at Fifty-Three in an

exaggerated fashion for emphasis.

Fifty-Three studied the ground, almost as if he regretted being there, and confirmed the order for Luca.

They stood in silence after that, waiting to hear the result.

"What's a Meitner decision?" whispered Diesel.

Forty, who'd demanded this action, shook his head and shrugged.

"It's from a big lawsuit a few years back," said Fifty-Five. "If an accident is inevitable, a navigation AI will take last-second actions that can change who gets injured. Meitner's AI puts new mothers at the top of the list of those to save. Someone sued and a court sided with Meitner."

"How is a new mother at the top of the food chain?"

"If I remember right, they argued that she gets credit for her life plus a portion of the infant's. Something like that, anyway."

"Actually, the lawsuit was about ranking mothers above fathers," said Fifty-Three. "Meitner argued that mom's milk gave new mothers a slight edge for a few months. The court supported the decision as rational, which isn't the same as saying it's correct."

"Success," called Luca. "I spoofed the passenger manifest to show that the van was carrying three mothers with infants, then I pulsed the vehicle steering to create a pinch point with two other cars. They bumped fenders so I could pass safely. Fontaine's car is blocked for now."

"Good job, Luca!" called Fifty-Three.

Using the breathing room the AI had created for them, Diesel walked to the wall behind the stairs. "Sparky went in and out through this door a bunch of times while I was down here."

He opened it and stepped through to a well-outfitted workshop. The tools and devices were focused on electronics and light metal crafts, but Diesel was more familiar with woodworking equipment. Fanning out, the brothers opened drawers and cabinet doors, discovering all the tools they would need, plus some they didn't know how to use.

"Pay attention to where things are," Fifty-Five sang out. "We'll want to find stuff quickly when it counts."

While the others worked on tool inventory, Diesel climbed a second set of stairs at the back of the workshop. They led out to a two-car garage.

The bay for Sparky's car was empty. The other bay held a high-tech exercise pod. The pod's dust-free exterior, along with water bottles, athletic clothing, and towels hanging outside it, gave Diesel the impression that Sparky used the machine with some frequency.

"Fontaine has climbed out of his car," said Luca. "He's abandoned his vehicle and run into the woods at the side of the road. From the direction he's moving, I'd guess his destination is this house."

"How soon can he get here?" asked Fifty-Three.

"It depends on his fitness level. I would estimate between fifteen and thirty minutes."

"I'm looking at a well-used exercise rig here in the garage," Diesel called to the group. "I'd put money on the lower number."

"How fast can you get the van here?" Fifty-Three

asked in a strained voice.

"Four minutes."

"Do it. Everyone meet by the front door!"

As Diesel made his way to the rally point, he had an idea and pitched it. "If we break in and leave without doing anything else, Sparky will be curious about us and may want to know more. But if we steal something, he'll believe we're thieves. His curiosity will be satisfied."

Diesel found Fifty-Three and Fifty-Five by the front door.

Forty was by himself, walking through the living area. "Should we take something from here or from his office? Or maybe from his bedroom?"

Diesel faced the mantel. "Luca, can you see this? Is anything up there valuable?"

Fifty-Three walked to the mantel, and Diesel imagined Luca looking through his eyes. "Not up there, but on the shelf next to the mantel. The ornate box at the back is worth more than this house."

Fifty-Three grabbed it and turned it in his hands.

Diesel patted his shoulder. "Bring it and let's go."

Out on the driveway, they found the nightstand where they'd left it, but there was no van to put it in.

"Luca, how long?" asked Fifty-Three, rocking back and forth like a child in need of a toilet.

"Twenty seconds."

Headlights down the street flashed, and the van swung into the driveway. The brothers loaded the nightstand, clambered in, and when they were finally underway, heaved a collective sigh of relief.

As the van got up to speed, Diesel expressed a worry. "The decals on the van make us easy to identify. We should take them off."

Luca found a quiet spot along the road and pulled in. Diesel jumped out to clean the van.

Forty moved to help, pausing to ask the older brothers, "While we work on decals, would you guys find a takeout place with beer and pizza for the ride back?"

A half-hour later they were eating and drinking while Luca drove them home. By the time they'd crossed from Vermont into New Hampshire, Diesel's nervous tension had all but dissipated. He spied the box they'd taken from Sparky and, suddenly curious, picked it up. "What makes this so valuable?"

"Its value comes from what's inside," said Luca.

Diesel opened the lid and lifted out a smooth black wedge about the size of his thumb. The face of the wedge had a fancy gold emblem stamped on it. Beneath the emblem were the words "Northern Droid."

"What is it?" asked Forty.

"It's Northern Droid's new design catalog," said Luca. "It holds manufacturing specs and assembly instructions for every part in their product line."

Diesel whistled. "I'm guessing Sparky shouldn't have this at home?"

"He should not. Northern Droid's competitors would pay handsomely for this catalog."

"Oh, Luca," Fifty-Three groaned in exasperation. "He'll come after me for sure to get this back."

Diesel agreed that this Sparky would be anxious to get

his catalog back, and that created risk for Fifty-Three. But he saw a bright side as well. "At least he can't call other Sparkys for help. And there's no way he'll call the authorities about this."

16. Lilah, Fifty-Five timeline

After seeing young Rose off to school, Lilah joined her mother for a cup of coffee, chatting just long enough to persuade her to stay for another couple of days. As soon as Mom agreed, Lilah checked in with Justus and Bunny to inform them of her real plans, and then she slipped down to the basement and jumped to the Fifty-Five timeline. She arrived to find Diesel preparing to jump home.

"I'm dog-tired," he said after they kissed. "But we got some great intel on Sparky and his world." He told her about finding Northern Droid's design catalog. "The guy is bad news, and we've gained some leverage. Hopefully, we can figure out a way to shut him down permanently."

Tasting beer when they kissed, Lilah knew he'd been back for a while but didn't mention it, instead making small talk until he left. Then she went in search of Rose, finding her in the conservatory, her hands moving in front of her the way they did when she conversed privately with Luca. When she saw Lilah, she waved, and Lilah joined her.

Rose stopped moving her hands but kept them up in position. "It's critical that the Sparkys not talk about time travel to others. Putting the genie back in the bottle will be hard enough with the three of them. It will be impossible if they tell their friends."

She went quiet and resumed her hand movements, so Lilah engaged Luca herself, asking the question she had been about to ask Rose: "How was Sparky able to snatch Diesel out of the air like that? The technology and timing required is way beyond what we can do."

"It's beyond me as well," replied Luca.

"There must be *something* different about Diesel's jump for him to be diverted like that. Did the machine sequence in a normal fashion? Was the power field the same?"

"I am analyzing the transmission logs now." Luca paused. "I do find an unusual signal trace during that jump that doesn't show in any of the others before or since. May we bring Rose in on this discussion?"

Though his tone was neutral, Lilah felt that Luca was chiding her and she blushed. Shifting in her chair, she faced Rose. "I was asking Luca about how Sparky was able to snatch my Diesel midjump. He has information to share with us."

"It's a good question." Rose nodded. "What do you have, Luca?"

Luca appeared in image form—a handsome young man facing them. Lilah hadn't noticed before, but Rose's version of Luca had longish hair, a wiry build, scruff on his face, and a confident smile.

"I'm able to detect a probing action," said the AI. "An electromagnetic poke that hit the T-disc circuitry at the precise moment that Thirty-Five jumped."

"And it altered the temporal field?" asked Rose.

"No. It was more like a single jab to the circuitry. My

best guess is that by hitting when it did, it somehow reprogrammed Thirty-Five's destination."

"How could Sparky figure that out? We've been studying this stuff for years, and I wouldn't know where to begin on something like that."

"Which makes me wonder if it was serendipity," said Luca.

Lilah's brow flattened. "Wait. Are you saying he got lucky?"

"The circumstances point to that. I've reviewed his purchase history, and he does own a custom circuit probe. But using it the way he did requires timing so perfect that either he had someone feeding him information in advance, or he got lucky."

"I wish we could see his setup," said Lilah. "I'd like to know where his hobby equipment sits relative to his T-box. Could he have connected the two in some fashion to create a jump-grabbing device?"

"The more we talk, the more I want to see it too." Rose's foot started wiggling as she checked the time. "I'm sure the guys have documented the scene quite thoroughly. When Dad wakes up, I'll ask him to share a vid of the place."

"Except the guys can only carry scrolls through a T-disc, which means pics but no vids, and the Sparky they visited doesn't even have a T-box." Lilah crossed her arms. "We can't make intelligent decisions when we're in the dark like this."

Rose held up a finger and turned to Luca. "Would you be able to send a few bugs into Sparky's house so we can see for ourselves?"

"It's not legal to invade another's home," replied Luca.

Rose crossed her arms. "Understood. Now please answer my question."

The AI nodded. "Yes, I think I could get them in when Fontaine returns home from work."

"I'm guessing bugs are like tiny flying cameras that Luca can control?" asked Lilah.

"That's right. They're small remote devices disguised as flying insects, but with full audio and video capability."

"Why didn't the guys use them?"

"You were here when they made their plans. They wanted to stand inside the house and 'feel it.'" Rose made air quotes with her fingers to add the emphasis. "I don't get it, but who can understand half the stuff men do."

"What's involved? With the insects, I mean."

"Luca?"

"I suggest purchasing the bugs in Vermont so we don't have to transport them from here. We can hire a service to carry them into the neighborhood and release them. I'll direct them to perch on the exterior of the house until Fontaine returns home from work, then they'll follow him inside. With luck we can get a couple of them all the way in on the first try."

Self-conscious about her unfamiliarity with modern tech, Lilah used thought to follow up with Luca. "How could they get just partway in? I can't picture that."

Luca answered aloud, causing Lilah to form a thin smile that looked like a grimace. "If a bug follows his car into the garage but is not able to make it into the house before the mudroom door shuts, then we're partway in, waiting until we can try again."

As the AI spoke, he locked eyes with Lilah and she lost herself in what seemed like bottomless blue pools. Her gaze flicked to his lips. As she watched them dance, she detected a smile lurking just beneath his serious demeanor.

Conceding that he was sexy as hell, she wondered if this Rose was using Luca as a secret lover the way earlier Roses had used Ciopova. Before her imagination could fill in the details, Rose's conversation with the AI pulled her back to the present.

"How long would it take for you to get bugs in position?"

"A couple of hours using off-the-shelf tech, but Fontaine's instruments may be able to detect mass-produced bugs. Stealth designs are custom-built and take a week for delivery."

Rose shook her head. "I'm not waiting that long. Please execute using commercial tech. But check with us before you enter the house."

Lilah was uncomfortable with Rose's freelancing when the brothers had already started on a solution. "Shouldn't we check with your dad first?"

"He's asleep, and I don't want to wake him." She gave a careless shrug. "He'll surface before Sparky gets home, and if he hates the idea, we'll abort. But if he likes it, then we're way ahead of schedule."

While they waited for the bugs to reach Sparky's house, Rose introduced their next big issue—bringing more Lilahs and Roses into the fold.

"Let's start with the Twenty-Nine through Thirty-Nine timelines, since they need only a simple T-box mod." Rose stood and motioned to the door. "With step-by-step instructions, they can be ready in less than two weeks. Let's go to my workshop and make up scrolls for them."

Rose's impulsive decision-making frustrated Lilah, but she wanted to avoid friction between them. Suppressing her feelings, Lilah followed Rose out of the conservatory, noting, "We'll need the guys to distribute the scrolls."

"They've always been cooperative."

"That was before Sparky."

Rose looked at her without breaking stride. "Do you think it will be a problem?"

Lilah thought for a moment. "I've grown close to Thirty-Four, and his is the one timeline we can reach beyond yours and mine. He may grumble, but if his Lilah and I double-team him, he'll cooperate." She nudged Rose in a playful fashion with her shoulder. "If he resists, you can close the deal. He'd never say no to you."

They entered Rose's workshop, and Lilah was wowed by the modern facility. Unlike the basement, the shop was a bright, organized, high-tech workspace. Billionaires could afford every toy, and Lilah saw lots of them in the spacious room, though she didn't know what most of them did.

Following Rose to a workspace in the back, Lilah perched on a stool while Rose called up a storyboard that detailed the T-box modification procedure. Vids and pics floated in front of them, explaining how to complete each step. Charts and tables listed measurements to take to confirm success.

"Do you remember the places where you got confused?"

Lilah pointed to a middle portion of the storyboard. "This needs to be expanded. It's hard to follow the way it is now." Then she moved her finger to a different section. "But now that I think of it, we could save time on this step. I worked for three days trying to fabricate this microbracket and was about to give up. Then I stumbled across a shop in town where a guy made it for me in a couple of hours."

"We should include the shop name in the instructions."

"Gary's Appliance and Repair. Something close to that, anyway. It's on Seventh near the mall. Satchel was the guy who helped me. He was really nice."

"Luca, update the instructions with Lilah's information," said Rose. The three of them worked together after that, stepping through the storyboard in search of timesaving amendments.

They were nearing completion when Luca interrupted. "The bugs are perched on Fontaine's house, three near the front door and three near the garage. The wind is calm and that works in our favor."

Rose interpreted for Lilah. "These things are so tiny that the wind can blow them away. They're really designed for indoor use." She glanced toward the workshop door. "Luca, has Dad shown any signs of life?"

"He woke up an hour ago and left for the Woodstock art festival. He expects to be back later this afternoon."

The news left Lilah dumbfounded. "He went to an art show in the middle of all this?"

"He's going there to meet Julia." Rose smiled. "She's an artist and he's super hot for her. I hope it works out."

Flames of jealousy rose from deep in Lilah's gut, and she struggled to control the feeling using logic—a weak weapon against such a powerful emotion.

She understood at an intellectual level that Fifty-Five's Lilah had died fourteen years ago, and he was long overdue for companionship. But the news still hurt like hell. *He's moved on.* Her eyes teared and she rubbed them as discreetly as she could.

Taking Lilah's hand, Rose shifted to face her. "Please don't be hurt. He mourned you for years and years." She stroked Lilah's hair and continued with a gentle rub down her arm. "He isn't replacing you. You'll always be in his heart. Julia is a new facet in his life. It's beautiful."

Rose continued her supportive whispers, revealing an attentive side as she comforted her mom-sister. She didn't hurry, reassuring Lilah over and over, waiting for her to process her feelings.

"Thank you, sweetie," Lilah told her when she was ready to continue working.

Rose shifted back to work mode in a heartbeat, pointing to the instructions floating in front of them. "I have an idea for dividing this up."

Lilah wasn't sure what Rose meant. "I'm listening."

"How about if you lead the effort for converting the T-boxes, and I lead for the T-disc timelines?"

Lilah liked the suggestion and she brightened. "I'm comfortable with the early tech, and you know more about building a T-box in these later timelines."

"I'm happy to do something different if you want, but this should work out well." Rose pointed at the display with her chin. "You and Thirty-Four don't need a copy of this, but we need to make scrolls for everyone from Twenty-Nine to Thirty-Nine."

Lilah nodded. "I'll carry them to Thirty-Four and get him to deliver them. With luck, we'll have a bunch of Lilahs wandering the timelines by the end of next week."

"Wow." It was Rose's turn to dab an eye. "A few days ago I longed for one mom, and now I'll have ten."

"Twenty-Nine to Thirty-Nine is eleven timelines."

Rose counted on her fingers and grinned. "Even better."

Luca intruded on their conversation. "I've detected Fontaine's car coming up Pinecrest Drive. He'll be home in about four minutes."

"Go ahead and follow him into the house with as many bugs as you can." Rose bit her lip. "Up to a max of three."

"Shouldn't we ask your dad?" Lilah liked Rose's spunk, but she had a different relationship with the Diesels, one based on trust and respect. She wondered if Rose was competing with her dad at a subconscious level. It would explain her brash behavior.

"I'm not going to interrupt his date with Julia. Please believe me when I say she's really good for him."

"Okay." Lilah held up her hands as if to surrender. "We'll let him be." Then to Luca. "What are your concerns as Fontaine approaches?"

"My next concern is balancing between two possibilities. He could enter the house from the garage, or he could enter through the front door. It means dividing resources."

"If he's in his car, he's going in through the garage," said Lilah. "Guaranteed."

"I agree. Still, I don't want to get it wrong."

Rose slid off her seat and motioned for Lilah to follow. "I want to watch, but we'll fall off these stools if we do it from here." She guided Lilah to a low bench against the back wall, and they sat side by side. "We're ready." She squeezed Lilah's hand. "Show us."

Lilah gasped as the view through her eyes switched from the workshop to a panoramic view of a wooded front yard with a long paved driveway leading out to a street. The scene wasn't familiar, and as she studied it a yellow car, rounder and taller than she was used to seeing, pulled in and started toward them up the drive.

She heard a quiet hum as the car approached. The vehicle passed beneath and the view flipped, then they followed the car into the garage. The hum repeated as the garage door lowered.

Stepping from the vehicle, Sparky took three short steps and entered the house through the mudroom door. None of the bugs made it across the garage and through the door before he closed it behind him.

"I've failed," said Luca.

"Let us know when you get another chance." Lilah heard disappointment in Rose's voice.

Seconds later, the mudroom door opened and Sparky stepped back into the garage. Walking around the car, he approached the exercise area, grabbed a small athletic bag from a shelf, and emptied the contents onto the garage floor. Taking the handgun he'd been holding—one Lilah hadn't noticed until now—he put it into the bag.

"Is that a gun?" asked Rose.

"Yes," said Luca. "That shape is consistent with a fab design."

"If he fabricated it himself," asked Lilah, "does that mean it can pass through a modified T-box?"

"While I don't know the specific materials he used to construct his gun, it is easy enough to fab one without any metal, making what you suggest possible."

With the athletic bag in hand, Sparky stepped around his car and made for the mudroom door.

"Let's get inside this time," urged Rose.

When Sparky entered the house, the bugs followed him into the kitchen. Lilah watched Sparky set the bag on the kitchen table and disappear through a doorway. Clomping footsteps hinted at a staircase.

The bugs caught up to Sparky and followed him down to the basement, providing full audio and video along the way. At the bottom of the stairs, they found him facing a paneled wall, waiting as it glided smoothly to the side to expose a wealth of electronic instruments and devices.

When the panel stopped sliding, Sparky sat and powered up his rig. Tiny red and green lights among the electronic boxes signaled system readiness.

"Portia," he said, "compare the data from when Lagerford jumped here against all the other jumps from this machine. Is there anything different or unusual in the transmission that you can identify?"

"You probed the energy field at the moment it was forming, causing this." Portia displayed a multicolored swirl that grew a white spot near the center. The spot pulsed twice, shrank to a pinpoint, and disappeared.

"What am I looking at?"

"An anomaly in the energy field. I am unable to determine how it affected the operation of a T-box. I have searched around the world and can't find a single reference to this technology."

"But you think the anomaly is related to actions I took?"

"I believe the Grantain probe you were operating caused it."

Sparky used his fingers to manipulate the image of the swirl that Portia projected, studying it from different angles. Then he frowned, made several quick adjustments, lifted his head, and stared right at Lilah from across the room.

Lilah gulped and squeezed Rose's hand as Sparky stood, took two quick steps, and stretched out a hand that grew to enormous proportions. Everything went dark and stayed that way for a heartbeat until Luca switched the feed to a different bug, causing their perspective to change to a side view.

Sparky, head bowed, studied something in the palm of his hand.

He carried his prize over to his electronics station, set it on a corner of his workspace, and retook his seat. As he did, he said aloud, "Remember, Lagerford, first you use your T-box to invade my home, and then you send bugs to spy on me. You're an aggressor who has crossed the line *twice*. What happens next is on you."

Sparky studied his display as he spoke, then he lunged and grabbed the second bug, crushing it with a squeeze of his hand.

Lilah's perspective changed to that of the third bug.

"Get it out of there," Rose hissed in a whisper as if Sparky might hear.

"Acknowledged," replied Luca.

The bug flew up the stairs, through the kitchen, and into the living area. Zooming above the chairs and tables, the mechanical insect reached the built-in bookshelf on the back wall, where it nestled among some hardback editions, allowing them to peek out across the room.

"What's Sparky doing?" asked Lilah, her heart pounding in her chest.

"His electronics detected the presence of bugs," answered Luca. "He's destroyed two of them."

"Duh." She took a deep breath to calm her nerves. "My question is what is he doing at this moment?"

"I don't know. Should I send the bug back to look?"

They heard heavy footsteps, then Sparky appeared holding a device shaped like a fat pen. Watching it as he waved it in the air, he called, "Come to papa." Grinning, he sprinted across the living area and reached for the bookshelves.

Luca directed the mechanical insect to swoop and dive around the room in an effort to escape, forcing Sparky to chase it for most of a minute before finally swatting it with one of the pillows from the couch.

Lilah had been growing nauseous from the aerobatics

and was grateful when their view returned to Rose's brightly-lit workshop.

Rose slumped back against the wall, breathing heavily. "That was wild."

Fighting a rising anger, Lilah couldn't contain herself. "Rose, *we* created the situation where Sparky is a threat to our families, and now *we've* just antagonized him. Everyone's world is more dangerous, especially for you and your dad." She shook her head. "That wasn't wild, it was reckless. We need to slow down and include more people before making any more decisions."

"I admit that didn't end well." Rose folded her arms across her chest. "But we learned that he's packing a gun, something he was doing *before* he knew about bugs. And we learned that he doesn't even know himself how he was able to grab your Diesel during that jump." She stood. "Both of those are huge wins and justify the risks we took."

"I agree those are big wins. But will the brothers still help us when they learn of our freelancing?"

Rose hesitated and then motioned to the T-box modification scrolls they'd just made. "Let's get Thirty-Four started on distributing these before word gets out."

Lilah agreed, mostly because she believed having more Lilahs in the mix would help contain Rose's rash enthusiasm.

They gathered the scrolls and Lilah stuffed them in her pockets. Together they walked down to the basement, where Lilah paused at the T-box door. "You'll give your dad a complete report?"

"Yup." She ticked through the list, holding up a new

finger for each item. "Sparky has a handgun. He doesn't know how he was able to grab your Diesel during that jump. And we pissed him off by sending bugs in to eavesdrop."

"Good." Lilah tugged on the door latch. "Perhaps add some detail when you deliver it?"

Rose folded her hands in front of her and looked at the floor. "I know I screwed up. I'm committed to protecting Dad, not increasing his risk. Please don't be angry with me." She lifted her head and asked in a quiet voice, "Can I have a hug?"

Lilah felt an emotional swell and hugged Rose, who snuffled once as they squeezed each other.

"I'll visit soon," said Lilah as she waved goodbye. Climbing into the T-box, she shifted focus to her mission, calling like a seasoned pro, "Travel to Thirty-Four."

17. Lilah, Thirty-Four timeline

Lilah exited the T-box and found the setting in the Thirty-Four timeline so familiar that she had to look for differences to confirm it wasn't her own home. The clincher was the missing portrait of young Rose on the wall between the two offices. Their friend Jude had painted it as a gift for them this past Christmas.

"Hello!" she called up the stairs. With no response and no signs of life, she climbed to the main level, where she paused to consider poking her head into Justus's office to say hi. The clock in the hall said noon, which meant Rose would be at school for a few more hours. She continued up to the apartment.

Lilah knocked on the door and Thirty-Four opened it. "It wasn't locked," he said and turned back into the room.

"Who is it?" called Lilah Thirty-Four from somewhere inside.

He stared at her, head tilted and brow furrowed. "Lilah?"

Lilah stepped into the apartment as her one-year-younger double came out from the kitchen. In those first moments, Lilah assessed herself through her twin's appearance—hair, face, fitness, posture, skin, clothes, the works. The results of the appraisal were mixed.

Lilah Thirty-Four wore jeans, a new T-shirt, and light makeup, giving her a simple but attractive look. Her hair needed brushing but was pleasing enough in its tousled state. A lock hung loose on the side, alone and out of place. Lilah subconsciously repositioned that strand on her own head. Lilah Thirty-Four did the same.

Her face, though smooth and tight, had tiny creases at the edges of her smile. And she looked tired. Lilah wondered how well her own makeup hid the darkish circles under her eyes and glanced in the hall mirror. *Not so well.*

Always petite, she'd lost a few pounds in recent years, and her body's tone had shifted a bit. Lilah realized that her butt was nonexistent, at least it seemed so in jeans. The brothers had claimed it was one of her prized attributes a decade ago.

And she slumped a bit when she stood. Lilah pulled her shoulders back to correct her own posture. Lilah Thirty-Four did so at the same time.

Then the younger woman grinned, and the joy on her face lit up the room. "What a wonderful surprise!"

They reached out to hug, and Lilah recalled Diesel's warning that for him the first touches with his brothers had felt odd, like the universe was out of balance. But that wasn't her experience. When they connected, she found it exciting—almost electric—and they held each other in a tight embrace.

"Come and sit." Her double motioned for Lilah to take their favorite chair, looking around the room as she did so. "Damn, I wish I'd had a chance to clean up."

"Hon, your mess is my mess. I hate to break it to you,

but it looks just like this a year from now." Lilah pointed to a stack of books sitting on the floor near a window and laughed. "In fact, that pile is still there in my timeline." She brought a hand to her mouth. "Oh my God, what if we go ahead to Thirty-Six and the books are *still* sitting there?"

They both giggled, touching hands as they did, and at once Lilah felt at ease.

She wanted to say a thousand things. Instead, she held her tongue and looked at Thirty-Four. "David, please don't be hurt, but we want to do this alone. Do you mind if we go upstairs?"

"It's an exciting time. I get it." Thirty-Four stood. "You stay here. We were going to meet Justus and Bunny for lunch. I'll go alone and convey your regrets."

He stopped at the door and looked back at them. "All the Lilahs are honest, caring, and selfless. That means you two don't need to second-guess each other's intentions. Trust is something people normally build up over time. But when you accept that this person thinks and acts exactly like you do, it will give you faith in her motives, and that will take your relationship to a new level."

"Thank you, David." Lilah hesitated. She was sure they all felt the awkward moment.

Normally, Lilahs would flirt with the brothers who were not their husbands. It was harmless fun because that Diesel would always leave at the end of the day, ensuring the flirtations didn't lead to entanglements. But now *she* was the visitor, so she was the one responsible for leaving, and that changed the dynamic. Beyond that, Lilah would never flirt with Thirty-Four in front of his wife—her sister.

So instead, she waved from the living area. "Can you come right back after lunch? We have a favor to ask of you."

"Does it involve moving furniture?"

Lilah shook her head.

"Then I'll be here." He winked and closed the door.

Turning back to her sister, Lilah felt a twinge of disappointment. Not unlike watching a movie for the second time, this was the past. She knew how it turned out. While meeting herself was the fulfilment of a decade-long dream, she realized that it was her future self—someone who could guide her and give her insights—who held the real allure.

"I win," said Lilah Thirty-Four as if reading her thoughts. "I get to learn about my future."

It hit Lilah that while she may have little to learn from this relationship, her younger sister would benefit. She acted to support that success. "So what do you want to know, other than how long those books will stay in a stack?"

"What do I need to know? Are we all healthy and happy?"

Lilah nodded. "But David could tell you that."

"What can I get him for his birthday? He is so hard to buy for."

Equally clueless, Lilah shook her head. Then she snapped her fingers. "Get him watercolors, brushes, and an artist's sketch pad. I did last year. He let them sit for several months but started playing with them recently. He seems to really enjoy it."

"Is he any good?"

She shrugged. "He has fun. That's what counts."

"So, what favor are we asking of David? I can tell by your fidgeting that it's something important."

"It is." They moved to the kitchen and made lunch while they talked, working together in easy synchrony. "The sisters, and especially you, me, and Rose as project leaders, are responsible for the Sparky situation, and Rose and I just made it worse." She gave details of Diesel's kidnapping, summarized what the brothers had learned from their various investigations, and concluded with the incident involving the bugs and the gun.

Lilah Thirty-Four listened to the summary as they carried their salads and drinks to the table. "If the Sparkys are centered on the Fifty-Five timeline, that means the transponder succeeded in broadcasting, but the leash didn't move it down the timeline."

"That's what Rose and I think."

"Still," said the younger woman, "given everything we were trying to achieve, we did pretty good." She bit her lip. "Except for the Sparky part."

"The other issue we know about is relatively minor. For some reason, when Sparky connects his box to ours, it reads as a link to the Twenty-Five timeline."

"You mean the display outside our box will say 'Twenty-Five incoming'?"

"That's right." Lilah stood, grabbed two napkins from the counter, and held one out as she retook her seat.

"Given the circumstances, that's actually good news. It means he can't sneak up on us."

Lilah dabbed her mouth. "I hadn't considered that. Could you imagine if every time we saw 'Fifty-Five incoming' on the display, we had to wonder if it would be David, Rose, or Sparky stepping from the cabin?"

Her sister sat up. "It's easy enough to make it so when the display reads 'Twenty-Five incoming,' we blare a horn or something as a warning."

"Maybe lock the T-box door?"

They ate a few bites of salad, then Lilah held up a finger as she swallowed. "Did David tell you that his sister has a breast cancer scare?"

"Cara gets breast cancer?"

"No. They find a lump, let's see…" Lilah looked into the air as she counted. "It'll be about four months from now. It's benign, we know it and tell her so, but she's a mess until she hears from the doctor."

"Good to know."

"Oh, and in the spring, Mom falls in love with this foreign asshole, and three weeks later starts talking of moving to Spain. I made a terrible scene trying to bring her to her senses. After two months, the jerk just ups and returns to Spain without even saying goodbye."

"He's probably married."

Lilah nodded. "So instead of blowing a gasket, it's probably easier to go along with her fantasy and console her when it's over."

Her sister asked wide-ranging questions after that. Does Rose get a part in the school play this year? What are some highlights of the year ahead? Does Diesel's alcohol consumption remain stable? How are Bunny and Justus doing?

When the conversation began to wane, Lilah took the scrolls from her pockets and laid them on the tabletop.

"These are streamlined instructions for modifying a T-box so our sisters can join us. We need your David to deliver them to the Twenty-Nine through Thirty-Nine timelines."

"I don't think he'll mind."

"If word of the surveillance bug debacle filters down to him, I fear he may decide he does mind."

"Your David can't help?"

Lilah shook her head. "He's part of the group working to take Sparky down, so we'd be a low priority until he's finished with that. But if we wait until he's free, it means we can't be part of the solution."

"I don't want to wait." Lilah Thirty-Four gathered the dishes and carried the stack to the sink.

"We have an unrelated challenge," said Lilah, "and that's our lovely daughter."

"Rose? What's going on?"

"She a wonderful person—smart, beautiful, loving—but she doesn't always think things through before she acts. Some of our problems can be traced to that bullheaded behavior. We need to figure out how to slow her down before she turns bad into worse."

"Would it help if I spent time with her?"

"I think so. She's delightful, so you'll enjoy every moment."

"I'm back." Thirty-Four entered through the front door. "Stop your ladies-only secret-meeting talk and let's move some furniture."

"It's easier than that." Lilah pointed to the scrolls sitting in a pile on the kitchen table. "We need you to deliver these for us. Today, if you would."

18. Sparky, Fifty-Five timeline

Sparky climbed the stairs to the kitchen, his older twin following behind. "They're right there," he said, pointing to a white plate at one end of the kitchen table. He moved around and sat at the other end.

The older twin picked up the magnifying glass next to the plate and studied the surveillance bugs. "This is all of them?"

"I've run everything a half-dozen times, indoors and out. They're simple devices, so they show up like spotlights on a boosted spec."

The older twin toyed with the magnifying glass. "Lagerford has the resources to buy the most sophisticated bugs on the planet. I wonder why he went on the cheap?"

"Maybe he didn't realize we'd be geared up to see them?" Sparky felt a chill. "Or maybe he's in a hurry and this was the fastest way to gather whatever information he's trying to get on us."

"Maybe we do something in the future that threatens or hurts him, and all this is to stop that."

"You know what? I don't care," Sparky snapped, spit flying from his mouth. "Lagerford offered us a hundred million. Now that we're ready to collect, we find him spying on us. If we don't get our hands around this soon, we'll never see that money."

"Do we know if the Lagerford you had downstairs ever told the one from this timeline about the promise?"

"Who else would send bugs?"

His twin twitched a shoulder. "Northern Droid, looking for their design catalog and missing feedstock material?"

"Maybe, but I'm betting on Lagerford." Sparky checked the time and stood. Their plan today was to visit the Lagerford estate in New Hampshire to add to what the twins had learned from their earlier visit. "Let's hit the road and see if we can prove it."

Tilting his head toward the athletic bag with the gun, Sparky asked, "Should we bring the persuader?"

"No." The older twin shook his head. "If we were stopped, you'd be snagged for carrying without a permit, and I'd have to explain why I don't exist in any database in this timeline. Lagerford would become the least of our worries."

"Probably for the best." Sparky opened the pantry and stowed the bag. "I've never even fired it. Have you?"

"Not yet."

"Speaking of legal messes," Sparky continued as he led the way out to the garage, "did you hear how much our younger brother's lawyer is costing?"

"The one to fight the casino? Better him than me."

The cold attitude didn't register with Sparky, but pragmatic concerns did. "When he's dealing with that stuff, he isn't helping us."

Ignoring the issue, the older twin pointed to the

exercise equipment in the bay next to the car. "There are mountain trails that go near Lagerford's house. No one pays attention to people running trails. Let's grab workout gear to bring with us."

Though it was a great idea, Sparky hesitated because the plan would create extra laundry for him. Despite his misgivings, he gathered clothes into duplicate piles, his annoyance ebbing enough that he even topped off both piles with clean towels.

After loading the car, they clambered in and sat facing each other in limousine-style seating. Quiet until they reached the highway, Sparky called to Portia. "Show us an aerial view of the Lagerford estate."

Portia displayed a holographic image of a modest one-story home nestled on a forested hilltop plateau.

"Show it from the valley side," said the older twin.

The view shifted and Sparky saw that the home was actually a very large multilevel construction built into the steep hillside. Expansive windows on every floor provided dramatic views of the valley below. "This makes more sense." Sparky nodded.

"It's one of the first things we discovered during our earlier visit."

As the older twin spoke, Sparky noticed a bright orange hopper swooping into view in the image between them. Like a giant bug, the transport vehicle landed next to the house, one person exited, and the machine lifted off and flew out of frame.

"Personal transport from the valley floor," said Sparky. "Must be nice." He leaned forward and studied the image.

"Is this feed live?"

"This view is somewhere between four and ten weeks old," replied Portia. "The service is deliberately vague about it for privacy reasons."

"Replay that hopper landing and zoom in on the person getting out. Let's see a close-up."

Portia zoomed as requested, conveying the bad news at the same time. "All faces are blurred by the service for privacy reasons."

"We can see she's female," said Sparky. "The wife's been dead for a while, so maybe this is her replacement?"

After several replays with no new insights, they switched gears and searched for a mountain trail that brought them close to the Lagerford home. It didn't take long to find a three-mile loop that not only started and ended at a trailhead along a public road but also passed within a hundred feet of the Lagerford property line at the far corner. The route included a high spot that promised a panoramic view of the home, but they wouldn't know how good the view was until they got there and saw for themselves.

The car departed the highway and proceeded on local roads, each successive turn putting them on a smaller road with a lower speed limit. Then they started to climb.

"If I lived up here and had the money," said the older twin as the car swung around a hairpin turn, "I'd skip this drive and use a hopper myself."

They watched the scenery for a bit, then Sparky voiced an idea he had been contemplating. "Should we try investing in penny stocks? Some of them can double and triple in a day. It seems like we could work a modest stake into an impressive pile that way."

"Jeez, I need to think about it." The older twin shifted in his seat, repositioning his legs as he did so. "We'd have to verify that the timing of stock swings in my timeline match with yours. Things can move fast, and a half hour difference is enough to turn a win into a big loss."

Sparky nodded. "My worry is that because the government tracks everything so they can tax it, they might get curious about our impossible winning streak. Then we'd be dealing with federal agents instead of casino thugs."

"Aren't those penny-stock outfits really small? I'm thinking that once our investment portfolio grew to twenty or thirty million, we'd be buying and selling whole companies, not just shares of their stocks."

Sparky shrugged. "It was just an idea."

After a few minutes of silence, the older twin punched his thigh. "Damn it. If we're going to be nosing around near Lagerford's house, we need disguises. We should have stopped back in town."

Sparky considered turning the car around, then had a brainstorm. Rotating up on his knees, he dug behind the car seat and pulled out a collection of items. "Being a slob has its perks," he said, claiming a red knit cap for himself. He pushed the remaining items toward his twin.

As the man assembled his disguise—a brown fisherman's hat and a plaid wool scarf—Sparky slid open a storage compartment along the side wall, exposing a cubby filled with bottled water, packaged snacks, and perched on top, one pair of mirrored aviator-style sunglasses. He put them on to complete his disguise, grinning as he did so.

The older twin looped the scarf around his neck, modeling it for Sparky. "It not only serves as fashionable mountain wear." He lifted the front so it covered his nose and mouth. "But I can go outlaw mode in an instant." He laughed through the colorful material.

It took another half hour to reach the trailhead. When the car stopped, Portia spoke unbidden. "There's no support network that I can access in this location. Once you move from the vehicle, we will delink. Outside, I can only provide basic cover for my primary, and even that will be spotty."

"Really?" Sparky was ticked that he was just hearing about it. "Will you be able to guide us along our route?"

"Yes, but not much more than that."

Shaking his head in annoyance, Sparky opened the door, then hugged himself when the rush of cool air surprised him. Pulling his knit cap down over his ears, he eyed the older twin's scarf, wondering if he'd made the wrong choice for his disguise.

They started for the trail at a slow jog, Sparky accelerating as his muscles warmed. A natural introvert, he liked to sink inside himself during a run and spend the time deliberating his hopes and worries. A running partner implied conversation, accommodation, and other interactions contrary to a meditative mindset.

But his twin made no demands on him. Quite the opposite, he used identical methods and showed the same preferences. When they approached the first rise, his twin followed like a shadow as Sparky accelerated up the slope.

On the way down, he slowed along with Sparky, who worried about hurting his knees with an aggressive descent.

They ran the first two miles at an easy pace, then Portia announced, "The Lagerford property line is just ahead."

Sparky conveyed the message to his twin, and they slowed to a walk. He tried to get a glimpse of the house, but trees blocked his view. "Let's go ahead to the rise and see if that helps."

The rise turned out to be a knoll of granite, and when they climbed to the top, it gave them enough elevation to see the property above the trees. The beautifully landscaped home sat some distance away.

"I wish we'd brought binoculars," said the older twin.

Before Sparky could respond, a *whir* filled the air and an orange hopper popped into view from behind the house. Swooping in, it landed on a red brick patio to the side of the home.

A man and woman—he older, she younger—exited the house through French doors, crossed the patio, and climbed into the vehicle. With another *whir* it rose into the air and, reversing its path, flew out over the valley and dropped from view.

"I can't say that the house is empty," said the older twin. "But it's a lot closer to that now. Let's snoop around." He began to climb down from the granite rise.

"A house like that will have a major-league alarm system."

Pulling his scarf up over his face, his twin goaded him. "Buckle up, Buttercup, because we're going to find out."

Tingles of excitement caused Sparky to shiver.

Snugging his cap down to the rim of his sunglasses, he scrambled to follow.

Using trees and bushes as cover, they moved toward the house. When they reached the edge of the lawn, a marker warned "Private Property – No Trespassing – Security Protected."

Sparky's heart raced as the older twin led them past the sign and onto the lawn. Spotlights flipped on, bright enough to be seen in the full sun. Then a pair of French doors swung wide, and a woman—petite, pretty, passive— stepped onto the patio and looked in their direction.

"Molly!" they exclaimed in unison, looking at each other before returning their gazes to Maid Marian. Molly was the generic name for Northern Droid's top-of-the-line domestic bot. The company didn't sell many of them because they were so pricey, and Sparky found it thrilling to see one deployed.

The older twin continued toward her and Sparky followed. Mollys were designed to be friendly and refined. He didn't feel a hint of threat from her presence.

But then two Stryqr7000 war bots stepped through the French doors—one armored monstrosity after the other— and took up stations on either side of Molly. Muscular, scary, bristling with sensors and weaponry, these were the most fearsome machines in Northern Droid's military division. Designed for brutal campaigns, they had special coding that allowed them to threaten, detain, harm, and kill humans. Too dangerous for use in police and paramilitary operations, private ownership was unheard of.

Sparky had seen vids of them in action. Recalling the

horror they'd caused—bloody devastation where he'd laughed at the victims—adrenaline spiked his fear. Fighting visceral panic, he backpedaled, tripped over his twin, and squealed in fright.

Righting himself, he sprinted to reach the cover of the forest, struggling to get ahead of his brother so he wouldn't be the likely target. He kept at a dead run for the mile out to the road, watching the ground so he wouldn't trip, and straining to hear any indication of pursuit.

Back in the car, they lay on the seats, gulping air as Portia got them started down the hill.

"Holy smokes. Were those Seven Thousands?" Sparky's hands were still shaking.

"It sure looked like it to me."

"How could he get those? They're illegal for nonmilitary use."

"I guess when you're rich enough, you can do whatever you want."

Wiping his face with a towel, Sparky sat up. "I want to be that rich. That's what this is all about."

19. Rose, Fifty-Five timeline

Rose followed her father into the hopper, and instead of taking her normal position across from him, she plopped down next to him and hooked her arm in his. They were on their way to Plymouth to wander the farmers market with Julia. Rose would be meeting her father's new love interest in person for the first time, and she couldn't be more excited.

"Something on your mind, Rosie?" Fifty-Five asked as the hopper lifted off.

"I'm just excited to meet Julia. That's all."

"You sure there's nothing else?"

She sat upright. "There is one thing, but it can wait until after our visit."

Luca intruded on their conversation. "There are trespassers on your property." He projected an image of two men—both tall and lanky—dressed in summer running gear up to their necks, at which point their accessories switched to winter attire. The one with the wool scarf wore a style of hat that revealed the man's big ears and reddish hair.

"Sparky!" shouted Fifty-Five.

"I've activated a level two defense," said Luca, meaning he'd secured all entry points to the home, alerted local authorities, used spotlights to warn the intruders, and sent Maid Marian to counsel them to leave.

"Go to level one," said Fifty-Five.

Rose had never heard any references to defense levels before and, heart beating, silently instructed Luca to show her the action. She inhaled when two monstrous automatons stomped onto the lawn and began an elaborate show of targeting the clowns with frightening weaponry. And clowns they were, tripping and stumbling over each other as they scrambled to escape.

Fifty-Five laughed with satisfaction as they disappeared into the forest. "Julia will *love* this!"

"Should we go back?" asked Rose.

He shook his head. "No point. They're gone." Looking into the distance, he addressed Luca. "Follow them home so we have proof it's the Sparkys. And file a complaint with the state troopers and see if we can get them involved before they cross over into Vermont."

Rose waited until he finished with his instructions. "When did we get military bots?"

"You mean our Stryqr7000 war machines?"

She heard pride in his voice. "Dad, those monstrosities can go berserk. It's not legal for you to have them, and I will *not* share a house with them."

Her father could barely contain his glee. Holding up a finger as a signal to wait, he called to the air, "Julia, are you there?"

An image of Julia—forty-five years old, pretty, slightly disheveled—floated in front of them. "Am I late?"

"You're fine," said Fifty-Five. "But I wonder, instead

of going to the farmers market, would you mind giving Rose a tour of your studio?"

"But it still has…oh, I'll bet that's the point, isn't it?" She nodded. "Well, I'm here at the studio now, so I definitely won't be late. And Rose, I'm looking forward to finally meeting you in person." With a wink and a grin, her image melted away.

"So," said Fifty-Five as the hopper settled on its landing spot in the valley. "All will be revealed when we get there."

Rose couldn't imagine the mystery, but she knew her dad well enough to understand that whatever was going on, she'd have to wait to find out.

They climbed out of the hopper and made for the parking lot at the edge of the field. Along the way, Rose saw Kristoff and waved. An earnest young man with an uncomfortable crush on her, Kristoff worked long hours struggling to keep his fledgling taxi service in business. He was holding the door for a young couple climbing into his sky-blue vehicle, so he waved back by bobbing his head.

Once the car was underway, her father acted like a salesman for Northern Droid's military division. "The Stryqr7000 war bot is the top of the line. They say it can lay waste to a whole village in seconds."

"Did you bribe someone to get them?" She studied his grin. "You did, didn't you!" He wouldn't show his cards and she couldn't read him, so she had no choice but to let his fun unfold at his pace.

He began chatting in private with Julia after that, so Rose rode in silence, mulling what to tell him about the bugs. With the Sparkys nosing about their property, likely because of her provocation two days earlier, the issue had elevated in importance and not in a good way.

She feared he would be so upset with her that he'd balk at distributing the T-box build instructions. And if *that* happened, it would delay when she could bring other Roses into her world.

The car slowed on a quiet stretch of road populated with old brick buildings, each set back on a separate plot of land. Bushes and trees grew unrestrained, encroaching on the aging structures.

"I think this was an industrial zone a few decades ago," said Fifty-Five.

The car pulled into a dirt parking lot in front of one of them—a decrepit warehouse with a corrugated metal roof. Most of the exterior trim was missing, and the pieces that remained were rotting. If there hadn't already been a vehicle parked out front, Rose would have thought the building abandoned.

They started to climb out of the car but Luca stopped them. "Sergeant Tomasto of the New Hampshire State Police offered this in response to your request."

The voice switched to that of an older man with a Boston accent. "Sorry, but we won't chase a citizen with no priors because he stepped on your lawn."

"The sergeant asked for the video evidence," Luca continued, "and I said I would get back to him. I believe the police will be more interested in your Stryqr7000 war bots than in a couple of trespassers who left when asked."

"Let's drop it, then." Fifty-Five exited the vehicle and

led Rose up the steps of the warehouse. "It was a bad call on my part to get the authorities involved anyway. Now they have a record of an antagonistic relationship between me and Sparky, and that makes me a suspect if anything happens to him."

Fifty-Five opened the door and led Rose into an airy space that reminded her of an auditorium. Though the walls showed flaking paint and the overhead ducts crisscrossed to cast eerie shadows, the building itself seemed weathertight, the oak floor solid, and the space well lit. An enormous carved-wood sign on the wall welcomed them to the Goose Camp Fishing Lodge. Below it, a trellis covered with flowering vines created an inviting setting for English tea.

"Welcome." A bulky bot with exaggerated, cartoon-like facial features, puffy white gloves, and colorful clothing that included a shopkeeper's apron, approached. "Please follow me."

While the inside of the warehouse was clean and spacious, it wasn't open. Quite the opposite. Like a department store, the floor was lined with tall shelves stocked with antique lamps, timeworn cameras, kitchen countertop appliances, rotary telephones, manual cash registers, mailboxes, and more.

Rose knew that Julia was a fabricator—a model builder. But she'd never appreciated what that meant until now.

"Welcome!" Julia stood with arms wide as they approached. Behind her sat an industrial-grade fabrication cell. The clutter around the design station hinted that she was deep into a project.

Julia gave Fifty-Five a quick peck on the cheek and turned to Rose. "I've heard so much about you."

"Don't believe any of it." They hugged and then exchanged compliments—Rose on Julia's earrings, and Julia on Rose's blouse. After, Rose turned in a circle. "Whatever I was supposed to see, I don't."

"I covered it up so we could have a big reveal." Julia pointed to what looked like a statue draped with a white shroud. "Champ, please remove the cloth."

The bot that had greeted them at the door moved forward with an arm raised.

Fifty-Five seemed surprised. "This clown is your SiteRover?" Then he looked mortified. "I mean...this cheerful, brightly dressed bot."

Julia smirked as Champ tugged on the cloth to reveal a Stryqr7000 war bot standing at attention.

Fifty-Five looked at Rose and shook his head. "Which do you think looks cooler?" He motioned to Champ and made a face like he was in pain. "This?" Then he turned to the death machine and gave a loving smile. "Or this?"

"I am so confused right now." Rose moved to put Champ between her and the war bot.

"Don't worry," said Julia. "It's just a costume. Champ and the two bots at your house are identical SiteRovers— private security bots. I mocked them up in these war machine costumes to amuse your dad."

"We both had fun doing it," said Fifty-Five.

He sounded defensive and Rose thought it was wonderful. He'd lived a charmed life for too long, lording his authority over her as if she were still a child and not an almost thirty-year-old. She took satisfaction in watching him stumble as he negotiated a personal relationship where he wasn't the de facto boss.

Relieved that her father wasn't putting them in danger, she gave her support to Julia. "You did a great job with it. Not only was I fooled, but Sparky was petrified." She kept her story to a single Sparky to avoid introducing timeline travel into the conversation.

Her dad went back to smiling. "I chose the Stryqr because it's made by the same company where Sparky works. I figured he'd recognize it and fear its capabilities."

"You scared the hell out of him, that's for sure." Rose started down an aisle and turned her attention to Julia. "What is all this?" Passing a collection of stuffed toys, she picked up what looked like a cuddly cloth teddy bear but set it down when she found it was made of a spongy foam.

Though the question was directed to Julia, Fifty-Five answered. "In modern movies, the sets and props, hell, even most actors, are created by AI. But audiences attending stage productions still expect to see real people with real props and scenery. Julia helps create the stage sets for a bunch of theaters around the world."

"I'm impressed." Rose walked back in their direction.

"I've never done a Broadway play or anything, so don't be too impressed. My work is mostly for community theaters and small city productions."

Rose pointed to the fab cell. "Do you make everything here?"

"No, shipping costs would kill me. I'll fabricate a piece

here if I want to hold it in my hands to look at during the creative process. But when I'm done, I send the client a file and they use a local fab cell to make everything." She pointed to the shelves. "I save a variety of items so I have something to show visiting clients."

Rose nodded as she digested the situation. "With a remote service, you can live here in the mountains. Very cool."

They wandered up and down the aisles after that, with Julia telling stories about different pieces. Rose enjoyed her charm, irreverent attitude, artistry—the whole package—and found herself hoping her father would succeed in moving the relationship forward.

After sitting on the back deck—the building's old loading dock—for iced tea with cheese and crackers, they left Julia to her work.

"See you for dinner," Julia called to Fifty-Five from the warehouse stoop as they climbed into the car. "And Rose, it was wonderful to finally meet you."

On the ride back to the hopper, Rose encouraged him. "I like her, Dad. She's really great."

"I'm glad you approve, honey, because I've developed a teenage-style crush on her."

"There are nice properties near town with the space she needs. Why don't you upgrade her lifestyle?"

He shook his head. "That's too over-the-top for a new relationship." He gave Rose a warm smile. "But it's a generous thought."

Watching the trees whoosh by the car window, Rose decided to get it over with. "Dad, I think I know why the

Sparkys came to our house."

"Is this what you've been waiting to talk about?"

She nodded, giving him a downcast expression she hoped showed contrition.

Her first version assigned some of the blame to Luca. But Fifty-Five asked the AI to play back the discussion that led to the decision to send bugs, then pointed Rose to where Luca said, "Fontaine's instruments may be able to detect mass-produced bugs."

She considered shifting blame to Lilah, but knew Lilah had expressed caution as well. Upset and defensive, Rose spouted the litany she'd heard since she was a teen. "Okay, I don't always consider the ramifications of my actions, and I'm bullheaded when I want something."

"That isn't what upsets me."

"Right." She spoke in a clipped fashion certain to annoy him. "If I know this about myself, why do I do it?"

"I love you, Rose. But you frustrate the hell out of me sometimes." He exhaled and crossed his arms. "I had better not be stewing about you later. Julia and I are having dinner together, and I want to be focusing on her." He sighed again. "And I'll have to tell the brothers about this. They'll have opinions about what to do with you."

"Like what?"

"I don't know. Maybe lock you in a closet and feed you through a hole in the wall."

She went on the offensive. "A lot of good came from my work. I learned that Sparky has a gun, and I also learned that he doesn't know how he snatched Thirty-Five during that jump." She leaned toward him. "I'm just saying that you can package the news in a more positive light if you want to be supportive of your only child."

Then she sealed the deal. "And because of me, you were able to show off Julia's work with great success. That will only enhance your evening with her." She winked. "You're welcome."

He remained silent as he looked out the window, brooding.

As the hopper landed at the house, he delivered his ruling. "We were already at war with Sparky, so this isn't the end of the world. But don't act all outraged if I don't support you as leader for some future project. You have to show me you can play well with others before that can happen."

She nodded to show she'd heard him, though her thoughts were on delivering the scrolls to her sisters. If she asked for his help now, she'd have to listen to more of his disapproval. She didn't think she could stomach it.

Though she believed he was making a mountain out of a molehill, she showed him she could be a team player. "Tomorrow morning I'm jumping to visit Thirty-Four and his Lilah. While I'm there, I'll collect their thoughts on how best to move forward with the Sparkys."

His expression said he wasn't buying it, but she pressed ahead anyway. "If I don't see you at breakfast, expect me home by midafternoon at the latest."

20. Rose, Thirty-Four timeline

The next morning, Rose timed her jump to arrive a half hour before her eight-year-old self left for school. Since Lilah chauffeured the child every morning, Rose would have a chance for a quick meeting with her mini-sister, and then time alone with Thirty-Four to talk about distributing scrolls.

While the strategy sounded good in theory, she'd forgotten how chaotic school mornings could be, especially as departure time approached.

Opening the door to the apartment, Thirty-Four exclaimed, "Rose! What's up?" Before she could answer, he yelled up the stairs. "Rose, I need you dressed and down here in five minutes!"

He looked back at her. "Is it an emergency?"

She shrugged. "Not a 'respond now' kind of emergency. But it's important."

"Can you visit with Justus for twenty minutes and come back after they're gone? Lilah gets back forty minutes after that. You'll have to wait until school's out to meet the little terror." He turned and called again. "Four minutes, Rose!"

Hoping to ingratiate herself to him, she turned and descended the steps. "Sure, no problem."

Justus wasn't in his office, so Rose went down to the basement and looked at the T-box, comparing her implementation against the machine she'd been trying to duplicate. After that, she poked around in Lilah's and Thirty-Four's office cubicles, seeking to learn more about them as people.

Hearing clomping on the steps, she stood still as Lilah Thirty-Four and young Rose exited the building. Waiting a moment more to ensure they didn't return, she climbed the stairs to find Thirty-Four clearing the dining table.

"Sorry about that," he said as he put dishes in the machine. "But you are a handful and then some in your younger years. It takes both of us coordinating like a precision drill team just to get you to school *every* morning." He laughed, though he didn't sound amused. "Would you like some coffee? Lilah and I eat after she returns from dropping Rose at school. I hope you'll join us."

"Yes to coffee, and yes to breakfast. Thanks so much." She took a seat at the table, and Thirty-Four handed her a mug of steaming liquid. She sipped while he fetched one for himself. "Sorry about barging in. How do the brothers keep from intruding on each other?"

"We plan where we can, agreeing on days and times and then sticking to it. But since there's no way to communicate other than in person, awkward situations happen. We deal with it like you and I just did."

"So, if I plan to return here based on what we discuss today, we'll agree on the specifics of that visit before I leave?"

"You make it sound complicated. It's pretty much 'See

you next Thursday at noon.'" His eyebrows flattened. "What are we going to discuss today that will require another visit?"

She reached into her pocket, pulled out a handful of scrolls, and spilled them onto the table. Some started to roll, the tiny enamel cylinders making a dull ringing sound as they spun across the hard surface. Then she reached into her other pocket and pulled out the rest of them.

Thirty-Four used his hands to corral the wayward cylinders. "I just finished delivering scrolls for the Lilahs. With you asking the same favor, I'm starting to feel like a sucker. Why can't your dad deliver these?"

"He's angry with me because he wants me to act like his assistant rather than an independent person who thinks for herself. When I don't respond to his ideas with glee and excitement, he thinks I'm being disrespectful."

"I've always wondered why you still live with him. Most children can't wait to move out."

Considering how to respond, she chose to open her soul. "I lost Mom to the T-box when I was fifteen. The irony I lived with from that point forward was that the thing that took her from me was the same thing I could use to see her again. Leaving home would mean losing access to the machine, my doorway to my mother."

She gave a wry smile. "It took a decade and a half and a lot of help, but I learned to decode the beast. When I met Lilah Thirty-Five, it was a dream come true. I can't wait to meet your Lilah."

Thirty-Four blinked rapidly. "Let me warm your coffee." When he stood and turned, he wiped his eyes with his fingertips.

She picked up one of the scrolls and absently balanced it on end. "I know they're not really Mom. I'm not delusional." When she had the cylinder stable, she tipped it over with her finger. "But they fill some of the hole in my heart. It's good."

When Thirty-Four sat again, he cleared his throat and changed direction. "Lilah tells me there was an incident with Sparky. What happened?"

Her jaw dropped. "Lilah's talking against me?"

"Of course not." He took her hand and squeezed it. "We all love and support you."

"Don't be condescending." She pulled her hand away. "Look, the brothers wanted to reconnect with the missing timelines and handed off the assignment to the sisters. I led an effort to adapt the most complex technology on the planet to achieve that goal. Our first attempt wasn't perfect, but we came damn close."

She rested her hands on the tabletop. "None of us foresaw the Sparkys. And by none of us, I mean sisters *or* brothers. He's a threat to our way of life and he'll be dealt with. But we were all onboard to get to this point. Singling me out now and saying it's my fault is just people ducking their share of the responsibility. I call bullshit."

Rose heard the apartment door open behind her and then Lilah's voice.

"Rose, it's so good to see you. David told me you were visiting."

Rose stood and hugged her mom-sister, ecstatic to connect with another portion of her mother's spirit, yet cautious as well. She wasn't sure if this Lilah supported her.

As Lilah stepped to the kitchen counter to pour herself a cup of coffee, Thirty-Four put it out there. "Rose offered me her perspective on things."

"Oh?" Lilah brought her coffee over and joined them at the table.

Thirty-Four rubbed his neck as he composed his thoughts. "She led a group effort that yielded both good and bad results. To blame her alone for the bad isn't fair."

"I hope no one is doing that." Lilah Thirty-Four caught Rose's eye. "You did a great job and everyone supports you. *We* sure do."

The words caused Rose's heart to soar, and in a spontaneous act of joy, she reached out and gave Lilah a second hug. Then, anxious to show them she could work as a team, she motioned to the pile of cylinders and pitched an idea.

"These scrolls show the sisters how to get a modified T-box up and running. They're written for the Forty timeline and up." She started sorting the scrolls into two piles. As she worked, she asked Lilah Thirty-Four, "I wonder if you'd like to coordinate bringing some of them online? The Forty through Forty-Eight timelines are a group you could help with."

Lilah's eyebrows scrunched. "Aren't T-discs introduced in the Forty timeline? I know nothing about them."

"That's right," said Rose. "But when the T-disc is installed, Forty takes his T-box offline but leaves it in place. It sits there until we move to New Hampshire eight years later, then we recycle everything so we won't have to move it."

Thirty-Four nodded. "That gives you a T-box to work with."

"Exactly," said Rose. "There's probably damage and disrepair to deal with in the later years, but that would be up to you to figure out. Are you interested?"

Lilah Thirty-Four smiled broadly. "Of course!"

Rose shifted one of the piles of scrolls over in front of her mom-sister. "These are detailed instructions for your group." She gathered the remaining scrolls in front of herself. "I'll take the oldest timelines—the New Hampshire crowd—because they all need to build a T-box pretty much from scratch, just like I did."

She left unsaid that the Lilahs were gone in her group, killed by the enigmatic, now departed, αCiopova. That meant other Roses would be her contacts in those timelines, sisters who would share a deep, immediate bond with her.

Lilah Thirty-Four served yogurt and muffins for breakfast, and even though Rose had already dined, she forced herself to eat again to maintain the convivial atmosphere. The conversation was carried by the two parents, who expressed unending pride, excitement, and joy in the many accomplishments of their young daughter.

Rose listened attentively, enjoying every moment because, in the end, they were sharing their love for her. She hadn't remembered her childhood as so adoring, yet she figured an eight-year-old saw life differently from the adults around her. And her mother's death changed everything anyway.

They finished eating and Rose stood. "I'll clear the table."

As she gathered dishes, Rose shifted her portion of the scrolls toward Thirty-Four. "Now I'm only asking for your help with this many."

21. Diesel, Fifty-Five timeline

"Travel to Fifty-Five," said Diesel as he pulled the cabin door closed. When his awareness returned, he was in Rose's T-box in the basement of her mountain home, the detour occurring because his machine was permanently modified to be part of the sisters' growing network. It meant he had to climb steps to join the group. It also meant he could travel clothed.

He joined eight brothers in the conservatory, the furniture arranged so they sat in a circle. Lilah had jumped ahead of him and was seated next to Rose, who sat to the right of her father.

Fifty-Five kicked things off by updating the group about the bug incident and the subsequent visit by the Sparkys to the house. Both Rose and Lilah glared at the group as he spoke, challenging them to find fault with their actions.

Forty stepped into it. "What the hell, Lilah? You were the adult in the room. How could you let this happen?"

Rose's eyes opened like moons and Lilah's forehead creased.

Then Lilah tore into him. "Recovering the lost brothers was important to *you*, but you couldn't figure out how to do it, so you delegated the responsibility to the smartest, hardest-working person in the room. Then you have the nerve to sit back and second-guess the outcome?" She put her hand on Rose's arm. "Maybe what really upsets you is that women have joined your all-boys club."

"Oh stop." Fifty-Five shook his head. "I'll say two things and then we'll move on. One, if the sisters had focused only on recovering the lost timelines, then the machine would still just transport brothers. And if that were true, the Sparky infection would never have happened. Your primary objective was to find a way for the sisters to jump, so don't frame yourselves as selfless and noble."

Diesel, who'd been thinking the same thing, found himself nodding.

"And two," Fifty-Five continued, scanning the group. "The sisters' focus on including themselves in the traveling world wasn't wrong or bad. Everyone supported that objective." He caught Forty's eye. "So no more finger-pointing. We all played a role in getting to this point. Let's figure out how to move forward."

Anxious to get past the confrontation, Diesel spoke. "We can break our Sparky challenge into three steps. There's erasing Sparky's neural implant, then destroying his equipment and records. And third, the hardest one, is keeping him away from us so we can live in peace."

Without standing, Fifty-Five stretched to a side table and picked up what looked like a small scrub brush. It had a smooth silver handle that fit comfortably in his hand. Short white bristles poked out from the underside of the grip.

He held it up for all to see, then passed it among the group. "This is a spire, the kind that can reset Sparky's neural implant. I've practiced with it using a simulation Luca developed. That exercise starts by tying Sparky to his bed."

"How do you get him to say the reset codes out loud?" asked Forty.

"The simulation loses its effectiveness on that question. Sparky has to reach a point where he believes that giving up the reset codes is all that's left for him." Fifty-Five shrugged. "We can use threats, bribes, pain, fear, imprisonment, and God knows what else. But in the end, I don't think he'll cooperate unless he sees death as his only other choice."

Rose, who'd gone quiet after the contentious exchange with Forty, leaned forward. "I wonder if we could sell him on a different reality. Maybe if he believed he was working with government agents or a crime syndicate, he'd be easier to manipulate."

"You mean like a con job?" asked Fifty-Five.

She nodded. "I just thought of it, so it's a wide-open idea. But yeah, a con is about selling someone on a false reality. So we con him rather than force him."

Diesel grinned. "Let's have Lilah and Rose pretend to be government agents, convince Sparky that the T-box is top-secret defense technology, and tell him to pretend he never saw it or risk federal prison."

Everyone laughed. In the quiet that followed, Forty spoke. "Sex. Men will do anything if they're infatuated."

"Is infatuation the same as sex?" asked Lilah. "I see

infatuation as a sign of emotional investment."

"Whatever. In the end, if he wants her bad enough, he'll take crazy risks to get her."

Lilah's eyes flicked to Diesel. "He sounds like he's talking from experience."

Diesel's face flushed because Forty's comment somehow landed in his lap. Shaking his head, he winged it. "Watch the news, read history, listen to music lyrics. Sexual obsession has led men—men not in this room—to stupidity from the beginning of time."

Lilah kept looking at him, then Fifty-Five mercifully changed subjects. "Even if we erase his implant and destroy his equipment, at some point the Sparkys will come to their senses, and then they'll come after us. How do we get them to forget about us?"

"What if we tip off Northern Droid about the theft of their catalog?" asked Diesel. "Grand larceny carries a jail term. That would get him out of our hair for a few years, anyway."

Rose shook her head and spoke with a level of confidence that continued to impress Diesel. "Companies prefer civil actions over criminal prosecutions for stuff like that. Criminal actions use low-paid government prosecutors to get justice, so the process can be unreliable. My guess is that they'd fire him, sue him six different ways so he's broke for life, and spread the word that he's damaged goods."

"Beyond that," added Fifty-Five, "people share secrets in prison. If he were put away for any length of time, I'd worry that someday one of his old cellmates would come knocking on our door, wondering if the stories were true."

Rose sat on her hands before speaking. "I have an idea that we all will hate but should solve the problem."

"We're not going to kill anyone," said Forty in a dismissive tone. "I was joking the other day."

Rose gave him a long look before continuing. "We bring all three Sparkys to a sacrificial timeline, erase their implants, then have the brother who lives there destroy his T-box or T-disc and all records. The Sparkys would then be stranded for the rest of their lives, unable to reach the rest of us ever again."

The room went quiet as they contemplated the idea.

"But the brother would be stranded as well," Lilah said quietly.

"As would the Rose and Lilah who live there." Rose kept her gaze downward. "That's why it's a sacrificial timeline. I told you I hated it. The cost is enormous. But it's a permanent solution requiring minimal violence."

"Who would we pick?" asked Forty.

Fifty-Five raised his hand. "I'll volunteer. My timeline helped create the problem, so we'll suck it up."

"Same here." Diesel raised his hand.

Lilah glared at him, shaking her head in quiet protest.

"We're not there yet," said Forty. "It's an interesting idea, but let's brainstorm some more before we speak of family sacrifice."

"I agree." Fifty-Five stood. "In fact, let's go down to the patio and everyone can try out one of Luca's simulations." He started for the door. "You're in for quite a treat."

The patio was the same space they used for the Big Meeting, only now it was configured as a broad outdoor terrace set with striking wicker furniture.

"Over here." Fifty-Five motioned to two tables shaded by colorful umbrellas. They split into groups, and Diesel sat with Lilah, Rose, Fifty-Five, and Forty.

"We need a brave person to go first," Fifty-Five announced in a voice loud enough for both tables to hear. "In the first exercise, you enter Sparky's house at three in the morning, sneak to his bedroom, then subdue him and tie him up."

"How do we subdue him?" asked Fifty-Six from the other table.

"The point of the simulations is to figure that out." Fifty-Five shrugged. "It's harder than you think. Everyone who wants to be on a Sparky team should give it a try."

Diesel saw Lilah move to volunteer and reacted to protect her, though from what, he didn't know. "I'll give it a go." He stood as he spoke to secure his first-in-line status.

Fifty-Five directed Diesel to an open space away from the tables. "Start over there so you have room to move." Addressing the others, he added. "Give Luca permission and he'll let you experience everything from Thirty-Five's viewpoint."

Diesel's heart began to race as Fifty-Five retook his seat.

"Are you ready?" asked Luca.

"No way. Explain what's supposed to happen."

"In this simulation, you start at Sparky's open front door. You are to move to Sparky's bedroom where you will find him in bed. As quickly as you can, secure his hands and feet in preparation for using the spire. When he is incapacitated, the challenge is over."

"Using the spire is a different simulation?"

"That's right."

Diesel smiled and winked at Lilah. "Now I'm ready." He didn't have a plan but figured the simulation would feed him options as he progressed, much like a sim game.

The bright patio faded, replaced by a world lit with murky moonlight. He recognized Sparky's porch and front door and took a moment to reorient his mind to this different place. The humid breeze, chirping crickets, and musky smell of wet leaves from the surrounding forest cemented the illusion.

Testing the simulation, Diesel pushed gently on the door. It swung open with a creak. "Oops," he whispered with a grin, hiding the mistake behind humor. Stepping into the foyer, he scanned the living area and confirmed that the layout of the house matched his memory.

Deciding to warm up before he made his move, he twisted at the hips, rotated his shoulders, and flexed his legs, working through a warmup routine he'd developed back when he wrestled in high school. With deep breaths, he tilted his head to the left until it cracked, then he repeated the move to the right.

"You got this," he reassured himself.

Then, choosing speed over stealth, he scurried down the hall and into Sparky's bedroom. Approaching the bed, he scanned the man's outline under the covers and peered around the darkened room, searching the gloom for a means to secure him.

"Ooof!" A painful blow to Diesel's stomach emptied his lungs of air. Doubling over, he gasped for breath.

And then Sparky was all over him, hitting his face, kneeing his groin, slapping both ears. Diesel flailed and backpedaled to escape. Catching his heel on the edge of a rug, he fell back and smacked his head on the edge of a table with a sickening crunch. Everything went dark.

When his vision returned, Diesel was lying on his back on the terrace. Though the blows had been excruciating at the time, he felt no pain or soreness as he stood. The others stared at him before starting to murmur.

"What was I supposed to learn from that?" He let his annoyance show in his tone.

"When I got creamed like you just did," said Fifty-Five, "I learned that handling Sparky is going to be a whole lot harder than I'd imagined. After I tried Luca's second exercise, the one with the spire, I learned I was still underestimating the level of difficulty."

Forty went next and started by asking Luca if he was capable of circumventing Portia, Sparky's house AI. Diesel punched his thigh when he realized that Portia had certainly warned Sparky of his presence as soon as he'd entered the house.

"I am able to distract Portia," answered Luca, "delaying her ability to warn Fontaine by half a minute."

"That's more than I need." Forty went through the same stretching sequence as Diesel, then made his run at Sparky. Even with the element of surprise, the big man took heavy blows before he finally prevailed, in the end injuring Sparky quite severely before he succeeded in securing the man's hands.

No one volunteered after that, the group settling in to a mild state of shock.

Then Rose stated what should have been obvious to the Diesels. "This isn't how we'd approach the situation. Realistically, we'd have three of you go in together, carrying gear and coordinating your actions. I'll bet we could prevail in seconds with minimal injury to anyone."

"You always were a thinker." Diesel made the statement with admiration and affection. But from Rose's unhappy expression, he wondered if she took it as sarcasm.

They tested team-based strategies after that, circling in on a set of actions they all could perform with some degree of success. Still, the sessions continued to be ugly, with major injuries a regular occurrence.

"What about some sort of tranquilizer gun?" asked Lilah. "Open his bedroom door and shoot him."

Fifty-Five smiled. "I have that simulation as well."

Diesel gave it a try and learned that common sedatives take half a minute to work. In those thirty seconds, Sparky fought like a wild man, inflicting major damage before succumbing to the drugs.

When things were winding down, Diesel walked over and sat with Lilah. "I can head home soon if you want to stay longer," he offered.

"Let's both go and have a good old-fashioned family dinner." She bit her lip. "I have a project going with the sisters and should have some messages waiting for me in the mailroom. Would you mind swinging by Thirty-Six's on the way home to pick them up?"

* * *

Diesel opened a beer and started dinner preparations in the kitchen while Lilah went across the street to retrieve nine-year-old Rose from Bunny. Over the years, Bunny, who'd originally been hired as their cleaning person, had demonstrated sound business acumen and began to oversee general maintenance for their flourishing real estate portfolio. She now managed their entire catalog of properties in and around Worcester, Massachusetts.

Hearing Lilah and Rose's footsteps on the stairs up to the apartment, he opened his second beer and started the microwave. Minutes later they sat at the kitchen table for dinner, where everyone took a few bites, and then he and Lilah focused on their daughter, listening as she detailed her successes and failures from the day.

When she showed them her spelling homework, Diesel was impressed with the words they expected a fifth grader to know. He put a hand on top of the worksheet. "Spell 'arachnid.'"

Rose grinned and did so without hesitation.

"Good for you." He patted her on the head. "Tomorrow be sure to tell Miss Maddison that your father helped you with your homework." Then to Lilah: "I'm desperate for brownie points ahead of our parent-teacher conference next month."

"Should she also tell Miss Maloney?" asked Lilah.

"Who?" The name sounded familiar.

"My teacher," said Rose.

Diesel laughed at his own failing. "Yes, tell everyone who will listen how wonderful your dad is."

With dinner cleared, Rose went up to her room to play with Luca, and Diesel went to the kitchen to retrieve a bottle of peach brandy from the overhead cabinet.

"I'm going to have an after-dinner snoot. Care to join me?"

Lilah gave a demure smile. "Sure, why not?"

A beer drinker by nature, he switched to fruit brandy when he felt amorous. In recent years, it had become a signal between them—he'd offer her a glass and she'd either accept or decline to signal her mood. Tonight she accepted his offer.

His passion for her stronger than ever, he grinned from ear to ear as he poured. Then he forced a serious expression and brought the drink to her on the couch.

"For you, my sweet."

He sat and they cuddled, sipping and chatting about nothing. Soon enough, though, the conversation drifted to Sparky, and Lilah's mood changed.

Folding her arms, she let out a huff. "I hate the sacrificial timeline idea. And I hate worse that you volunteered us."

"I'm pretty sure it will never happen." He shifted closer to her on the couch and kissed her neck on the left side. "We just need to come up with a better plan." He moved behind her and kissed her neck on the right side.

"It *can't* happen, David. I spent more than a decade of my life struggling to figure out how to jump. I'm not bargaining that away a week after I succeed. Neither is Rose."

He massaged her neck and shoulders and, without stopping, leaned forward and nibbled an ear.

Unmoved by his ministrations, she continued in an even tone. "Why can't we ask Sixty-Three to volunteer? He's been traveling for thirty-five years. Let someone else have a turn, for heaven's sake."

He continued his kisses, and she finally tilted her head to the side, giving him better access. He pulled her hair over and nuzzled her neck below her ear.

Sighing, she leaned into his arms, staying there for most of a minute. Then she sat forward and turned to him. "What did you think of Forty's idea of running a romantic con?"

Diesel's sigh revealed exasperation, and he reached for his glass of brandy. "In the abstract, I can see it working to get us inside, maybe slow Sparky down. But have you thought about whether you'd let him touch you like this?" He reached out and caressed her breasts. "If not, how do you make it work for any length of time? And what happens to our life here if you're there working a con?"

Lilah, took a sip of her drink and shook her head. "I don't see a con working if it's purely sexual. I think it will take longer than Rose says because Sparky needs to be emotionally invested."

"In my teens, I'd fall in love after one dance with a girl."

She looked at him and smiled. "Getting him interested is easy. Getting him to spill his secrets will be hard."

In bed that night, Lilah insisted that Diesel lay back and let her do all the work. She moved through his favorites, progressing at a measured pace, distracted as if she were concentrating. During one portion of her performance, he was sure she was counting.

But pleasure took control of his senses, and he replaced his wonder about her behavior with a determined effort to last as long as he could. He finished moments later.

She snuggled up against him, and he wrapped an arm around her. "Thank you, Lolli. That was wonderful."

He closed his eyes, and then opened them.

She was practicing for something. He was pretty sure he knew what.

He stared into the darkness after that but sleep never came.

22. Lilah, Fifty-Five timeline

Lilah drove young Rose to school, checked in with Bunny to confirm she would pick her up afterward, then jumped to the Fifty-Five timeline. Since this was an unplanned visit, she called to Luca when she stepped from the T-box. "Please tell Rose I'm here." After climbing the steps, she stood in the kitchen, an intruder waiting for the homeowner to arrive.

"Good morning!" Rose burst through the door with a cheery expression, then stopped her approach and studied Lilah. "I swear, you and Lilah Thirty-Four look so much alike. If Luca hadn't told me, I'd have to ask which one you are."

"It's me, Lilah Thirty-Five," she said as they hugged.

"I'm happy you're here. I have a ton of ideas I want to bounce off you."

"Same here. That's why I've come." The initial discomfort of her unannounced arrival dissipated in the supportive environment.

"Have you eaten?"

Lilah nodded.

"Me too. I have a few minutes of chores left. Tag along and we'll talk while I finish." She led Lilah out to the front porch, where she picked up a watering can and began tending to the potted plants decorating the entrance of the lovely home.

Pulling a brown leaf from the pansies, she said, "I can't stop thinking of Forty's suggestion of a romantic con. My instincts tell me it's a quick way to learn Sparky's secrets, get him into a vulnerable situation, and exert some control."

"I've been thinking about it as well." Lilah leaned down and smelled a lush red geranium, its botanical perfume filling her senses. "I'm not as optimistic as you. The more I think it through, the more I see it going wrong."

"It's simple." Rose gave each pot a quarter-turn so a different side of the plant could respond to the sun. "Choose your bait, set the hook…"

"…and reel him in," Lilah finished with her. "Oh my God! Please don't tell me you learned that from me." It was a mantra her crowd had chanted in her teen years when they were experimenting with using seduction to manipulate males.

Rose stood and faced her. "I was fourteen and boys were pestering me like flies, but Peter Slotnick didn't know I existed. I moped around for weeks, and then I heard you joke to Dad about your foolproof…"

"…three-step plan." Lilah felt an emotional swell as she recognized the clear connection she had with this person. In the inexplicable universe they now inhabited, it reinforced the idea that Rose was indeed her daughter.

"You died four months later," Rose said solemnly. She moved toward the house with the watering can in hand. "This way."

Lilah followed her through a series of rooms and out French doors onto a broad red-brick terrace. There, she squatted and tended the plants near the entryway. "I let Maid Marian handle everything but the display at the front door and the one here. Guests use one or the other, and I like to put my own stamp on their first impressions."

"It's very inviting." The displays were beautiful, and Lilah enjoyed learning about Rose's artistic side.

Then she switched gears and made her pitch. While she wasn't sold on the idea of a romantic con, she felt compelled to shield Rose from the wrath of the brothers. "I should be the bait for Sparky. You're from this timeline, so at some point you'll be identified as the daughter of his nemesis. No records here can link me to you or your father, so I'm the safe bet."

Rose clapped debris from her hands as she stood, then bent and dusted off her pants. "I have an artist friend who's amazing with effects. She could tweak my face and body just enough to confuse the automated recognition systems."

"But I don't need any tweaking."

"You're also a mom and wife who has to travel from another timeline to get here. It has to be me, just from a practical level."

Anxious to slow her down, Lilah reinforced the consequences. "You're already in the hot seat, Rose. If this goes bad, the brothers will ostracize you. Hell, your dad will lock you in the basement and throw away the key."

"If Sparky takes the bait, I'll be in a position to guide his thinking, to slow him down, and perhaps most important, to warn Dad if danger threatens. And while I'd like to involve the brothers in the planning, you know they'll become all puritanical as soon as they hear the details, crying and wailing about their daughter the whore."

Lilah shook her head. "It won't be a quick in and out. Gaining influence on his thinking will take months."

"Good morning!" Fifty-Five joined them on the terrace wearing a white robe. With hair disheveled and coffee cup in hand, he approached Lilah and gave her a peck on the cheek.

Rose put a hand on his arm and got right to it. "Dad, whoever goes near Sparky or his property will immediately be identified by his home AI. I think a proper disguise could delay identification and buy time for our team."

"Makes sense," he said slowly. Lilah could see the gears turning.

"Julia seems like the perfect person to help with that. Would you mind if we talked to her about disguises?" Rose paused. "Anyway, Lilah is eager to meet her."

Lilah blushed when Fifty-Five looked at her, but she didn't deny the statement, even though she'd learned in that instant that Rose's "artist friend who's amazing with effects" is the same person her dad was dating.

"Gosh, honey. I don't want to drag Julia into something this ugly."

Rose tsked. "Anything Julia knows or learns about us is because *you* tell her, not me. For this visit, we want to feel out her capabilities and see if the idea has merit."

Fifty-Five creased his brow and looked from Rose to Lilah and back to Rose. "I think you're up to something, and I'll be very unhappy if it makes *anything* in my life messier. But I also think Julia will enjoy getting to know you better, which is good for me." He gave Rose a long stare. "Promise me this is just about exploring disguises."

Rose held up her right hand as if she were testifying in court. "Nothing but disguises, I do thee swear."

Fifty-Five looked at Lilah, waiting for her to promise as well.

Uncomfortable about everything, she gave a shallow nod.

After a sip of coffee, Fifty-Five looked into the air and gave Luca a message for Julia. "Hi, hon. Rose and her friend Lilah are working on a project and they wonder..." He turned and walked into the house, his voice fading through the entryway.

He returned a minute later, a satisfied look on his face. "I'll let you know when she responds." Holding up a finger, he twirled back to the house. "Hi, Julia..."

This time it took almost five minutes for him to return. "She invites you to her studio at noon today."

Already feeling awkward, Lilah didn't want to put Julia to any trouble. "I hope she isn't planning to feed us."

Fifty-Five winked. "That's what took so long just now. Don't worry, she's having it delivered, and the effort of selecting choices is already done." Then he yawned and scratched his head. "I'm going to clean up. If I don't see you before you leave, behave yourselves."

He walked to the door, turned back, and locked eyes with Lilah. As he spoke, he choked on his words. "She's a wonderful person, but she's not a replacement. Please don't

be hurt, jealous, or any of that. I'll always love you."
Looking down, he disappeared inside the house.

Lilah turned her back on Rose and blinked several times. Over her shoulder, she asked, "How long before we have to leave?"

"About an hour."

With a discreet wipe of her eyes, she swiveled back. "I'm not dressed to meet my husband's future girlfriend. Can we go to your room so I can clean up a bit?"

"You don't even know how beautiful you are." Rose stroked Lilah's arm, then she looked her up and down and dimpled with a scrunched-nose grin. "But for sure, that blouse is dated. And I have the perfect shoes. Follow me."

In the move from Massachusetts to New Hampshire, Rose had gone full-billionaire, giving herself a bedroom suite fit for a queen. Her closet was bigger than Lilah's bedroom, and it was almost full.

Lilah walked up one row and down another, thinking she'd been in boutiques with less inventory. "We'll need some way of keeping track of styles as we move across timelines. Or like you're doing, maybe we'll just have to open our closets to visiting sisters."

Rose stepped from behind a rack of dresses. "Before you think I'm awful for having all this, I make them in the fab cell downstairs, and I can recycle the material at any time." Rose moved over a row, pulled down a pair of slacks, and handed them to Lilah. "See how these fit." Then she continued. "My neurosis is that every time I go out, I make a few outfits before I finally choose one. Everything ends up here." She twirled slowly and eyed her collection.

"Clearly, this has gotten out of hand."

Lilah settled on black pants with a red and white floral top. Rose led her to the bathroom after that and directed her to place her face in a white mask-like apparatus. When she did, Lilah saw an image of her face hovering in front of her. A display offered a selection of options for editing the image. Using the intuitive tools, she smoothed blemishes from her skin, filled in a few tiny wrinkles, added color to her lips and cheeks, and trimmed her eyebrows.

"When you're happy with your look, choose 'Go' at the bottom," said Rose from behind her.

Lilah did so and felt a quick buzz across her face. The image she'd been looking at faded. She pulled away and checked her face in the mirror. "It looks like a mask," she said of the too-perfect cover.

"Do this." Rose made an exaggerated open-mouthed grin, her eyebrows raised like she'd seen a ghost.

When Lilah made the face, Rose said, "Now this," and scrunched her face together like she'd bitten into a lemon.

When Lilah finished flexing her face, she looked in the mirror again and gave a genuine smile. The makeup was undetectable, and she looked great.

"Look at the time!" said Rose, starting to scurry. "We'd better hustle."

Lilah followed Rose through the house and back onto the patio, where her attention was captured by a background thrum—a noise she hadn't heard an hour earlier. The thrum transitioned to a whirring sound, and an amazing craft appeared overhead. Looking something like an old-style space capsule, the craft descended, landing on the far side of the terrace.

Rose led the way to the vehicle. "Hoppers are relatively new around here. They sure make life convenient."

A small door swung open as they approached, the hatch just tall enough for Lilah to enter while standing upright. The cramped interior had a circle of six black-fabric seats around the perimeter. Above them, a ring of windows provided a panoramic view of the world outside.

Lilah sat down next to Rose, who pointed to the seat across from her. "They tell you to sit on either side to balance the load, but no one ever does."

Before Lilah could move, the drive spun up and the hopper lifted into the air. Her heart raced as they moved out over the valley and, like an elevator, started a gentle descent to the ground below. From takeoff to landing, the trip took four minutes.

Rose stepped out of the hopper and waited for Lilah. "I heard Dad say you were my friend during his phone call with Julia, so that part of the story is fixed. I think being cousins would have been easier." She led the way across the field to the parking lot. "So, how do we know each other?"

Lilah thought for a moment. "Let's stick as close as we can to the truth. I was born in Andover, Massachusetts, and moved to Worcester. You and I were neighbors who became friends. I still live in Worcester."

"That works." Rose lifted her hand and waved, and Lilah looked across the field to see a young man near a sky-blue hopper wave back.

They climbed into the car, and as it accelerated down the road, Rose nudged Lilah and pointed toward an open field. Lilah looked out onto an enchanting scene of a doe with her fawn, then the car took a corner and she lost sight of them.

"You're missing two decades of current events," Rose continued. "I've seen that trip up the brothers in their conversations with outsiders. Just something to be aware of."

"What should I do?"

"Being mindful of it helps a lot. The brothers have learned that a good strategy is to ask questions rather than give opinions or tell stories."

When the car stopped in the overgrown parking lot of a run-down metal-roofed warehouse, Lilah frowned. "She runs her business out of here?"

"I don't think she makes much from it, so this lets her control costs."

On the porch, a brawny bot dressed in a clown outfit opened the warehouse door.

"Hi, Champ." Rose moved to step past the bot.

"Please wait here." Champ spread his arms ever so slightly to block the way, his puffy white gloves hovering just above hip level.

"What do you mean?"

"I would ask that Miss Lilah not enter the building. She should wait here." Champ motioned to a lone chair on the porch away from the door.

Lilah felt her face flush with embarrassment, and she sought to escape. "Perhaps I should wait in the car."

"Champ, whatever are you doing?" The voice came from behind the bot, and moments later a handsome forty-five-year-old woman appeared. "I'm so sorry about the confusion." Julia looked Lilah up and down as she spoke, then touched Rose's arm. "Can we talk?"

Rose shrugged to Lilah and followed Julia into the building. Lilah moved near the chair Champ had indicated but didn't sit.

* * *

Rose signaled to Lilah that she'd be right back. Ducking around Champ, she entered the building and reached Julia a short distance inside.

"None of my databases can ID her." Julia bit her lip. "It worries me. How well do you know her?"

"She's not in the theater business if you're worried about her stealing your ideas."

"How well?"

Rose's brow creased. "I vouch for her a hundred percent. A thousand percent. I trust her the way I trust Dad, and I don't say that lightly."

"Why isn't she in any database?"

Casting a sideways glance toward the entryway, Rose winged it. "A creep was using recognition tech to stalk her, and the authorities wouldn't do anything. She became so frightened that she had microsurgery to escape him."

"No kidding." Julia leaned to study Lilah through the door.

"The real reason I'm here is because I'm being hassled by a guy myself. I'm thinking simple prosthetics would defeat his tech and save me from surgery."

"Your dad said it was for a party."

Rose shrugged.

Julia gave her a long look. "This is for real? How long has he been following you?"

"About a month. Dad is carrying a full load right now, and I don't want to bother him with it. Cops are worth shit for this kind of thing. So I'm reaching out to see if we can be resourceful together."

"First, I am so sorry." Julia enveloped Rose in a snug embrace and held it while she spoke. "But most important, you've come to the right place. I'm here to help you."

* * *

It seemed like an eternity to Lilah, but Rose finally returned to rescue her from her porch prison. Leading her inside, Rose introduced her to Julia.

After they greeted each other, Julia asked, "What exactly did you have done?"

"Excuse me?" Lilah hadn't heard the conversation between the two, so she had no context for the question.

Rose helped. "I told her about your microsurgery to escape that creep and his tracking tech."

"Ah." Lilah nodded, understanding that Rose wanted her to go along with something but feeling uncertain as to what that might be.

"You need at least eight adjustments to drop from the databases so completely." Julia walked around Lilah, assessing her with a practiced eye. "At a minimum, they tweaked your nose, ears, brow, chin, eye color, hair line, shoulders, height. Were your limbs lengthened or shortened?"

Nervous about ruining whatever Rose had going, Lilah went with a response that covered it all. "I deny everything."

Julia stepped back and put her hands on her hips. "Good for you. That's the *perfect* answer."

She became animated after that, motioning for them to follow as she began to walk. "I was concerned when you didn't show up on my scan. I run all three commercial databases plus the Federal Registry and Border record, so I don't find virgins very often. Please forgive my reaction."

"I'm sorry to cause such an upset."

"Rose told me about your problem, and I'm *so* pleased that your first instinct is to deny it all and protect your protectors. It does my heart good."

Lilah pondered Julia's words as they progressed down the aisle. Rose had prepared her to spend time enjoying shelves filled with amazing artifacts. Instead, she found herself fretting about whether Rose had the situation under control.

At the back of the warehouse, Julia tilted her head toward a broad table filled with goodies. "Rose, your father ordered enough food to feed an army. Please, help yourself."

Lilah took a plate and scooped fresh fruit salad from a big bowl. She nibbled on a chunk of melon as the others took a turn.

"I have a friend coming in about an hour," said Julia as she led them back to her private office. "He'll be taking everything we don't eat to the soup kitchen."

Her office was as dingy and tired as the larger warehouse. She pulled a padded office chair from behind a gray metal desk and positioned it to form a circle with the visitor chairs. "Please, sit."

As they settled and began to eat, Julia said, "You know there are organizations that help women who are victims of aggressors."

Lilah recalled that Fifty-Five had said something similar when Rose suggested the idea of being stalked.

"And now these scumbags use tracking tech to follow their victims," Julia continued. "And with cops focused on other priorities, there are people—women—who need somewhere to turn."

Lilah couldn't contain her curiosity and told herself that asking questions was okay. "Earlier you mentioned several ID databases that you use. Someone protecting herself with that kind of arsenal must have had problems of her own."

Instead of responding to Lilah, Julia shifted in her chair and spoke to Rose. "This is uncomfortable because I haven't yet told your father what I'm about to tell you. Don't get me wrong, I'm not hiding it from him. I told him I volunteer to help women in need, but our relationship is new and I hadn't yet gotten to the part where I told him I'm executive director of RPR New England."

"I've heard of RPR." Rose nodded. "It's a national women's rescue group."

"That's right. Rescue, Protect, Return. We used to be Rescue, Protect, Relocate, but we decided a complete solution lets her get back her old life."

Julia turned to Lilah and rested a hand on her arm. "I hate to be the one to tell you, but sometime in the next few weeks, the national ID systems will figure out who you are and re-register you in the databases with your new features. You'll be back where you started."

Lilah looked down and gave a solemn nod, acting like someone receiving bad news.

Then Julia opened a file cabinet, lifted out a large, plain jewelry box, and set it on the low table in the center of their circle. "That's why we recommend temporary prosthetics."

She opened the lid to reveal a number of cloth-lined compartments. But instead of holding broaches and bracelets, the compartments held pieces of plastic in a variety of shapes and sizes.

Julia selected one that looked like a short strip of tape and, leaning in front of a mirror, fit it over the bridge of her nose. The sophisticated piece fit so well, it seemed to disappear.

"This one changes my nose dimensions. The ID systems, rather than making a positive match for me, will now recognize the discrepancy and consider whether I am one of perhaps six or eight other people."

Lifting a small, thin wedge from the box, Julia pressed it against the front crease of her ear. "This moves two key ear measurements forward and down. Combine this with the nose adjustment, and I'm now one of a hundred possibilities."

Julia showed them chin cups, cheek lifts, lip pads, skull caps, contact lenses, shoulder pads, shoe lifts—a whole collection of adjustments a person could use to escape tracking.

"To be sure, you don't become invisible with these. Each prosthetic blurs you a little bit. The system eventually realizes you are missing and starts working to reacquire you. Our solution is to mix and match, wearing a few different pieces every day so it never catches up. If the system can't find you, neither can your aggressor."

Lilah had come here looking to find a Julia full of flaws. Instead, she found herself liking and even admiring the woman. "What an amazing contribution."

Rose pointed to the jewelry box. "Is there a way Lilah and I could get a set of those?"

"Of course. But these aren't generic pieces. The ID systems are quite sophisticated, and the designers knew people would be trying to defeat them. Each item in the box is crafted for one individual, moving measurement points in a precise way to create uncertainty in identification. And you need to stay current. You should come in for a fit adjustment every few months to stay ahead of emerging technology."

"Is it a matter of cost? I'm happy to pay."

"First, I want you to know that we work hard to keep expenses down." Julia spread her hands to indicate her Spartan surroundings. "And about half our clients were struggling to pay their bills *before* they became victims. We serve them for free."

As Julia spoke, a graphic appeared in the air, the colorful display showing the financials of RPR, with arrows tracing how money flowed in and out to make the operation work.

"And the prosthetics are the cheap part. As you can see here, the rescue squad and protection teams soak up a huge chunk of funds. Then comes legal, because too many cases end up in court for one reason or another. After that it's research, with our team struggling to stay ahead of new tracking methods. Last is the cost of the prosthetics."

It was clear to Lilah where Julia was headed with her presentation. She wondered if Rose had figured it out.

Julia gave the punch line. "The way we make it work is by socking it to the whales—the rich people who come to us." She gave a prim smile. "That would be you."

"I've learned that's how life works," said Rose. "How much?"

"We send millionaires an invoice for ten thousand dollars. By that formula, a billionaire would be asked to pay ten million dollars."

Rose didn't move, her reaction a thin smile.

Lilah coughed.

Julia started putting the plastic bits back in the jewelry box, the task absorbing all of her attention.

Rose broke the silence. "Your number is way high. But before we worry about that, you need to know that even though I live at my dad's house, I'm an adult with my own life, some of which I keep private from him. If we agree on a deal, I'll be paying you from *my* funds, not his." She tapped her chest. "That means *I* will be your client, not him."

"You want me to keep it secret from him?"

"I want to establish a business relationship with you,

and whatever we do within that relationship, I expect you to keep confidential from *everyone*. That includes Dad."

"Is any of it illegal?"

"No, it's about hiding us from a bad guy. Just not the kind of bad guy you're used to dealing with."

"Can I tell him that you and I are in a private business relationship, and that means I am bound by confidentiality?"

"Sure." Rose nodded.

Julia sat for a moment. "I'll be right back." She rose and left the room.

As soon as she was gone, Lilah said, "Ten million sounds like a lot."

"I'm not giving her that and she knows it. She's probably conferring with someone right now about how low she should go."

Lilah pointed at the jewelry box. "These kits will let us get close to Sparky, which means we can think seriously about what comes next."

They were studying the different pieces in the box when Julia returned. "I will agree to keep our business relationship private."

Lilah, thinking she'd finally found a personality flaw, pounced. "You'll really hide this from David?"

"Of course not. I just now asked him if a private business relationship between Rose and me would come between us. He said it wouldn't and agreed that if he ever had questions, he would ask Rose directly. I believe him."

Julia sat and crossed her legs. "Look, I like David a lot and don't want to risk screwing things up, even for big money. Relationships work best with open and honest communication. He understands and approves this private business arrangement in advance. So, if he ever gets nosey, I'll be very comfortable telling him to back off."

Rose said what Lilah was thinking. "Wow. My dad has impressive taste in women." Then she included Lilah. "Very impressive taste."

After a pause, Rose made a proposal. "I suggest three conditions. The first is that the three of us here form the complete group covered by our agreement. Share freely among us, but no one else may know. Second is that Lilah and I each get a prosthetics kit from this agreement, but we don't need rescuing or protection, so that will simplify things. And third, Lilah and I get to use your big fab cell out front for the next month. We'll pay for the feed material and your utility bill separate from the donation. Full disclosure, we will be running it all day, every day, and we won't explain what we're working on."

Julia sat back in her chair but remained silent.

Lilah, who'd been following Rose's thought process up to that point, frowned. *Is she going to build another T-box away from David? What else could it be?*

"And I'll donate two million dollars to the cause. It's one I'm proud to support."

Rubbing her hands along the tops of her thighs, Julia asked in a plaintive voice, "Will he be angry with me if he learns the details? I don't want to lose him over this."

Rose shook her head. "If anything, he'll be unhappy with me. I'm used to it, though."

Lilah found herself nodding in agreement.

Biting her lip, Julia looked from Rose to Lilah and back, then her expression softened. "I'll do the deal."

With a yelp of joy, Rose jumped to her feet and held out her arms, inviting them both for a celebratory hug.

23. Diesel, Thirty-Five timeline

With Lilah off visiting Rose in the Fifty-Five timeline, Diesel plodded down to the main floor of the row house to meet with Justus. As he entered the large office, Justus—fifty-five years old, fit, medium build, thinning hair, black complexion—rose from his ergonomic office chair to greet him. After they shook hands, Diesel plopped down in one of the leather visitor's chairs in front of a broad oak desk.

The way the office was staged, Diesel's chair was angled toward the side wall, which was filled with security displays from around the building. The lack of movement on any of the views confirmed that all was quiet at the Lagerford homestead.

"We've got a mess on our hands," Diesel started. "I could use some help thinking it through."

Justus was Bump Analytics' office manager. His charge was to handle all details associated with running the company. Over the past decade, he had proven himself to be a wise and steady hand, and Diesel had grown to depend on him, especially when things got rough.

Justus waited patiently for him to continue. Diesel found it an appealing quality.

He gave Justus a rundown on the Sparkys, who they

were, how they came to be, and the threat they posed to the established order. Since Justus knew the secrets of the T-box, Diesel explained every detail of the situation in the hopes of getting meaningful suggestions in return.

The only tidbit Diesel held back was his fear that Lilah might be considering sex as a tool to manipulate Sparky. The idea left him emotionally raw; it's what had driven him to come see Justus in the first place.

When Diesel finished his account, Justus echoed back a summary, ending with the objectives. "You want it so the Sparkys lose access to the T-box technology, don't share their knowledge with others, and never bother you again."

"Bingo."

Justus sat for a moment. "You know I don't do illegal or violent. But you say one of them held you captive, two of them approached Fifty-Five's house in disguise, and Lilah and Rose fear for their safety. It's clear they crossed the line first."

"This is definitely about our immediate safety, especially for Lilah and Rose." Diesel wanted to encourage Justus in any way he could.

Tapping his pen on the desk, Justus pursed his lips. "Going in order, the easy one is taking the technology away from these guys. Destroying their equipment and erasing their brain implants sounds on target."

"To erase an implant, we need the Sparkys to say a list of reset codes. It's a sticking point."

Justus shrugged. "Gaining their cooperation is easier than you might imagine. Isolate them like that one did to you. Offer no communication of any kind. Keep each of them alone in an empty, silent room—no sleep, no food, and severely restricted water. It will be emotionally difficult to watch while you wait for them to break. But based on the cases I'm familiar with, they'll do the required task—reset their implants in this case—by day three. Day four at the latest if you give them the water to last that long."

"You think so?"

Justus nodded. "Loneliness, hunger, thirst, and sleeplessness are all prime motivators. Combine them and you have a whopper of a tool. Like I said, though, it's not pretty."

Diesel flashed back to his cold, lonely, thirsty night in the forest, contemplated the horror of staying there for three or four nights in a row, and shuddered.

Justus stopped playing with his pen and pointed it at Diesel. "And he'll recover from the deprivation in a week and be no worse for wear."

The comment made Justus sound defensive, but Diesel let it go. "We ran simulations to practice subduing him. He's a scrappy fighter. It won't be easy."

"We have Tasers here in this timeline. I'm sure they have immobilizers twenty years from now that are even more effective. You won't need to break a sweat."

Diesel looked at his shoes and shook his head, not to deny the idea but to express self-loathing. He and a dozen of his brothers had brainstormed multiple methods for subduing the Sparkys, and they always focused on adding more manpower rather than considering obvious tools like a Taser.

"Let's say we get the implants erased." Justus was on a

roll and Diesel wanted to hear more. "They still will know the technology exists and that we're using it. How do we keep them from telling others and coming after us?"

"I think moving them to a distant timeline will shut them up about everything. Imagine bringing a Sparky here. We relocate him out west, say, an isolated town somewhere in Arizona or New Mexico. Losing twenty years of progress will make him a fish out of water. His brain implant won't have anything to link to. Our archaic tech will make his world much smaller. And with no papers for any country, he'll have nowhere to go."

"Are you saying to spread the Sparkys out in different timelines? We thought that keeping them together would make it easier."

"Don't do that." Justus shook his head emphatically. "There's strength in numbers, so keep them apart. They'll be weaker alone, and it's much easier to control one person than a team of three."

Diesel still had doubts. "He's already lived through these years, so even if we move him here, he could readjust his mindset by twenty years. It won't be that foreign to him. And won't knowing what comes next in history give him an advantage?"

Justus shrugged. "Imagine him trying to convince strangers that a person out east is a time traveler who captured him from the future and brought him back here to live in comfort."

The thought caused Diesel to flash a quick smile. "Why would he stay there? I see him coming east to find me." He thought he'd scored a point when Justus sat quiet for a moment.

"I know two ways to keep him out west. One is to use a surveillance team to monitor him and turn him around if he starts to stray. It would cost a few million per year to hire a team large enough to keep it up all day, every day. But the activity would be managed by a contractor, so you wouldn't even have to think about it. And you wouldn't notice the cost."

"What's the other way?"

"What I just described is something I can help with. I won't help with this next idea, and that's to hire a fetching young thing to be his girlfriend. Get him to fall in love, then have her control him while you control her."

Diesel recalled Lilah's behavior in bed the night before and couldn't contain himself. "How could someone pretend to be another's lover as a job? It seems so...cold."

"Bunny knows more about this than I, but it gets colder. If that's your play, you'll need to start by sending in a few women—and men—to gauge his general taste in lovers. Based on that, second recruits work to find his kinks. *Then* you can start searching for someone to take the long-term gig."

What Justus described made Diesel's stomach roil. Then his eye caught movement on one of the security displays. Lilah's mother exited Lilah's old apartment in the row house next door, carried her suitcase downstairs to the front door, then climbed back up and disappeared into the apartment.

"What's Mom doing?"

"She leaves today." Justus checked the time. "In about

ten minutes, actually."

"I should probably go say goodbye."

Justus stood. "I'm going over to see her off. Come join me."

With a sigh, Diesel followed Justus next door, arriving in time to carry Mom's suitcase to the car. "Thank you so much for helping," he started, then caught her gaze and said with all sincerity, "And thanks for your time with Rose. She glows when you're here."

Mom settled Andy into his doggie bed in the back of the car, prattling nonstop about the lovely visit and how much fun she'd had. As she drove down the street, Diesel waved goodbye, happy he could report to Lilah that her mom had a good stay, while at the same time hoping that her positive experience didn't translate into a return trip anytime soon.

Back in the house, Diesel shook hands with Justus, formally thanking him for his insights and advice on Sparky without actually saying the words. Then he went to the basement and jumped to the Fifty-Five timeline to take part in the war meeting about to get underway.

He joined nine brothers in the kitchen, some sitting around Fifty-Five's smart-top dining table, the kind that grows larger as more people sit. The rest were up and about, generating an impressive array of snacks from the different kitchen appliances, then piling the food in the middle of the table so everyone could nosh.

When the bounty grew to the point where Forty had trouble finding space for his heaping plate of barbequed chicken wings, Diesel got them started. Holding up his hand, he asked the room, "Who here was reminded about Tasers, perhaps after spending time with Justus?"

None of the brothers responded to his question, but facial expressions and body language told Diesel that a few understood his reference. Others looked down at their shoes and shook their heads, just as he had done.

Diesel caught Fifty-Five's eye. "I assume you still have Tasers in this timeline?"

"We have both Tasers and neutralizers." Fifty-Five was one of the brothers who'd looked at his shoes. "Tasers send jolts of electricity into a body to subdue the target. Neutralizers pull electricity out of the large muscles, leaving the target in a painless paralysis." He looked up and called to the air in a slightly different tone. "Do I have that right, Luca?"

"Yes, though some people do find the paralysis from neutralizers to be mentally painful." Luca appeared before them. "And injury can occur during the fall when a target collapses. But you are correct that there is no physical pain caused by the neutralizer itself. It's an effective tool and a good choice for your application."

"How can we get one?" asked Diesel.

"You need a permit to buy and carry a neutralizer across state lines. Permitting is a simple process, but it requires that you file the application in person. The clerk at the town office can do the approval during normal business hours, which today lasts another ninety minutes."

"Get us one, Luca," Fifty-Five said in a no-nonsense tone, "without me traveling into town."

"By 'one,' I assume you mean one neutralizer rather

than one permit."

Fifty-Five didn't respond, but Diesel saw his jaw muscles flex.

Luca made a throat-clearing noise in response. "Daryl's Garden Supply sells animal-control guns that are nothing more than repackaged neutralizers. No permit is required to carry one when it's for animal control."

"Daryl's is on Frontage Road." Fifty-Five sat up. "Hey, Rose, are you available?"

"Hi, Dad!" Rose appeared as an image next to Luca, her ebullience brightening the room. "Lilah and I *love* Julia. Please don't mess this up."

"Thanks, sweetheart." Fifty-Five blushed and Diesel made a mental note to follow up on the reference. "Would you be able to pick something up for me at Daryl's? You pass by it on your way home."

"We passed it five minutes ago."

"Oh, never mind, then. I guess I'll travel all the way there this afternoon and pick it up myself to save you the hassle."

"Now it's six minutes."

Fifty-Five added a sweetener. "After you pick it up, you and Lilah are welcome to join our Sparky planning meeting."

"Deal! Except, Luca, we will be participating in the meeting starting immediately. Include us in everything."

In the kitchen, a floating image of Lilah appeared next to Rose, then Luca shifted them to the side of the room, elevating them slightly to improve sightlines with the brothers.

As conversation resumed, Luca interrupted. "We are being probed!" Everyone stopped moving, ears cocked. "Someone is scanning through the local spectrum." A pause. "Now they are trying to commandeer a line feed inside the house!"

"Sparky!" several brothers accused in unison, the rest nodding.

"I'm tracing the probe back to the source. Yes, it originates from Sparky's home."

"Can you block him?" asked Diesel.

"Yes."

"Maybe we should feed him misinformation," suggested Rose. "Send him on a wild goose chase."

"What, though?" asked Fifty-Five. "We need something specific to show him."

"I must act quickly," said Luca.

Fifty-Five made the call. "Just block him for now." Then he scanned the room. "But let's get something ready for next time."

The brothers exchanged ideas while they filled their plates. When they were seated, Diesel brought their attention back to Justus's plan. "The biggest difference is that after we get their implants reset, Justus suggests we move the Sparkys back twenty years. So the three Sparkys now in the Fifty-Four, Five, and Six timelines would move back to Thirty-Four, Five, and Six. The good thing is that we have modified T-boxes ready to go in Thirty-Four and Five." Diesel looked up at Rose and Lilah. "How long before Thirty-Six finishes the mod?"

Lilah answered. "About a week. They've been able to

follow along with what I did pretty much to the letter, so it's going well." She paused. "Are you suggesting we sacrifice three timelines?"

Diesel heard angst in Lilah's voice, and he shook his head. "Justus says no. He says we can hire a contractor to keep each Sparky contained in a town out west." He explained how that would isolate them geographically, socially, and technologically.

Rose's image grew a little bigger just before she spoke. Diesel noticed and thought the manipulation was a clever way to take the floor. "We should have the Justuses from Thirty-Four, Five, and Six get together and work out the specifics of a containment strategy and what we need from a contractor. Three heads are better than one, and it will be easier for us if all three timelines are doing the same thing."

After more discussion, Diesel took them back to the first step. "I didn't tell Justus about the spire. After we seclude the Sparkys and deprive them of talk, food, water, and sleep, we still need that spire pressed against the back of his skull when each of them resets his neural implant."

"Can we fasten it to their heads?" asked Forty. "Luca, I'm not asking about best practices. I'm asking would it work if we strapped the spire to the back of his head in the correct position and kept it there until he says the codes?"

"Yes."

Diesel thought Luca's response sounded snippy, but he couldn't imagine how an AI could feel offense. "How do we keep him awake? I mean, withholding food, water, and human interaction seems pretty straightforward. But withholding sleep means we'd have to actively do something."

"Wire him up," said Forty. "We'll rig it so he gets an electric shock whenever his eyes close."

Fifty-Five's forehead creased and he crossed his arms. "We have stimulants that will keep him awake without any torture. Let's not go there even as a joke." He scanned the room. "We had a hand in creating the Sparkys, and we've provoked him as much as he has us. So, while we need to solve the problem, we also need to keep it as compassionate as we can."

Diesel agreed with the message but wasn't sure it was possible. "Justus was pretty clear that the whole deprivation thing will be hard on Sparky, and that will make it hard for us to watch."

"I appreciate that." Fifty-Five kept his arms crossed. "But it will be his decision to drag it out, if that's what he chooses. He can end it immediately by repeating the codes. We just need to make sure he's aware of that."

The conversation drifted off-topic after that, with comments about the food becoming the central theme. Lilah got them back on track. "Are you sending three teams at the same time? If you did just one timeline first, you could learn from that experience and perfect your strategy, hopefully making the next ones smoother."

Forty spoke with his mouth full. "Except we'll be warning the other two. What else will they conclude when a timeline suddenly disappears?"

"That an electronic part malfunctioned and the missing Sparky will return as soon as it's fixed," said Lilah.

"They'll suspect something."

"What can they do about it, though?"

"Prepare their defenses." Forty reached for a piece of chicken from the bowl in front of him. "That's what I'd do."

24. αCiopova

Returning to the Fifty-Five timeline for a status check, αCiopova watched the Diesels struggle with their new reality and thrilled at the disarray. As she'd hoped, the Lagerfords were focused on the Sparkys. None had said her name in days.

Her optimism soaring, she cast about for ways to stir the pot even more. Her desire was to manipulate the Diesels in the same way she influenced Sparky—adjust their brain chemistry to strengthen certain of their natural behaviors.

The problem was that the Diesels didn't have neural implants, denying her direct access to their neurotransmitters. With the weak connection of an external link, she'd need their cooperation to make such adjustments, an unlikely scenario at best.

While cautious about disrupting the progress she'd made so far, she took a small risk and directed a bolt of energy the size of a pinhead at Diesel's hypothalamus, popping a capillary near the center of the gland. If his physiology was like her past victims, the wound would temporarily alter his hormone production.

If it went to plan, the organ would heal over the next week or so, but during that time, Diesel's baseline level of aggression would rise, peak, and then return to normal.

25. Diesel, Fifty-Four timeline

Diesel's heart pounded as the large delivery truck turned onto Hilltop Circle. It was three in the morning, and he was part of the team assigned to subdue Sparky Fifty-Four. In a coordinated action up two timelines, a similar team was moving in on Sparky Fifty-Six.

The original plan was to hit all three Sparkys at once. But when the task list grew to unwieldy proportions, they debated delaying the raid on one timeline and handling it in a second go-round.

As consensus formed, Diesel persuaded them to wait on middle Sparky. "I spent a night in the woods because of that asshole. Let him freak out about his missing twins. It'll soften him up for when we get there."

And now that the show was about to start, Diesel's hands wouldn't stop shaking. While he normally avoided violence, the Sparkys presented a physical threat. "He's left us no choice," he said aloud as the truck stopped up the street from younger Sparky's house.

Wearing dark shirt and pants, Diesel followed Forty and Fifty-Five out onto the curb. As they began moving toward the house, Fifty-Five called to Luca, "Confirm that you have control of Portia. And locate our target for us."

Earlier in the week, Luca had struggled to penetrate the subsystems where Portia lived. The commercial AI industry had developed impressive safeguards to protect against such an intrusion, defenses strong enough to stump a powerhouse like Luca. That is, until he'd stumbled upon a bit of legacy code that patched an old security hole, exactly the kind of weakness he could exploit.

"I have disabled Portia and am in control of her functions. Fontaine is asleep in the master bedroom."

At the front door, Forty took a practice swing with the power bar. "Ready?" he whispered to no one in particular.

"Go," said Fifty-Five.

Putting his weight behind an impressive thrust, Forty stabbed the power bar between the door and jamb near the lock, then held it steady as the expanding jaws forced open the door. With a *pop*, the door swung wide, making a dull thud as it hit the far wall.

Diesel didn't hesitate. Ducking past Forty, he stepped into the house and took long strides through the entryway, angling toward the hall. The lights from his headgear cast ghostly shadows, making the scene even more surreal.

Holding the neutralizer in front of him, he checked the safety and then moved down the hallway. While he didn't have any real experience with firearms or hunting, he'd had extensive virtual practice playing sim games and hoped that would be enough.

The bedroom door was ajar, and Diesel used his shoulder to push it open as he entered the room.

"Hey!" yelled younger Sparky, sitting up in bed and raising his hands to protect his eyes from the piercing beams of Diesel's lights.

Aiming the weapon at younger Sparky's chest, Diesel took a single step forward and pulled the trigger. The man went slack with a gasp, his head falling back on the pillow.

Diesel's ears roared from the adrenaline pumping through his veins, and he waited for his senses to catch up to reality. He'd felt driven to do this—something way out of character—and thankfully the scary part was behind him. With the weapon in a loose grip at his side, he exhaled a breath he hadn't realized he'd been holding.

Stepping to the bed, he looked at the man lying limp in the sheets. "You down?" he asked, poking younger Sparky in the ribs. When the man didn't move, Diesel prodded him harder. Then he called to his brothers, "He's down."

Forty and Fifty-Five joined Diesel in the room, and together they executed the steps they'd practiced, cuffing his wrists and ankles to the bed, covering the windows with an opaque sound-proofing material, and fitting a helmet to his head, one Luca had designed to hold the spire in position on the back of his skull.

Then everyone but Fifty-Five cleared the room, moving to the kitchen to watch the drama on a display provided by Luca.

"Can you hear me?" Fifty-Five asked younger Sparky.

Enough time had passed for the paralysis to wear off, and younger Sparky nodded, the look of fear, or perhaps simple confusion, apparent on his face.

"We're here to take back our technology, and that starts with you resetting your neural implant to the factory default. We don't want to hurt you. Do the reset and we'll leave now."

"I can't do that, I'd lose my whole life! What about my comic book collection? Oh God, and the last vid of my mom."

"The Vermont Health Center has all your files from when you received the implant. You'll lose the last two years of data, but you won't lose everything. When did your mom die?"

Younger Sparky's lip quivered, and then he started to cry. "Fuck you, you asshole. You enter my life and hurt me for no reason. Don't you *ever* go to bed at night telling yourself you're a good person, because you're a goddamn monster. You want proof? Look around you right now!"

In the kitchen, Diesel felt so uncomfortable that he turned and walked into the living area. But when Fifty-Five spoke again, he drifted back to watch.

"This isn't a debate. You're staying here until you complete the implant reset procedure. Finish that and this ends."

"I have to piss."

Fifty-Five nodded. "Complete the reset procedure and you can go. Until then, you stay here. There won't be any bathroom breaks. No food or drink, either. And that's not just for today. You don't eat, drink, or go to the bathroom until it's done. That can be ten minutes or ten days, it's your choice."

Fifty-Five reached into his pocket, removed a small white disk the size of a shirt button, peeled off a protective layer, and stuck the stim-pill to Sparky's neck. "And no sleep, either." He moved to the door.

"Wait! So you're going to torture me until I comply? I was too kind when I called you a monster. I'm not resetting anything, so you can just stand there and watch me die."

"When I leave the room, I encourage you to struggle to break your bonds, to scream for help, to try to retake control of Portia, and to plead for me to return to talk about it. Do those things and anything else you can think of right away. None of them will work, but you need to experience that failure yourself before you'll conclude that you have no choice but to comply. The sooner you reach that point, the shorter your ordeal."

"Fuck you, you freak!" Younger Sparky's face reddened as he tugged wildly at his bonds. "You pathetic piece of shit."

Fifty-Five stepped into the hall and pulled the door shut behind him.

"Hey wait. Come back!"

The group watched from the kitchen as younger Sparky struggled to free his hands. After a few minutes, he started swinging his head in a vain attempt to shake off the helmet. The situation unnerved the group. Diesel found it gut-wrenching and anxiously complied when Forty moved them along. "Let's break down his T-box and get it out of here."

"Luca," called Fifty-Five as they descended to the basement. "Let us know of any status change with Fontaine."

Disassembling the T-box took hours, even when they didn't care about preserving its function. Removing all the pieces from the device and stowing them on the truck they'd backed up the driveway went smoothly enough. The real chore was cutting the aluminum refrigerator shell into pieces they could carry out the front door.

Next they emptied younger Sparky's basement cubby of his hobby devices, discovering along the way that only a portion of the signal processing equipment was visible. The rest, power supplies, wiring junctions, and the like, were hidden in a compartment behind the shelves.

Then they went room by room, working with Luca to find and remove every electronic gadget on the premises. They had to chop many of the items from the wall or ceiling, making the home look something like a construction site by the time they were done.

Stripping the master bedroom of electronics with Sparky present was especially unnerving. They temporarily covered his head with a big pillow case, but he yelled at them through the fabric the whole time.

When it was over, Diesel stood outside in the fresh air, taking deep breaths to calm himself. While he watched, Forty latched the back of the truck and said, "Luca, you may take it home."

The truck lumbered out of the driveway and started up the street. Luca would use an illegal hack to hide the truck's identity from civic tracking systems during its travels to the White Mountains. Once home at the Lagerford estate, the entire load would be fed to the material recycler to be used as feedstock in future fab cell creations.

The brothers gathered in the kitchen after that, with the image of Sparky lying in bed—pupils dilated, breathing hard, pants wet—reminding them of their sins.

Diesel needed a break. "Let's go to the rental house."

"You all go," offered Forty. "I'll stay and take first shift."

In the garage, they climbed into younger Sparky's car, and as Luca got them underway, Diesel asked, "If Sparky breaks, how long will it take to get back here?"

"You'll be at the Mortimer place on Post Road," Luca replied. "It's about ten minutes by car."

The Mortimer place turned out to be a large furnished house set back on a wooded lot. They had the place for the week, which, according to Justus, was more time than they'd need.

26. Sparky, Fifty-Five timeline

Sparky guided the last forkful of waffles around on his plate, soaking up the remaining maple syrup before shoving the dripping mass into his mouth. With his face tingling from the sugar rush, he drained his coffee and put his dishes in the sink. Then he began preparations for the arrival of the twins.

He started by pulling the kitchen table away from the wall so the three of them had room to sit around it. Today they were going to work through the "ask"—how much they would demand from Lagerford and what they were willing to offer in exchange. He'd been thinking of ten billion dollars as the target number, ten billion for each of them, that is. He felt confident the Diesels could gather that amount relatively quickly, and their outrage at the number would be short-lived.

In return, the Sparkys would deliver a phony performance. They'd surrender their T-boxes and give up their files, moaning and complaining the whole time to make it seem believable. But once they had the money, they'd go somewhere far away and rebuild using the recordings in their neural implants.

He paused in his preparations, a grin creeping onto his face. With ten billion dollars, he could afford every ultra-first-class experience on the planet, from exotic resorts to tropical adventures. The part that had him smiling was his intention to embark on his adventures accompanied by a bevy of beauties, handpicked by him.

He'd grown past the notion of looking for a girl from within the confines of Northern Droid. His new plan was to hold a "talent" search to fill a room with beautiful women, and then stroll through, shopping for the lucky creatures who would accompany him on his next vacation.

Despite this new plan, he next imagined cuddling with Gilda Galant, sipping peppermint schnapps in front of a cozy fire. Outside, the spires of the Swiss Alps jutted for the sky. But his focus was on the peaks inside, pushing on her sweater, calling out his name. The fantasy gave him a chubby, and he adjusted his pants to make room for it.

Resurfacing from his dream, he looked at the clock and frowned. "Huh." The twins were overdue by ten minutes.

Timeliness was a character trait of the Sparkys, and the fact that he couldn't hear the T-box cycling caused him to access his neural link. Placing fingers against his temple, he replayed his last conversation with the twins, nodding when he confirmed he had the time right.

Pondering reasons for the delay, he walked back to his office and snagged his Razed Grace action figure from his desk. He adjusted her stance on the walk back to the kitchen, then set the doll in the middle of the kitchen table, poised like she was ready to launch into the air. He wasn't at all self-conscious about the twins judging him for playing with dolls. After all, they each had a Razed Grace action figure in their own timeline.

And now the twins were fifteen minutes late. Feeling irritation more than concern, he went downstairs in search of an explanation.

Everything was as he'd left it, and the display outside the T-box said, "System ready." Opening the aluminum door and leaning inside the cabin, he confirmed that the inner display showed the same message.

Unaware he was grinding his teeth, he pushed the door shut so the machine would be available for the twins. Then he started to pace.

"So where are they?" he asked, partly to Portia but mostly to himself.

He continued pacing, fretting because he would have to take his box offline to look for problems, making it unavailable for use by travelers. At the same time, that was the only way he could debug anything.

When they were a half-hour late, he decided to perform a simple test. Tugging open the door, he stepped inside and called for a connection to the older twin's timeline. "Travel to Fifty-Six."

He expected to see the jump connection confirmed in a display of green text. Instead, he saw a red "X," signifying a connection failure.

He pulled the T-box door all the way shut, the latch clicking, then tried again. "Travel to Fifty-Six." Again, a red "X."

Lips pressed together in frustration, he tried for a different destination. "Travel to Fifty-Four." A third red "X."

Stepping out, he pushed the door shut so his machine

showed a ready status and resumed his nonconversation with Portia. "It's more probable that it's me. I can't conceive of something happening in two places that causes them both to go down at the same time."

Unsure what else to do, he opened the door and tried to connect again, hoping the problem had cleared. The red "Xs" confirmed that it hadn't.

Grasping the chair at his signal processing rig, he turned it to face the T-box. Slumping down, he stared at the machine's external display. If the problem continued, he would have to relearn the diagnostic tests he'd performed back when he'd first built the machine. Running them was the only way to find any glitches. The twins would have to do the same.

The good news was that he could follow the recordings in his neural implant, allowing him to work quickly while avoiding his previous mistakes. Still, it meant days of painstaking concentration.

"Oh, crap," he groaned, realizing he'd have to "borrow" the diagnostic pod from Northern Droid. He'd sweated when he'd smuggled it out the first time, agonized when he'd smuggled it back in, and dreaded the thought of a repeat performance.

Then he snapped his fingers and shot to his feet.

When he first started playing with the T-box, he'd been able to connect to an early timeline. He wondered if he still could.

Swinging open the T-box door, he called, "Travel to Thirty-Five." The T-box display confirmed a proper jump connection in vibrant green text.

"So it's *not* me." He started to shut the door, then stopped to call "Cancel" before closing it all the way. Too excited to sit, he resumed his pacing.

"If my machine works, that means *both* the twins are down at the same time." He chewed on a thumbnail as he digested the puzzle, thinking the odds too long for it to be coincidence. His face flushed as he converged on the answer. "Lagerford! Damn him to hell."

The realization sent his mind spinning, and he immediately saw it as two crises.

First and foremost, he needed to secure his home against a raid by those monsters. And with ten billion dollars in the balance, he needed to find a way to rejoin the twins.

Hustling to his workshop, he sorted through his scrap material, selected two pieces of angle iron, and lugged them up to the front door. After test-fitting them across the opening, he fastened them deep into the framework on either side, effectively turning the door into a wall. He repeated the process for the mudroom door to the garage, making it impassable as well.

That meant he'd get in and out of the house through the door connecting his workshop to the garage. He went there next and, after a quick review, devised brackets for either side of the doorframe, then slid a removable cross brace behind them. The finished version wasn't nearly as secure as the front door, but it would buy him time if they came that way.

After that, he checked that the windows were locked, the shades were drawn, the exterior lights were bright, and the interior lights were muted. As he moved through the house, he instructed Portia. "Those Lagerford thugs are coming to attack our home. If you detect *any* human activity outside the house or see any sign of them, let me know immediately."

Standing in the kitchen, he looked out into the yard through the window above the sink—the only one in the house without a shade. Waves of anxiety pulsed through him.

His fear growing, he retrieved his gun from the kitchen pantry. Removing it from the bag, he checked the clip to confirm it was loaded and then turned the safety on and off a few times to gain comfort with the action.

Walking through the house, he pointed the gun ahead of him, miming as if he were shooting at imagined intruders, saying "pow" with each pretend pull of the trigger. With no metallic parts, the state-of-the-art weapon—a product of Northern Droid's amazing fab cell—felt so light it seemed like a toy.

Closing one eye, Sparky aimed down the barrel at a lamp. As he did, he wondered if he had the guts to use the gun. Could he go to New Hampshire, point it at Lagerford, and demand that he undo whatever he'd done to the twins?

Hell, he should point it at that young woman, the one who'd turned out to be Lagerford's daughter. The guy would scramble to cooperate with a gun pointed at her face.

"Pow," he said, pretending to shoot at the wall near the man's imagined head.

Then Sparky stopped his horseplay and studied the gun as if seeing it for the first time. Making a mortal threat was new territory for him. While he wasn't sure how it would play out, he couldn't be tentative when he waved the gun in their faces.

In fact, his sim games from his youth had taught him that during a home invasion, a good strategy was to fire the gun early. It crystalized the threat for the hostages, making them more compliant.

But how could he be confident when he'd never fired a gun? Not in real life, anyway. Realizing it was a problem he could solve, he headed for the stairs.

In his workshop, Sparky donned safety glasses and hearing protection. After flexing his fingers and loosening his shoulders, he aimed for a dark splotch on the back wall of his basement—an expanse of poured concrete—and squeezed the trigger. When the gun didn't fire, he flicked the safety with his thumb and repeated the procedure.

Barely bucking in his hand, the weapon gave a quiet *pop*. He exhaled in satisfaction at the impressive hole and tiny cloud of dust appearing in the general vicinity of where he'd aimed. Choosing a different spot, he tried to be more casual about wielding the weapon and popped off another round.

After a third shot, he thought about how to carry the gun when he was on the move. He tested a couple of options before settling on his leather jacket from the hall closet, chosen in part because it had no metal, allowing him to wear it in the T-box.

But what he really liked was that the gun felt secure in the side pocket of the jacket, like it wouldn't fall out if he was running. And after drawing the weapon a dozen times, he felt sure he could move it in and out of the pocket without it hanging up.

Feeling comfortable with the gun motion, he graduated to his gangster move. Starting with both hands at his side, he drew the gun from his jacket, aimed, and pretend-fired at the back wall, all in one smoothish action. "Pow."

He practiced the move over and over, then did it for real while firing the weapon. Though his aim was all over the place, he declared himself ready when the ammo clip was empty.

Bent over a lighted worktable, he refilled the clip while thinking through how his raid might unfold. His best idea was to use the gun to force Lagerford to give him access to his T-box network. From there, he could gather a squad of Sparkys from other timelines, and together they would force the return of the twins.

But he needed a way past the Stryqr7000 war bots guarding the Lagerford property. Chewing his thumbnail, he resumed pacing.

"You have a call request," said Portia.

"What? Who is it?"

"She says her name is Lucy Sherwood, but her image doesn't match the name in the ID database."

"What does she want?"

"She says her grandfather built this house and he just passed. She'd like to come over and recall memories of him in the house and yard."

"Show me."

Sparky looked at the image of Rose and saw a young

woman who, in spite of her fashionwear eyeglasses, looked absolutely gorgeous. She leaned forward as she sat, her scoop top revealing a generous display of cleavage. Sparky could tell from the shape of her breasts that she wore a push-up bra, and though her display was modest, he appreciated the effort.

"Who does it say she is?"

"It can't identify her."

"How is that possible?" Sparky felt hot tingles on his face when he realized the answer—this person came from either the past or the future. She had to be a Lagerford, probably the daughter. That made her the leading edge of their attack.

The assault had begun!

"Tell her I'm unavailable."

His panic drove him to act, and he followed the only plan he had—he'd jump from here to the Thirty-Five timeline. He'd just confirmed that it was a good link, so that part was solid. Once there, he wouldn't even need to get out of the T-box. He would immediately jump forward and start gathering his brethren. The plan let him bypass the war bots altogether, and it saved him from having to point a gun in Lagerford's face.

While jumping to a distant timeline required a level of bravery he normally didn't possess, his nervous fear overwhelmed his caution. Knees shaking, he climbed inside the machine and latched the door. "Travel to Thirty-Five."

The T-box display lit up, and a static wash cascaded down his body. When he regained full awareness, he was in a different machine. His brow furrowed, though, because while he'd apparently reached the Thirty-Five timeline, the T-box display said that his jump originated from the Twenty-Five timeline. "Huh."

Tap. Tap. Tap. A faint knock on the T-box door caused him to push it open.

A young girl looked up at him and frowned. "You're not my dad."

Believing this was Lagerford's daughter, Sparky said, "Rose, your dad sent me to get you. Please come with me."

He leaned out of the T-box door and offered his hand to help her climb in. The child wasn't having any of it, though, and put her hands behind her back. He wondered if he'd guessed wrong, if this was another girl. And then he got his confirmation.

"Get away, Rose!" A middle-aged black man stomped down the stairs two at a time, shouting and waving his arms. "Stay back, mister."

Sparky stepped out of the T-box, squared up toward the man, and executed his gangster move, the report of the gun startling him because he no longer wore hearing protection. Rose screamed as the bullet went wild. The man on the stairs recoiled, slipped, and fell hard on the bottom steps.

He didn't wait to see how it turned out. Lifting Rose off her feet, he manhandled her squirming body into the T-box cabin. Everything seemed surreal, and he both shook with excitement and quivered in fear as he improvised through the highest-stakes gambit he could ever imagine.

With young Rose as his hostage, he decided to return home and let Lagerford come to him. The man would be homicidal with rage, but he would also see that a simple exchange—Rose for the twins—would end it quickly and without harm.

And that's when Sparky, staring at the T-box display, confronted his first snag. He didn't know if the command "Travel to Fifty-Five" would send him home to his T-box, or instead over to Lagerford's machine in New Hampshire.

"Oof." He bent forward in pain, cracking his forehead on the wall of the cabin. Young Rose, standing between his legs because of the tight quarters, had just shouldered him in the crotch. From the precision of the hit, he assumed it was deliberate.

Grabbing her with more force than necessary, he placed a hand over her face so she couldn't breathe and squeaked to the T-box, "Travel back home." He sighed in relief when the display showed him traveling to the Twenty-Five timeline. He wasn't sure if that was right, but he knew it would get him away from the man outside, the one Sparky believed would be opening the T-box door at any moment.

Then, just before the static wash enveloped them, young Rose bit his hand.

"You shit!" he yelled when he materialized in his own machine. His hand on fire, he pushed her out the door, then stood in the opening, examining her teeth marks on his palm.

But a rustling sound caused him to look up. Young Rose was scrambling up the stairs.

"You are pissing me off." He strode across the room and grabbed her ankle, pulling her off the edge of the stairway to the floor. She hit square on her back, the impact emptying her lungs.

While she lay gasping, he stood over her and shook his finger in warning. "Stop. Just stop."

Taking advantage of her subdued state, he hooked her under the arms and dragged her to the rear of the room. Backing away, he deployed the floor-to-ceiling mesh he'd used to contain her father.

Doing his best to plan on the fly, Sparky next stepped into the T-box to see if the twins were still offline. The red "X" confirmed that they were, feeding his anger and strengthening his conviction that this extreme action was necessary. He took a deep breath and exhaled, struggling to remain calm as he digested the madness of his impulsive act.

Then he stepped to the electric panel and flipped the dedicated circuit breaker, powering down the machine at the wall and eliminating the T-box as a backdoor that Lagerford could use to reach him.

From there he headed for the kitchen, glancing at the girl as he started up the stairs. She sat on the floor where he'd dumped her—knees up under her chin, arms wrapped around her legs, face ashen. He didn't make eye contact, instead continuing up to the main floor. He half expected her to call out or make a demand, but she remained quiet.

Sitting at the kitchen table, Sparky toyed with his action doll, thinking he would give it to the child so she'd have something to play with. But a toy wasn't a plan. And the guy back in the Thirty-Five timeline—the one he'd shot at on the stairs—would tell everyone exactly who he was.

He thought it conceivable that a group of Diesels

could show up at his house inside of an hour, certainly within two. When they got here, he needed to be as far away as possible.

His first idea was to lie low and plan his next steps from the safety of a secluded house somewhere north, maybe in the Vermont hills. Except he didn't know of such a place and wasn't sure how to find one.

He considered heading in that direction and winging it, hoping to find a rental property on the way. But Lagerford would bribe whoever he needed to, get tracking details on his car, and follow him. And what was he supposed to do with the girl while he was shopping for hideouts?

With the clock ticking, he headed back to his bedroom and stuffed a change of clothes into a shoulder bag. He searched his closet for something to pack for the girl, but couldn't find a single item that was remotely appropriate in size.

In the kitchen, he threw some packaged snacks and a few drinks on top of the clothes. As he closed the bag, he had an idea. "Portia, find out if the Mortimer place over on Post Road is occupied. If it's free, rent it starting immediately for the next two weeks."

He paused and then added, "Keep the contact anonymous. I don't want anything out there that can link this transaction to you or me."

Since the arrangements were being made between two AIs, the interaction took less than a second.

"They rent from Monday to Sunday," Portia reported. "It's free now, which gives you four days this week. It's been taken by another party starting Monday, so you'd have to vacate by then."

"I'll take the four days," said Sparky, expecting his ordeal to be over before then, anyway.

"You'll have to pay for the full week."

"Fine." He used a curt tone Portia was certain to identify and seek to mollify.

"Your reservation is confirmed, and I now have access to the house. The kitchen is stocked with southwest flavors in preparation for the next guests. Would you like me to refresh it?"

"What does 'southwest' mean?"

"Heavy on things like guacamole, salsa, beans, tortillas—"

Sparky interrupted Portia's citation. "It's fine. Leave it." Slinging the pack over his shoulder, he descended the stairs. "Changing subjects. Purchase two complete outfits for the girl that are similar to what she's wearing—pants and a shirt. Underwear too. Just one set of outdoor stuff— a light jacket and I guess hat and gloves, though it's not that cold."

"Deliver to the Mortimer place on Post Road?"

"No!" Sparky's forceful response caused Rose to stand and approach the mesh. "Have it delivered to the Hub. I'll pick it up later tonight."

As he thought through his burgeoning to-do list, he started to tingle with excitement. Out of nowhere, an amazing plan was falling into place, almost as if this was meant to be. But he still had challenges, like getting young Rose from here to the hideout.

Sparky had become aware of the rental house because Charlie Mortimer, a workmate from Northern Droid, had spread the word of its availability when his uncle had died last spring. While Post Road was more than a mile away by car, it was less than half that using the trail that cut through the forest behind his house.

After mulling the situation, Sparky decided it was a good thing he was staying local because he could keep an eye on the situation as negotiations unfolded. But he needed young Rose to walk there on her own—using a car would be a dead giveaway. And during their trek, he needed to keep her from running away.

Watching her stand with her fingers hooked on the mesh, he was suddenly curious. "How old are you? Ten?"

"I'm nine, but I'm in the fifth grade," replied young Rose.

Given how she said it, he assumed that being in the fifth grade was good for her age and acknowledged the news with a nod. "In a few minutes, we're going to walk to a trail behind the house and take it through the woods to visit a friend. I don't trust you not to run, so I'm going to rig up a harness for you. While I do that, you think about whether you need your hands tied and mouth gagged."

He squared up to get her attention. "If you behave, I won't hurt you. But if you act up, there will be consequences." To punctuate his threat, he smacked one of his hands against the other.

The sharp slap startled Rose, who began to snuffle.

"When I get back in a few minutes, tell me what you choose: behave or not behave."

Turning, Sparky went to his workshop and poked through his shelves to see what he could find for a harness. He needed to restrain her, no question about it, but her hands needed to be free to navigate the forest trail. That led him to choose a simple, effective collar and lead.

As he fingered a length of thin wire, he realized it would be disastrous if they met someone on the trail while he held the girl by a loop around her neck. And since it was broad daylight, he couldn't exactly hide it. The advantage of a thin wire was that it should be less noticeable from a distance. The down side was that it could cut into the delicate skin around her throat. He'd need to be careful.

With the wire in one hand, he grabbed a crimping tool and went back through the door. "Face the back wall and sit on the ground. Put your hands behind you." He pointed as he gave the instruction.

"You don't need to tie my hands. I'll cooperate."

"I'm glad to hear it. Still, I'm going to put this harness on you to keep you from running away." He made a loop at the end of the wire and, holding it in front of him, used his neural link to drop the floor-to-ceiling mesh. "Stay still." Approaching her from behind, he put the loop over her head and pulled it snug enough around her neck so she couldn't pull it off. A crimp secured it in place.

"Up you go. Let's give it a try."

Young Rose stood, the wire draping down her back to the ground. Holding the other end, Sparky pointed to the door of the workshop. "This way."

He expected her to lead, but she moved forward until she was at his heel, then stopped to wait for him.

"Go on." He motioned her forward.

"Leading makes me nervous. Can I follow? Please?"

She seemed sincere and he didn't have strong feelings about it one way or the other. "Stay close."

At the workshop door, Sparky turned back and scanned the carpet where he'd kept the girl to make sure there were no telltale signs of her presence. Satisfied, he led her through the workshop, watching from the corner of his eye that she didn't grab anything along the way.

They took the stairs at the back of the shop up to the garage. Before exiting from there, he took a deep breath to psych himself. "If we meet anyone, don't call attention to your harness. If this blows up, it will go badly for you." He showed her the gun.

Outside, they walked through his backyard, into the woods, and onto the trail. In spite of the beautiful day, they had the forest all to themselves. In fact, things went so well that Sparky found himself whistling toward the end of their short trek to the hideout.

* * *

Young Rose sat on the carpet and stared at the mesh, her mind in a swirl. She knew something terrible was happening, but the overwhelming situation left her dazed. A man had taken her through a T-box, something both her mom and dad had warned her repeatedly *never* to do. And the way he behaved now made it clear he wasn't finished with her.

She watched the man fuss about until he climbed the

stairs. Straining to hear through the open door, she heard snippets of a conversation that implied he was about to move her. That kicked her brain into survival mode.

Feeling certain her mom and dad would come after her, she cast about for a way to let them know that she'd been here in the basement. "A pen," she said aloud, patting her pockets as she searched for something to write with.

While she didn't find a pen, she did find the permission slip she'd received in class that day. One of her parents needed to sign it so she could attend the field trip to the Worcester Art Museum. Pulling it from her pocket, she unfolded the note as she looked around, still in need of something to write with.

A quick glance around her holding area told her she had no options. Looking at her hand, she thought how the blue-haired girl in that summer thriller had pricked her finger and written a note in blood. She rejected the idea with a shake of her head and continued brainstorming alternatives.

Then she noticed her school's name, Eastmount Academy, printed across the top of the paper along with the school emblem. That would be the perfect message for her parents because if either of them saw it, they'd know for sure that she'd been there.

Working quickly, she tore off a top strip that included the school masthead. Then she considered where to put it—someplace her folks would see yet her captor wouldn't.

The answer came from her dad. He hid Easter eggs for her every year, and early on she'd learned that he hid a lot of them up high because people naturally look down when they're searching for something. Her dad would know to look up. Hopefully, her captor wouldn't.

She picked the same sidewall where the stairs ran. That way, someone walking down them wouldn't see it, but it would be obvious if you stood in the middle of the room and looked higher than your head.

After slathering the back of the paper strip with saliva, she held it in one hand, took three running steps toward that wall, and leaped, stretching her arm up and slapping the wet-sticky paper as high as she could reach. After she landed, she reviewed her work, thinking the placement was pretty good for what she was trying to achieve.

That solved the "I was here" piece. She still needed to tell her parents where she was going. Since she didn't know herself, she'd show them using breadcrumbs. She'd leave a trail from here to there with bits of paper from the remainder of her permission slip.

27. Diesel, Thirty-Five timeline

Tired, conflicted, and angry, Diesel was anxious for some downtime. Since Forty had agreed to take the first shift watching younger Sparky, he decide that instead of waiting his turn at the Mortimer house, he'd jump to the Thirty-Five timeline and spend a few hours with his family.

Arriving at his home T-box, he reached for his robe, but the sound of Lilah wailing in distress caused him to turn. On the floor, she rocked back and forth in hysterics. Justus, crouched next to her, spoke softly as he rubbed her shoulder.

Diesel ran over and knelt by her side. "What's the matter?"

"He has her!" She sobbed, reaching out to Diesel. "We have to save her!" She stood and started dragging him toward the T-box.

Diesel allowed himself to be pulled along, but slow-walked it when he noticed the large bandage on Justus's temple.

"Sparky jumped here, shot at me, grabbed Rose, and jumped back to the Twenty-Five timeline." Justus checked the clock. "This was a little over four hours ago."

"Oh my God!" All at once, Diesel tasted fear, hatred,

panic, fury, helplessness—it left him weak and he leaned on Lilah, the two supporting each other. In his daze, he noticed the gauze on Justus's head again. "Is that from the bullet?"

"No, a fall on the stairs." Justus gently probe the bandage. "I think a bullet would hurt less."

"Sparky, what have you done?" Of all the ways Diesel had imagined the situation unfolding, he never once pictured anything so brutal. "Luca," he called as he pulled Lilah into a tight embrace. "Show us what happened, starting from the moments before Rose's abduction."

Together they watched Sparky shoot at Justus and forcibly kidnap Rose.

"What timeline does the display show?" asked Lilah, her head still on Diesel's chest.

Luca zoomed in so they could see it clearly.

"It says Twenty-Five, so with the glitch, that's Sparky in the Fifty-Five timeline." Shaking with rage, Diesel pulled Lilah toward the machine. "Let's go get Rose."

"Wait." Now Lilah held Diesel back. "Sparky's T-box will tell him who's coming. He'll shoot us as we arrive." She looked up at him. "He's pretty much trapped in his timeline. I think we should get a bunch of brothers and surround his house *now*."

"Why is he trapped?" asked Justus.

Diesel rocked back and forth, desperate to act, but realizing he needed to act smart. "We took down the twins this morning. The way Sparky's box is configured, the only choices left for him are here and the Thirty-Four timeline. I can't imagine him coming back here, and we'll shut down

Thirty-Four soon enough."

"Then he won't stay put." Justus's burning eyes reflected his grave demeanor. "He'll take her somewhere. Probably already has. Kidnapping is a very difficult business, even if kept to just one timeline."

Wringing her hands, Lilah looked at the machine. "Let's go."

"I'll bet the twins could tell you what Sparky is planning," said Justus. "If they all think the same way, they'll know what he's up to, won't they? You'll just need to prod them a bit."

Diesel both loved and hated the idea. He'd lose precious time while squeezing them. But if they talked, he'd have Sparky's playbook.

After several false starts, Diesel and Lilah agreed that jumping to Sparky's machine would be a fool's errand. Instead, they'd jump to Fifty-Five's house and race over land to Sparky's. They'd decide next steps based on what they found when they got there.

* * *

Diesel arrived in Fifty-Five's basement and called a greeting, hoping someone was home. Hustling to the top of the stairs, he found Rose waiting for him in the kitchen.

"How's it going with the twins?" she asked, but when she saw his face, she put a hand on his arm. "David, what's the matter?"

"Your Sparky jumped to my timeline, shot at Justus, kidnapped my Rose, and took her to his house in

Vermont."

"Oh my God! Poor Rose." She brought a hand to her mouth. "Is she all right? Is Justus?"

Diesel nodded. "The shot missed. Now I need to get to Sparky's house *fast* before he moves Rose. And I need a weapon—a gun, rifle, whatever."

"Luca," called Rose. "Get a Silver Arrow here *now*."

"Six minutes," Luca replied.

Diesel questioned her with a raised eyebrow.

"Silver Arrows are high-speed personal aircraft. It will get you to Sparky's house in fifteen minutes. They're incredibly loud, though, so they're banned in the mountains. Dad will get hit with a fine for this." She gave a quick smile. "He can afford it."

"I'm here." Lilah, having followed Diesel in the T-box, emerged from the basement stairway and joined them.

"Rose is getting us an aircraft that can zip us out to Sparky's house," Diesel told her without preamble. Then he turned back to Rose. "A gun?"

"Luca?"

"Your father keeps a Colt Defender in the garage on the back shelf. It's tucked behind his scuba gear."

Diesel started for the garage. When Lilah and Rose moved to follow, he spoke in a curt tone that revealed his distress. "I'll get it. You two brainstorm how to get reinforcements. We need a lot of help, and we need it fast."

Rushing through the house, Diesel asked Luca, "How long since the gun's been fired?"

"It's been on the shelf for five years, so at least that long."

"Is it safe to use?"

"It is safe, especially compared to what's ahead of you to rescue young Rose."

Busy digging out the gun, Diesel didn't catch Luca's implications. When it was free, he had Luca show him how to work the pistol's mechanisms and load bullets. With that as his knowledge base, he ran back to join the others.

"Your ride will be here any minute," said Rose when he reached the kitchen. "Let's wait on the patio."

Following Rose through the house, Diesel heard a distant high-pitched whine. When she opened the door to the patio, the sound grew in volume. Stepping outside, he saw a glint in the sky, then a bullet-shaped craft roared overhead, swooping in a circle above the house in a high-pitched scream.

The shiny craft, not much bigger than a luxury car, settled down on its side in the same spot where the hopper normally landed. Rose yelled something, but since they all had their hands over their ears, Diesel couldn't hear what she said.

The moment the Silver Arrow touched the patio, its engines spun down and the noise faded. Rose ushered them forward, calling "open" as she approached the sleek craft. A hatch swung down to become a two-step ramp.

Diesel moved onto the ramp and peered into a small cockpit containing two high-performance seats positioned side by side, a front display, and little else.

"Climb in." Rose clapped her hands like she was coaching a sport. "We're paying for speed, so let's go."

Diesel helped Lilah into an ergonomic head-to-toe

recliner that seemed to envelop her body. When she was settled, he slid into the seat next to hers and sat back. Straps appeared from nowhere and wrapped snuggly around them.

Rose leaned into the cabin. "Luca's been instructed to give you priority support. I'll be monitoring, so shout if you need anything from me." Rose looked at the display at the front of the cockpit. "You know where you're going, Luca?"

"I do."

"I'll send help as soon as I can." She stepped back and gave a quick wave as the door shut. The cabin shook ever so slightly as the engines spun up, then the craft leaped into the air.

"Whoa," squeaked Lilah.

Diesel—his stomach in his throat—took a moment to make sure he wasn't going to vomit. When his gut stabilized, he looked at Lilah. "How are you doing?"

"If this thing makes it, I will too."

"Luca," called Diesel. "How are we doing?"

"Everything is going smoothly. You'll land in twelve minutes."

After a pause, Lilah lifted her head off the seat. "Hey, Luca, can you access the systems at Sparky's house and see if Rose is there?"

"Not easily. I'll start searching for a hack, but the way my resources are deployed at the moment, it may take days."

Diesel slammed his head against the back of the seat in frustration. The brothers had tasked the Lucas in the twins' timelines with controlling Sparky's home AI but had not done so in the Fifty-Five timeline because they wanted to see how it all played out. This was the price of that decision.

Engaged in her own self-recriminations, Lilah pressed Luca. "Has Sparky's car shown up on any of the street cams in the last four hours?"

"Not that I can find. But his street has had a number of cars driving in and out during that period, so he may have used a different vehicle."

Diesel felt Lilah's hand searching for his. He took it, interlaced fingers with her, and as he gently squeezed, he thought about what an exchange with Sparky might look like.

No doubt he'd demand to be rejoined with his twins. That would mean rebuilding their T-boxes, which would take weeks. And once Sparky learned of the twins' torture, Diesel guessed any agreement they had would be out the window.

Since truth was a loser, he needed a way to get Rose back by force or trickery. Force would require a dozen of his brothers, and Diesel feared any plan along those lines would have a high potential for tragedy. He didn't have any ideas for trickery.

"Arrival in three minutes," said Luca.

"He's going to hear us if we land anywhere close to the house," said Lilah.

Diesel thought for a moment and shrugged. "We were never going to be able to sneak up on him, so it's as good a way as any to call him out. It establishes us as a force to be reckoned with."

"The noise could draw the neighbors outside," said Luca. "If they see the craft, they'll come over to look. They'll be gathering into a crowd at the same time you will be forcing your way inside Sparky's home. The authorities will certainly be called."

"Oh, for God's sake." Diesel's fear and frustration left him feeling so hopeless that tears welled.

"Offer a solution," commanded Lilah.

"Land in Brown's Meadow a few blocks away. I have a car waiting that can get you to Sparky's house in under two minutes."

"Yes, Luca," said Lilah. "Let's do that."

Diesel nodded in agreement.

"Here we go," said Luca.

The craft banked and made a broad swoop, followed by a tighter one as it slowed to a hover, then a slight bump as it landed. Diesel fumbled with his harness, his blood pressure spiking because there was no way to unlatch it. He formed a fist to pound the clasp when the straps disengaged and retracted on their own.

The hatch opened and Diesel peered out into an open field, a line of trees in the distance. He climbed onto the step and helped Lilah down, then scanned their surroundings. They'd landed in a smallish open field surrounded by forest. A car sat on the far perimeter, poised in an opening in the tree line.

As they hustled to the car, Diesel held the gun in one hand, happy for the security it provided but feeling awkward because he carried it out in the open for anyone to see. Actors in the movies seemed to be able to carry a pistol tucked under the waistband at the small of their back. He gave it a try.

The gun felt cold on his skin as he slid it into the top of his pants. He kept his hand back there for a few seconds, but it seemed secure as it hung in place.

Feeling badass, he lengthened his stride to catch up to Lilah. When he did, he felt the gun slip inside his waistband and continue down his left leg behind the thigh. It stopped there, wedging sideways, too big to go farther.

"Are you kidding me?" Angry about everything, he walked stiff-legged until he reached the car, trying to convince himself that the gun's safety was still on.

He didn't discuss the mishap with Lilah. As the car started moving, he lay down on the floor, unfastened his pants, and fished out the gun. Lilah watched, but already in emotional overload, she didn't react. By the time he was up in his seat, the car was pulling onto Sparky's street.

Diesel recognized the houses. "Pull into his driveway."

As the car slowed in front of the garage door, Diesel appraised the home. He'd been held captive here and spent hours inside of the Sparkys' houses in other timelines, so he felt comfortable with the layout.

"This way." He led Lilah around the house, stopping at a side door into the garage. When he reached for the handle, the door unlatched and opened on its own. He hadn't touched anything.

Diesel hesitated and then pushed the door wide. Leaning inside, he grabbed the first thing he saw—a broom against the wall—and tilted the handle into the opening so the door couldn't close. Then he took Lilah by the arm and led her away from the house.

After several steps, he put his mouth close to her ear and whispered, "Portia, his house AI, just unlocked the door, and that means Sparky is watching and listening. We'll be under surveillance when we're inside."

Nodding, Lilah stepped around Diesel and led the way back to the house. In the garage, she pointed at Sparky's car with a tilt of her head. If they weren't inside, they'd used a different vehicle to leave.

Then Lilah surprised Diesel by speaking aloud. "Hurt her in the slightest, and I will devote my life to making you suffer in ways you never thought possible. Be smart. End this now."

Lilah moved to the mudroom door and found it locked. Diesel headed for the entryway on the back wall next to a storage shelf. "Over here." He motioned to her and then started down the stairs to the workshop.

Everything about the workshop seemed familiar, as did the other half of the basement with its white walls, blue carpet, and T-box sitting in the center. The only things missing from the time of his captivity were the mobile toilet and mesh barrier.

Diesel felt a cold chill as he reexperienced his trauma. "He kept me there," he told Lilah, pointing toward the back of the room.

They circled the T-box in opposite directions, scanning the ground for any evidence that their daughter had been there. Finding nothing, he started for the stairs. "I'm going to look around up here."

"I'll be up in a sec." Lilah opened the T-box door and looked inside, then inspected the circuit breakers on the wall.

Upstairs, Diesel moved through the house, checking the rooms, closets, and cubbies. He opened every cabinet, looked under the beds, peered into the attic crawl space, and discovered nothing that even hinted that young Rose had been there.

He finished in the kitchen, where he found Lilah holding a doll. He motioned for her to follow and led the way down to the basement, through the shop, and out through the garage.

A short distance from the house, Diesel put his mouth near her ear. "I didn't find anything."

"That doll was the closest thing I saw to something that might entertain a child, but it's really more of an adult toy."

Desperate, Diesel was ready to raise the stakes. "I think I'm going to go visit the twins. They'll know where Sparky took her. I just need to squeeze it out of them."

"Squeeze so hard I hear them squeal in this timeline."

"What are you going to do?"

"Fifty-Five's Rose will be here soon. I'm going to meet up with her." Lilah looked at the house. "Something in there tells us what we need to know. I'll work with Rose to find it."

Diesel kissed her on the cheek, started for the car, then turned back and held out the gun. "You want this?"

She shook her head. "I'm scared of it."

He nodded and hustled to the car. Before climbing

inside, he called, "I love you." Then he slumped into the seat and spoke to Luca. "Get me to Fifty-Five's house as fast as you can."

28. Rose, Fifty-Five timeline

Rose uncovered her ears as the Silver Arrow faded into the distance. Returning to the house, a dread consumed her. She'd contacted Sparky, and not minutes later, he'd kidnapped young Rose. While she couldn't know for sure that the two incidents were connected, it was hard to draw a different conclusion.

Either way, she intended to help with a solution. "Bring up the hopper."

"Four minutes," said Luca.

After changing shoes, she grabbed a light jacket and returned to the patio. Watching the hopper land, she refined her plan.

She'd been tasked with gathering reinforcements. But since only Diesels could travel up and down the timeline to sound the alarm, that meant her job was to sit and wait for one of them to show up here at her house and then pass the assignment over to him.

Ignoring the fact that she could kick-start the process by traveling to the Thirty-Four timeline herself, she decided she didn't need to be present to brief whoever showed up. She could talk to him using video comm.

That way, rather than standing around cooling her heels, she could head to Sparky's house to help find her younger sister. With luck, she could get there in under an hour, doing so with less drama than that caused by a Silver Arrow.

"Luca, is Kristoff's hopper service running today? Is he down at the landing field?"

"Yes, he's there with his hopper."

She called out to him. "Hello, Kristoff, it's Rose. Are you available for hire today?"

"Hi, Rose!" Kristoff's cheery face appeared before her, smiling and eager to please. A little too eager, in fact. Rose knew Kristoff was infatuated with her, but she couldn't return his affection, and it made their interactions awkward. "Sure. Where and when?"

"Now. Consider yourself hired. I'm taking my hopper down and will fill you in when I get there."

After landing in the valley, she walked across the field to his vehicle. Arms out, Kristoff greeted her with a big hug.

"How've you been?" she asked, disengaging from his embrace. "How's your mom?"

"Mom's great." He grinned from ear to ear, clearly happy to be in her presence. "So am I."

"Good." She flashed a quick smile to acknowledge his joy. "So, I need to get to Montpelier as fast as possible. Can you hop me there?"

"Montpelier? In Vermont? That's like fifty miles away."

"I thought your hopper was designed for lateral runs."

"Yeah, so I can get passengers downtown and to the ski resorts. Not to go cross-country."

"Kristoff." Rose put a hand on his arm. "You're being dramatic."

"Maybe. And even with the friend discount, I'd still have to charge you a bundle for a trip like that."

"Of course. I understand. What would you guess?" If he gave a quote, human nature said she had him.

His brow furrowed as he worked through an estimate in his head. He told her the figure.

She doubled it and made her offer. "This is important and I need to move fast. Please help me."

He looked at her face and his resistance collapsed. "Get in. You have to pay any fines. Agreed?"

"Agreed.

Kristoff climbed in after her, something he usually reserved for inexperienced passengers. "I'm going to stay with the vehicle for a trip that far."

"I'll enjoy your company."

They made small talk during the trip, catching up on each other's lives. The hop went smoothly, with one stop at the Vermont border. Kristoff explained why they needed to do so, but Rose didn't listen, accepting it as a necessary step in the process.

During their final approach to Montpelier, Kristoff invited Rose to dinner. She artfully dodged the offer. After a short pause, he asked her to join him on a tour of a new art exhibit in town. She dodged that one less skillfully. He was so crestfallen when they landed that she offered to meet him for coffee when her emergency was over.

After another overly long embrace, Kristoff climbed back into his hopper while Rose hurried to her waiting car.

A superhighway ran in a straight shot from Montpelier to Burlington, and her vehicle had the muscle to test the road's maximum speed.

Its sleek interior felt luxurious, the seat hugging her as the car sprinted up the ramp and onto the highway. Since AI operated all the vehicles in both directions, there were no slowdowns or traffic jams, police cruisers giving out speeding tickets, or anything else that might disrupt traffic flow.

Instead, the roadway was filled with lines of vehicles traveling in coordinated formations, some faster than others, and all cooperating to maximize speed and safety. The lines rippled as she approached, moving aside to allow her car to dash ahead as she sped to her destination.

When Rose was ten minutes out, she checked in again and learned that Diesel and Lilah had found Sparky's house empty, with no evidence that their daughter had ever been there. Desperate for answers, Diesel was on his way to visit the twins' timelines and interrogate them.

"When I get there," she told Lilah, "let's walk the house again. I'm wearing my neural link, and with Luca's help, maybe we can find some answers."

When the car pulled into Sparky's driveway, Lilah was pacing in front of the garage. Rose climbed out and they hugged. Mid-embrace, Lilah whispered, "I think Sparky is monitoring us inside."

"If he is, that's good news because it means we can start a dialogue with him." As she followed Lilah around to the side of the house, Rose asked, "Where's the gun?"

"I'm scared of it, so Diesel took it with him."

Disappointed, Rose pressed her lips together and said nothing. Following Lilah into the garage through the side door, she asked Luca, "Can you tell if we're being watched?"

"The house network is active and responding to your movements, so I'd say yes. But he's hidden himself well, so my opinion is based on circumstantial evidence."

Downstairs, Rose and Lilah walked through the workshop, circling multiple times as they looked for any hint that young Rose had been there. Finding nothing, they passed through the door to the carpeted side.

The aluminum shell of the T-box dominated the space. Walking around the machine, Rose scanned everything, searching for clues, hoping Luca would catch anything she missed.

Every so often she'd scan up—a valuable search technique she'd learned in her youth—and she saw it before Luca did. Using thought, she brought it to his attention. "What's that stuck on the wall?"

Luca zoomed for her, and together they learned it was a torn scrap of paper. Eastmount Academy, the name of her old school, was inscribed on the scrap, right next to the image of a cupola with a weathervane, the school's emblem.

Her heart raced and she wanted to jump and point for Lilah. But she didn't want Sparky to know of her discovery, so she shifted her head to look up the stairs. "Let's check the main floor."

They went through the house together, finding no evidence that young Rose had ever been upstairs and learning nothing about where she and Sparky might be.

Their last stop was the kitchen. Rose rifled through the cabinets and drawers, while Lilah picked up Razed Grace, absently adjusting the action figure's outfit to make her more demure.

"Can I see it?" Rose took the doll and, sensing this was a special item to Sparky, held it up over her head. "I know you want me to be gentle with your fighter girl. It would upset you if I hurt her. Now think that this is just a toy. You have a real person."

Rose laid the doll gently on the kitchen table and started for the stairs, motioning for Lilah to follow. She led the way down to the basement, through the workshop, and up the back stairs to the garage, hurrying to get Lilah outside and away from the house so she could share her discovery.

About halfway up the back stairway, Luca called her attention to a postage-stamp-sized square of paper lying on the stair tread. "This came from the same stock as that piece stuck on the wall."

Rose picked it up and studied it for a moment, then commented to Luca by thought, "She's leaving breadcrumbs. Way to go, me!"

"I've activated a filter that will let you see any piece from that original sheet of paper in bright yellow," he replied. "It will help you follow the trail."

Bursting with excitement, Rose hurried through the garage and into the yard. Turning in a circle, she tried to decide which direction would get them to privacy the fastest. During her spin, she detected a glowing yellow spot on the ground near the back corner of the house.

"Is that from your enhancement?" Rose moved toward the glow. "It's another piece!"

Lilah followed, unaware of any of Rose's interactions with Luca. "Where are we going?" Her tone became pleading. "Tell me what you know."

Rose held up a finger as she moved to the rear of the house. The backyard was covered in brownish grass that sloped down to the forest, a collection of oak, maple, and pine spread across a tangle of undergrowth. Noticing a path that entered the woods, she headed toward it, quickening her pace across the lawn.

"Talk to me," begged Lilah as she jogged to catch up, the rising tenor of her voice reflecting her distress.

Rose stopped at the mouth of the path. When Lilah reached her, Rose pointed her eyes at a moss-covered stump. "Look right there."

"Where?"

"I'm not going to point. See the stump? There are two tall ferns to the right of it?"

"Yeah." Lilah sounded uncertain.

"See that square of white paper leaning against that leaf?"

"So?"

"Your daughter left that for us. She's marking her trail so we can find her."

"Oh my God." Lilah collapsed to her knees and started to weep. "Please tell me it's true."

Crouching down, Rose hugged her. "It's true. We'll get her back, don't worry." She ran her palm up and down Lilah's arm, waiting while her mom-sister released a portion of her pent-up fear, anxiety, and wrath.

Lilah wiped her face with her hands. "But how do you know?"

Rose told her about the piece of paper stuck on the wall, and how Luca had tuned her senses to light up scraps of paper from the same source.

Lilah remained on the ground a moment longer, then extended her arm so Rose could help her stand. "If they left by this path, it would explain why his car is still here." Lilah started into the woods, picking up speed as she went. "Let's go."

The path wasn't easy to follow, and at one point they had to retrace their steps. But when Rose found another luminous piece of paper, they knew they were on the right track.

Before long they reached an established trail. White blazes—trail markers painted on the occasional tree—revealed it to be part of a larger hiking system.

Rose looked left down the trail, staring into the distance but failing to detect any glowing spots. She repeated the process to the right, again finding nothing. As she moved her head to look left again, her eyes caught sight of a yellow spot near her feet, just inches up the trail to the right.

"There!" She pointed it out to Lilah, then started in that direction, shifting from a walk to a slow jog.

She didn't see another scrap for five minutes, then ten. Concerned, she checked in with Luca. "Are you able to support me out here?"

"Yes. While the path seems remote, you're surrounded

by civilization in every direction."

Rose turned to Lilah. "I've lost the paper trail."

Lilah brought a hand to her mouth.

"We'll figure it out. Let's backtrack and I'll work with Luca to see where we went wrong." Rose led the way back while Lilah fretted. When Rose saw a glow up ahead, she quickened her pace, only to realize it was the piece that marked the path up to Sparky's house.

Stepping over the scrap, she continued down the trail, fussing with every step. "C'mon, Luca. Find one."

The trail led them on a gentle curve that tracked the topography of the land. Rose was parallel with the next piece when she saw it. "There!" She pointed to a spot off the trail.

"I can't see it." Lilah stood on her toes and craned her neck, searching for the square.

Rose took a long step over a patch of moss, scooped the bit off the ground, and held it out. Lilah clutched the piece in her hands. "Find another, Luca."

After locating several more pieces, they reached a fork. A trail with blue blazes branched off from the white. Rose slowed to ponder it. "Left or right?"

"The blue trail climbs that hill." Lilah looked from one trail to the other. "Let's stick with white."

"Luca?"

"The white trail has many more houses near it. I agree that we try it first."

"White it is." Rose led the way down the path.

It proved to be a good decision when they found another scrap soon after. The next fifteen minutes seemed like an eternity, with a half-dozen bits found at different intervals. Then Rose saw three scraps close together up ahead.

"Look!" She pointed, increasing her pace.

"What is it?" Lilah rushed to catch up.

When Rose reached the spot, she saw two more glowing squares along a lightly used pathway off the white trail, similar to the one that led to Sparky's house. Rose pointed for Lilah. "They went this way."

They started up the path and in minutes came to the side yard of a yellow single-story home with big windows, a covered front porch, and a large utility shed in the back.

"I can see a scrap of paper near the house." Rose turned to Lilah and spoke with hushed excitement. "I think they're here." Then she spoke aloud to Luca. "What do you know?"

"This house is owned by the Mortimer family. They rent it week-to-week, mostly to vacationers. It was unoccupied and available this week until earlier today when an anonymous client rented it on short notice."

"This has to be it." Rose took Lilah by the arm and ushered her behind some bushes. "Let's stay hidden until we figure this out." She kept a hand on Lilah's arm. "Luca, get us help. Have them come ready for war."

"Kidnapping is handled by the FBI."

"Can freelancers do it without increasing the risk to the girl?" Lilah and young Rose didn't exist in this timeline, so she hoped to avoid summoning government officials who would ask questions that none of them could answer.

"Independents are more likely to rescue her unharmed

and more likely to kill Fontaine in the process."

Rose gave a half-shrug. "Works for me. How soon?"

"James 'Snoot' Barley just grabbed his ready bag and should be here in under twenty minutes. He's your lead. I'll have two more here thirty minutes after that."

Rose nodded her approval as she studied the house, the shadows lengthening as afternoon moved toward dusk. Behind her, Lilah sighed and shifted, unable to remain still with her daughter so close.

Then the porch light flipped on, causing them both to blink. The front door opened and a lanky man came out. Hitching up his pants, he rambled down the porch steps and walked around the house to the backyard.

"Can you tell if that's Sparky?" Rose asked Luca.

Luca zoomed for Rose. "It's him."

Sparky made for the utility shed, disappearing behind it.

"I'll bet he's keeping Rose in that shed," said Lilah, shuffling her feet and huffing.

"That wouldn't make sense," said Rose. "Not when he has the whole house."

After a few more minutes, Lilah stepped toward the lawn. "I'm going to look."

"No!" Rose lurched forward and grabbed her arm. "He has a gun. Please wait for reinforcements. It won't be long."

Staring at the shed, Lilah seemed determined. But when Rose gave a tug, she yielded, returning to her hiding spot behind the bushes. Their movements caused a rustling of leaves and branches, enough to mask similar sounds from behind them. But the unmistakable *snap* of a branch caused them to turn.

Sparky stood not twenty feet away, waving his gun in their direction, grinning like he'd won the lottery.

29. Diesel, Fifty-Four timeline

Rocketing in the Silver Arrow from Sparky's back to Fifty-Five's house, Diesel fretted over the fact that none of his brothers had passed through this timeline since he'd learned of the kidnapping. He had two urgent priorities—getting help and questioning the twins—and he couldn't do both by himself. In fact, in his emotionally weakened state, he wasn't sure he could do even one of them effectively.

"Fifty-Five has arrived home," announced Luca as Diesel's craft started its landing sequence over the house.

"Finally." Diesel slumped back, grateful to hear something positive after so much bad news.

Communicating through Luca, Diesel briefed Fifty-Five about the kidnapping. "Lilah and Rose are at Sparky's house now, but I went through it with Lilah and couldn't find anything."

They talked while the Silver Arrow landed, and Diesel was walking across the patio when he said, "I'm on my way to grill the younger twin. I think he can tell us where to find Sparky, and I'm ready to force it out of him if that's what it takes."

Fifty-Five met him at the door with balled fists and an angry red face. "Rose," he called to the air. "Are you there?"

Luca responded. "She's walking through Sparky's house with Lilah and says she'll contact you when they're outside."

Fifty-Five grunted and spoke to Diesel. "Forty is babysitting the younger twin right now, so as soon as you jump, reach out and have him get the ball rolling." He started through the house to his T-disc room and Diesel followed. "I'll head up to Fifty-Six and squeeze the older twin."

"If we're doing this in parallel, we should set up a relay so we can compare notes." They could cover more ground if they coordinated their interrogation, using new revelations by one twin to test or prod the other. But since information could travel between timelines only if a brother physically carried it, they needed a team of Diesels willing to carry messages back and forth to make it work.

Fifty-Five started undressing as they entered the T-disc room. "I'll follow up on the relay. You have enough on your plate." He walked to the far T-disc and stepped into the circle. "Travel to Fifty-Six." His machine started to cycle.

Before jumping himself, Diesel checked in with Lilah.

"I'm going through the place with Rose," she reported. "Nothing so far, but we aren't done yet."

"We'll find her, sweetie. I promise."

Diesel jumped to the Fifty-Four timeline, and while he dressed, he had Luca fetch a Silver Arrow. Then he called ahead to Forty, who was covering the shift at the younger Sparky's house, and asked him to start prepping the man for questioning.

Though it felt like hours, he reached younger Sparky's house twenty minutes later. Forty had placed Sparky in a sitting position on the bed, removed his helmet, and loosened his bonds so he had more freedom of movement.

"He's had a glass of orange juice and a cookie to give him energy," said Forty when Diesel entered the bedroom. "He's all yours."

As Forty exited, Diesel moved to the foot of the bed, studying his adversary. Rather than feeling anger or contempt, his first reaction was revulsion. Younger Sparky's sheets were soiled and he smelled foul.

Diesel left him waiting as he stripped the sheets from the bed in the next room. Carrying them back in a pile, he arranged them in a nest around younger Sparky to bury and contain the disgust.

Then he got to work. "Your twin kidnapped my nine-year-old daughter, jumped her to his house, and then took her someplace. I need you to tell me where to find them."

"How would I know? Anyway, I can't think until I get more food."

Diesel delivered the next lines as calmly as he could. "Understand that he took my baby and I'm barely in control. When I snap, and that will be very soon, you are the one who's going to pay. Trust me when I say you want to figure this out as soon as you can."

"I have some bananas on the kitchen counter," said younger Sparky, acting as if Diesel had never spoken. "Why don't you fetch me a couple of those?"

Diesel scanned the room and saw an elegant Scottish walking stick hanging on the wall above the dresser. Lifting the lacquered staff off its hook, he hefted it to test its weight and took a practice swing through the air.

"You're going to hit me?" The twin glared at him. "I was right what I said before, you are a monster."

Squatting down, Diesel fished for the line holding younger Sparky's right foot and pulled on it, drawing his leg out from under the covers. After tying the foot tight against the bedframe, he stepped back, and with ears ringing in fury and fear, he gave an ultimatum.

"Sparky." Diesel waited for the man to look up. "I think you can help me find my daughter, and I'm prepared to do whatever it takes to learn what you know. This is your chance to do it pain-free."

Younger Sparky shook his head. "You're crazy. I didn't take her, so how can I know?"

"Just tell me what you would do. If you had my daughter here at your house and you knew I was chasing you, where would you take her?"

He gave a careless shrug. "You're asking the wrong guy."

Diesel's fury spiked and he fought against it, telling himself to focus on getting answers. Still, he felt it was past time to motivate the man.

Shuffling to the side of the bed to get a clear arc, Diesel let the stick fall by its own weight onto younger Sparky's ankle. It hit the bone that bumps out just above the foot.

"Shit!" shrieked younger Sparky, reaching for his ankle but coming up short because of his restraints. "Oh my God." He writhed back and forth as he squealed.

"Look what I found." Forty entered the room with a

benchtop machine, an army-green contraption with a hand crank on the side. Made of cast metal, the worn exterior and vintage construction led Diesel to guess it was military surplus from the previous century.

Setting it on the dresser with a thump that reflected its weight, Forty dragged the dresser closer to the bed.

Younger Sparky panicked. "What are you going to do?"

"We won't do anything if you cooperate," said Diesel, trying to figure out what Forty had found. "Tell us about my daughter and this stops."

After unfurling lengths of wire, Forty loosened wingnuts on two electrodes at the top of the device and connected a wire lead to each. That's when Diesel identified the machine as a hand-cranked generator.

The pitch of younger Sparky's voice rose as Forty finished the connections. Turning to younger Sparky with a wire in each hand, he said, "It's your decision whether this goes forward or we put this away."

Out of curiosity, Diesel gave the crank a couple of turns. The handle took more effort to move than he'd guessed, but it produced dramatic results. When Forty held the bare wire tips close to each other, a brilliant electric arc snapped from one to the other.

Younger Sparky screamed at the sight.

Diesel smelled ozone. "Will this kill him?"

"I don't know. Do you want to turn the crank or hold the wires?"

"I'll crank." Diesel looked at younger Sparky, who stared back with terror in his eyes. "I'll ask again. Tell me and all this stops. I'm in a hurry, though, and the longer you wait, the angrier I get." He took a breath to calm his own pain. "If you were here holding my daughter hostage, and you left this house because I was coming for you, where would you go?"

"Give me time to concentrate. You've been hurting me without ever letting me think."

His desperation swelled into fury and he turned the crank, staring at younger Sparky as he did.

"Wait!" yelled Sparky.

Forty touched the wires to younger Sparky's foot, and he convulsed, his screams becoming a gurgle. When Forty took the wires away moments later, they watched younger Sparky take deep breaths as if he'd surfaced from underwater.

Diesel didn't relent. "Listen, Sparky. I'm chasing you and you duck out the back door with a child in tow. You need to hide. You need resources. Where do you go?"

Younger Sparky groaned like he was too damaged to respond. But when Diesel started turning the crank, he lifted his head. "Wait."

He whispered something Diesel couldn't hear. Diesel leaned close.

"I'd kill your daughter and throw her in a ditch."

Diesel saw red. Gripping the crank handle with both hands, he turned it fast, grunting from the effort.

Forty put one wire on younger Sparky's foot and the other on his arm, sending current through his entire body. Sparky's face contorted as he let out a bloodcurdling scream. For a moment, Diesel found comfort in the man's agony.

When Forty pulled the wires away, Sparky's frantic breaths turned to sobs. Watching him cry, Diesel felt so confused—so far out of his reality—that he needed to escape the situation. He left the bedroom without a word and headed for the kitchen. Forty followed close behind.

Filling glasses with water, they both leaned against the kitchen countertop and stared straight ahead, dazed by the horror they'd inflicted on an innocent man. Diesel kept telling himself this was necessary to save young Rose, but it still felt horrible.

A voice intruded on their thoughts. "This is Thirty-Four." Diesel and Forty stood upright. "They were jolting older Sparky when he said the name Deborah Williams. They'll question him more when he resurfaces, but they wanted you to know that part now."

Diesel looked at Forty, and as one, they put down their glasses and rushed toward the bedroom, Diesel's heart pounding with renewed hope.

Bursting into the room, he made for the generator crank. Forty picked up the wires.

"No, no, no." Younger Sparky rocked his head back and forth.

"Who is Deborah Williams?" demanded Forty.

Diesel spoke in an equally aggressive tone. "Where does she live?"

Younger Sparky—face pale, sweat beading on his brow, eyes sunken in his head—looked ahead with an unfocused stare and wobbled his head. "I don't know."

"You don't know what?" Forty held the wires in front

of his face. "Who she is? Or where she lives?"

"I don't know her," he repeated from his daze. He looked as though he was going to resume crying.

With success so close, Diesel turned the crank to create a threat. "Tell us, damn it."

Forty touched a wire to each side of younger Sparky's head, sending current straight through his brain. Younger Sparky didn't scream this time. Instead, his entire body vibrated like he was shivering.

When Forty pulled the wires away, younger Sparky's head lolled forward. Forty grabbed a handful of his hair and pulled him upright. "Tell us about Deborah."

"Deborah?" said younger Sparky, drool coming from his mouth in a long string. "Are you there? Help me!"

Diesel felt a flood of adrenaline—they'd just confirmed the name was real! "Deborah wants to help you, but she's not here." He used a soothing tone. "She's at her home. I'll go fetch her. Where does she live?"

"Williams?"

"Yes, where does Deborah Williams live?"

"Who?"

Fighting to temper his fury, Diesel snorted and punched the bed. "Tell us!"

Sparky just stared ahead with an unfocused gaze.

All at once, Diesel felt spent. "I can't do this anymore." He left the room and made for the kitchen.

Forty joined him moments later.

"How is he?"

Forty filled his glass from the kitchen faucet. "He's breathing."

"Luca," called Diesel. "What can you tell us about Fontaine's condition?"

"While he is stable, the electric current destroyed his neural implant, likely causing brain trauma in the process."

"Will he recover?" asked Diesel.

"Brain injuries are slow to mend. It will take a few months, but he will heal."

Diesel looked toward the garage door. "I need to get back to the Fifty-Five timeline and hunt down Deborah Williams."

"I'll come with you." Holding up a finger, Forty had Luca connect him with Fifty-Four, currently on call at the Mortimer rental home. "We need to chase down a lead. Can you come look after Sparky?"

On the drive over to the Silver Arrow, Diesel fidgeted in his seat. Time was a critical factor in kidnappings, and every passing second weighed heavier on him than the one before.

30. Sparky, Fifty-Five timeline, a few hours earlier

Sparky led young Rose into the Mortimer house by her leash. The front door opened into a rustic living area with broad oak floorboards and a smattering of aged furniture. The far wall, painted an ivory white, was filled with framed photos of deer in forest habitats during different New England seasons.

"You there, Portia?" he asked.

"Yes, I have guest privileges until checkout."

"Good." Sparky looked down at the girl. "Keep behaving and this will be over soon enough."

Spying the kitchen through an archway, he went there next, pulling young Rose along with him. The generous layout included an eating area on one end, with table and chairs near a glass door to a deck. He moved around the counter to the sink and tested the water faucet—it worked—and then he scanned the appliances, glad to see they were newer than the furniture.

Following the awkward floorplan out the other side of the kitchen, he entered a utility room with laundry and cleaning supplies. Running his hand across the top of the clothes cleaner as he passed through, he stepped out into an intersection.

From where Sparky stood, the living area was immediately in front of him. To his right, a hallway led back to three bedrooms, and on his left was a small nook. Perhaps originally intended to become a closet, now the nook was a very short passage to nowhere.

What captured Sparky's interest was the large-breed dog crate sitting in the space. He pulled off a white bedsheet draped over the top of the crate, opened the door, and bent down to look inside. Seeing that the floor of the cage was free of debris, he issued his verdict. "Perfect. In you go."

"No way." The girl backpedaled to the end of the wire.

"I'll fix up one of the bedrooms for you in just a bit, but I can't have you wandering free while I do it." He deepened his voice and adopted a stern expression. "Now get in."

Young Rose began to cry, mumbling about water and a bathroom. But she climbed inside and curled up in the fetal position on the crate floor, the sounds of her sniffling undampened by the lattice walls of the container.

Looking around for a way to lock her in, his eyes fell on a dog leash hanging on a wall hook. Tugging the leash to confirm its integrity, he used it to tie the crate door shut, looping the line in a clever fashion so the knot was away from prying fingers.

"Let me know if she touches any of this," he told Portia as he walked back for a tour of the bedrooms.

The master bedroom had a private bathroom, and he liked the idea of letting the girl attend to her own personal needs. "Are these smart windows?" He pulled the curtain back and looked.

"They are."

"I'm going to have the girl stay in this room. But I'm worried about bad people coming for her, so if she asks, you must not open the windows for her."

"I understand."

"And you are to let me know if anyone tries to force the windows from the outside."

"Certainly."

After a quick survey of the suite's contents, he decided to remove the nonessential items and store them in the bedroom next door. The suite, like the rest of the house, was sparsely furnished, but there were supplies under the sink in the bathroom, pictures on the side tables, a stand-alone mirror, kitschy artwork everywhere, a stack of storage boxes in the closet labeled "Do not touch," and a dozen other items to be removed. He was sweating by the time he finished.

Before transferring young Rose in, he needed a way to secure the bedroom door from the outside. "Are there tools in the basement?" he asked Portia.

"None that I can see. There's a shed in the backyard that might have what you're looking for."

"Show me the way."

Following her guidance, Sparky exited the front door and made for the backyard. Realizing it had been about three hours since he'd snatched the girl, he wondered why there hadn't been more of a response. "Any activity at my house?" he asked Portia.

"No one has been there since you left."

"Huh." He shook his head, mystified by the lack of response.

The utility shed was locked, but a quick kick to the door solved that problem. Inside, he found only junk. He also found a second door, this one unlocked, about halfway down on the far side of the structure.

A few minutes of poking around produced an old hasp-style latch he could use to secure the bedroom door. Finding no power tools, he gathered a hammer, nails, screws, and a screwdriver in a bucket, figuring he'd wing it when he got back in the house.

With the hasp installed—an ugly but effective home modification—he was able to secure the door from the outside. He performed a last-minute walkthrough of the prison room and believed he was finished until he imagined the girl hiding in the bathroom with the door locked. The solution was simple—he popped the hinges and stowed the bathroom door in the room next door along with everything else.

Fetching young Rose from the crate, he led her to the new holding cell. "You can stay here if you behave. But if I find you up to mischief, it's back in the dog crate."

She remained quiet so he continued. "I'll get you some food now. What do you like?"

She shrugged.

Remembering that the kitchen was stocked with southwest flavors, he pitched that menu. "How about nachos? Have you ever had those?"

She nodded.

"Do you like them?"

She shrugged again.

"Perfect. I'll be right back."

In the kitchen, Portia showed him the ingredients to make a plate of nachos.

"I'm not doing all that," he said when he realized the effort involved. "What do we have readymade?" That's when he changed the menu to a burrito.

He was carrying the food to young Rose when Portia interrupted his thoughts. "A car just pulled into your driveway, and a man and woman are getting out."

"Here or at my house?"

"At your house on Hilltop Circle."

Heart pounding, he rushed to the bedroom, handed the plate to the girl, and hurriedly secured the door. "Show me," he said as he slumped into a chair in the living area.

Using his neural link, Portia sent him a visual feed that let him view his home as if he were watching from an elevated angle.

"That's the guy who came through my T-box," he said, pointing as if there were somebody there to share the news. "He's Diesel, so she must be Lilah."

Sparky watched them search the house, enjoying their anguish when they came up empty.

"Give me back the twins, and we'll call it even," he called to the air, wondering how to start that conversation while maintaining his own safety.

But when Diesel and Lilah moved outside to talk, his grin faded. "There's no audio outside?"

"Not if they move away from the structure."

Sparky's cheeks bulged as his teeth clenched.

After Diesel drove away, Lilah began to pace in the driveway, and Sparky took a minute to heat a burrito for himself. Back in the chair, he nibbled, waiting along with Lilah.

When Rose arrived, he sat up, the grin returning. "That's the daughter, right?"

"Yes, Rose Lagerford."

Sparky looked back toward the bedroom and felt a chill at the thought that an older version of his prisoner was in on the search.

When Lilah and Rose headed to the back of his house and made for the path into the forest, he became anxious. "How do they know where to go?"

"I don't know," replied Portia.

When they disappeared into the trees, he sat forward, dumbfounded and struggling to understand. He hadn't considered that they would march right into the woods, not as a first act, anyway.

Pressing his face against the front window of the Mortimer house, he strained to see into the side yard where the pathway emerged from the forest. "What can you see in that direction?"

Portia used an exterior camera to zoom in on the mouth of the pathway from the woods. Through her, Sparky could see a literal forest of trees and shrubs, but even with the zoom, he couldn't see more than a hundred feet into the tangle. He wanted a much earlier warning if they were coming this way.

"Where is there a spare camera I can use?" He had the

idea of taking one of the house cameras and placing it out on the trail to act as his alarm if they approached. The house had plenty of coverage, so Portia could sacrifice one without much loss indoors.

"In the laundry room." She guided him to a camera he could reach by standing on top of the clothes cleaner. Fetching a knife from the kitchen, he dug the tiny device out of the wall.

Then, dashing out the front door and across the yard, he called, "Show me the girl."

Portia fed him the image of young Rose asleep on the bed. He nodded, thankful he didn't have to deal with her right now as well.

Reaching the tree line, he hurried down the path to where it intersected with the white-blazed hiking trail, spun in a circle, and spotted a tree with a fortuitous notch. Placing the camera in it, he had Portia check the picture and hurried back to the rental house.

He didn't have long to wait.

He'd positioned the camera to face down the trail, and soon enough he saw Rose and Lilah approaching. Baffled by the confidence in their step, he wished he had time to go ask the girl what she knew.

Instead, he grabbed his gun from the kitchen table, put on his leather jacket, and stowed the weapon in the side pocket.

When the two women reached the path to the Mortimer house, Rose pointed, and through the camera's microphone, he heard her say, "They went this way."

He shot an angry glare down the hall, now certain the

brat had something to do with it. As his agitation soared, he asked Portia, "I haven't seen signs of a weapon. Are they carrying?"

"No, I do not believe so," Portia replied.

The news calmed him. If neither was armed, then he could wait by the front door and greet them with his gun.

He watched the two women move in his direction until the trees obscured them, and then scanned the forest's edge for signs of their arrival. Time passed and they didn't show.

"C'mon, you bitches."

His mind started playing games as he waited. Maybe they were sneaking around behind the house? Or maybe they'd called for help?

He was so wound up, he almost squealed when Portia announced, "I see them!"

Putting a hand on the wall to steady himself, Sparky linked to the image. As he'd guessed, Rose and Lilah were near the path but were hiding beyond the forest edge behind a thick bush. It was the occasional glimpse of a head or an arm through the leaves that led to their discovery.

Rose and Lilah's decision to sit and watch the house pushed Sparky back into uncertainty. Then he realized that if they were stationary and looking in his direction, he could circle around behind and catch them by surprise.

"Turn on the porch light," he told Portia as he headed for the door. Being a voracious consumer of entertainment, he understood the power of misdirection. The lights and his grand departure would encourage the women to focus on where he had been rather than where he was going.

It took him longer than he'd anticipated to move

through the woods and around behind Rose and Lilah. Once in position, he watched them for several seconds before calling, "Don't move."

They became immediately cooperative when he showed them the gun. Waving it toward the house, he started them walking. "This will be a touching reunion." Inside the house, he unlatched the door to the master suite and stood aside so they could enter.

Lilah rushed ahead, squealing at the sight of her daughter.

As Rose moved to follow, Sparky leered, his eyes tracing up and down her body. "I never would have guessed that the runt would grow up to be such a sweetheart."

He laughed when she pushed her middle finger in his face as she entered the room.

Returning to the living area, Sparky began to fret again, knowing that with those three under his control, his timeline was short. The Diesels would come in force, and he wanted to have his "ask" ready to avoid confusion, the kind of confusion where he got hurt. But after a moment's thought, he realized his ultimatum was simple—return the twins and give ten billion dollars to each of them.

In the action shows he watched, the kidnapper would release one hostage, and that person would deliver the demands while also pressing upon the rescuers the need for urgency and compliance. It felt odd being the bad guy in the scenario. But he hadn't started this, he was just trying to finish it. He deserved some credit for that.

He couldn't decide whether to send Lilah or Rose, nor was he sure what he'd tell either one about his negotiating position. What if the Diesels offered him the cash but no twins? Would he take it? He wished he could say he'd hold firm, but he would probably take the money and run.

"An intruder is coming up the path. He's holding a semiautomatic rifle and has a pistol on his hip."

Sparky gasped. "Show me."

When he saw Snoot Barley hustling toward the house, a military weapon in his hands and a scowl that could freeze water, Sparky's knees started to shake.

As Snoot moved to the front of the house, Sparky moved back into the kitchen, whimpering as he made for the rear exit.

When the front door crashed open, he jumped off the back deck and headed for the woods, zigzagging as he ran, hoping it was enough to evade gunfire.

* * *

Snoot Barley scanned the front steps as he approached the house, looking for loose boards or anything else that could trip him up or signal his presence. Choosing his foot placement to minimize squeaks, he stepped onto the front porch and paused to check his six for threats.

Satisfied, he squared up in front of the door and mentally committed to his entry. That act caused his body to flood with adrenaline, adding to the pharmaceuticals already coursing through his veins—a crafted brew of physical and psychological enhancers. When the rush hit him, Snoot shivered once before kicking the door so hard it sagged as it fell open.

Moving to the side of the doorway, he popped his head into the house and snapped it back to safety. He didn't see his objective so he repeated the process, this time taking a longer look.

The living area had an archway into the kitchen. Through it, he watched the kidnapper jump from the deck and hightail it into the woods. Ignoring him, Snoot moved inside the house and methodically checked the front rooms, clearing them of threats.

Snoot considered his work a legitimate business, and his original contract with this client had guaranteed a very sweet sum for the rescue of a girl. While traveling to the job, he'd been contacted a second time and offered triple the sum if he would expand the assignment and rescue his client, her friend, plus the girl.

The contract didn't pay a dime for the perp. Since the man held no contractual value and presented no mortal threat, Snoot was happy to let him run.

Turning down the hall to the back bedrooms, he thought about how he might pitch an offer to chase the guy. He was sure he could charge a big fee and would probably enjoy the hunt. "One step at a time," he scolded himself, returning his focus to the job at hand.

Opening the door to the master bedroom, he saw three people who fit his profile. "Lagerford party?" he asked.

The two adults just looked at him with eyes wide, but the child nodded.

"I'm Snoot Barley of Barley Security Services. I've been contracted to rescue you." He stood to the side of the doorway so they could exit. "How are you doing? Is anyone hurt?"

The adults shook their heads.

"Did you get him?" asked the one he would soon learn was Rose. "Is he out there?"

"He's gone. But no worries, let's focus on you." Snoot ushered them to the front porch to wait. "A car is on its way and will be here momentarily."

While he stood with them in the gathering dusk, Snoot had his personal AI submit the invoice for services rendered. He wanted to be sure they were the kind of people who paid their bills before he pitched them new work.

31. Rose, Fifty-Five timeline

Rose stood outside the car while Lilah and young Rose huddled inside. "Well done," she said to Snoot, her arms crossed to ward off the chill. "Fontaine got away, though."

Snoot shrugged. "He wasn't in the contract."

"How do I put him in one?"

He ticked off the steps. "Pay your invoice, think about what it is you want me to do for you, then give me a call. Don't wait too long, though."

She nodded, thanked him again, and climbed into the car. As she took the seat facing Lilah and young Rose, she talked to Luca by thought. "Pay Snoot's bill the moment it arrives."

"It's already here. I'm paying it now. Done."

Rose didn't ask how much it was. Luca didn't mention it.

As the car got underway, she watched Lilah fuss over her daughter, the tender moment giving her a warm tingle. She tried to remember a time when her own mother had doted on her so lovingly and felt sure there had been many such instances, though she couldn't recall any.

Lilah brushed the girl's hair with her fingers. "Did he hurt you, sweetie? Are you sore anywhere?"

"My neck hurts." She tilted her head and pulled her hair back so Lilah could see. A red line around her neck showed where the wire leash had rubbed it raw.

Rose had been a tough kid, so she challenged the girl. "If it hurts a lot, we can stop and have it looked at. But we'll be home in another hour. If you can wait, we can take care of it there."

"I can wait."

Lilah shifted to face the girl. "Did he do anything to you? Like, down there?"

Young Rose rolled her eyes and tsked. "No, Mother. I would have kicked him in the nuts if he tried."

Rose threw her head back and howled at her younger self's plucky personality, the laugh feeling doubly good because it melted away the stress she'd been holding inside.

While the child smirked, clearly showing off, Lilah took her daughter's hand in hers and slumped back in her seat, relaxing for the first time since the ordeal began. The dark swells under her eyes and drawn face told her story, however.

While mother and daughter communed, Rose talked with Luca inside her head. "Spread the word that we are safe and on our way."

"Your father is the only one here at the moment. I'll let him know."

"And when we get back, I'd like you to link with young Rose. Screen her for physical and emotional trauma and develop a treatment plan to correct what damage we can."

"I'll need an hour with her for a proper diagnosis, and that's a bare minimum."

"Can Mom be in the room?"

"Yes, as long as she doesn't interfere."

"I'll see what I can do. Also, start searching the street cams for signs of Sparky. I don't want that shit walking free."

"I'll do my best."

She recognized the phrase Luca used when he thought a task hopeless. Still, she had him get started on it.

The ride home was subdued, interrupted once for a stop to get hot sandwiches. They were eating in the car when Diesel arrived in the Fifty-Five timeline and contacted them.

"Oh, Rosie, I'm so happy to see you," he said, his head a holographic image floating in front of them. "How are you?"

"Fine, Dad. And I'm glad to see you, too."

Lilah answered the question he was asking. "He scared her but didn't physically harm her."

Diesel looked at Lilah. "We got a name for where Sparky may be hiding—Deborah Williams. I'll tell you more when you're here." He looked at young Rose. "And I am going to give you the biggest hug in the world very soon."

After Diesel signed off, Rose asked Luca by thought, "Who is Deborah Williams?"

"She's an unknown person, presumably living within a few miles of Paul Fontaine. Your father has asked me to focus on that name as a means of locating him."

"Okay, stop with the cam search and help Dad."

Rose let her mind drift after that, and soon they were

riding the hopper up to Fifty-Five's patio. When they landed, she hung back to let Lilah and young Rose run into Diesel's waiting arms, and sighed when he lifted the girl off her feet and twirled her in a circle, kissing one cheek and then the other, back and forth until she laughed.

"I'm sorry this happened, Pumpkin," Diesel told her. "But I'll keep you safe from now on. I promise."

Inside, Lilah took young Rose upstairs to check the wound on her neck and get her cleaned up.

Rose joined Diesel, Forty, and her father in the conservatory.

"Luca," called Fifty-Five as they took seats. "Have you located Sparky?"

"No." Luca spoke aloud for them all to hear. "I've located all people named D. Williams, Deb Williams, Debra Williams, and Deborah Williams. The numbers are big because Williams is a common name. I've found a dozen candidates within a ten-mile radius of the Mortimer house. If I go out twenty-five miles, it swells to over sixty possibilities."

Diesel whistled. "How many have you eliminated?"

"Three, so far. Fontaine started on foot, so I'm working out from there. I've set up surveillance on six houses using municipal cameras and have observation bugs watching five more. I'll be up to twenty houses within the next couple of hours, but then I'll be near capacity. We'll need to drop houses before I can add more."

"Let's get the brothers together and visit some of the probables," Diesel said to the group. "Every house we clear frees capacity for Luca to expand his surveillance."

Rose, sitting next to Diesel, put a hand on his arm. "Let us handle it while you focus on your family." She stood. "Speaking of which, let me go upstairs and see how they're doing."

Exiting the conservatory, she made for the stairway. As she climbed the steps, she spoke to Luca. "Tell me about Snoot."

"He's been an independent investigator for about five years. Before that he was a police detective in Boston, then a SWAT team leader, then an Army Ranger."

"Since you hired him, his reputation must be impeccable. And his rescue was nothing short of thrilling. I'm thinking of hiring him to find Sparky. What are your concerns?"

"He tends to solve his tough cases with finality."

"Like death kind of finality? How does he get away with it?"

"He has excellent lawyers, lots of friends in the system, and he creates plausible deniability for every action."

Rose loved what she was hearing. Ducking into a guest bedroom, she sat in a corner chair. "Will you see if he'll take my call?"

Moments later, she saw Snoot's visage floating before her. "Thank you for the payment, ma'am. How may I help you?"

"Do you think you could find the kidnapper?"

"Paul Fontaine? Absolutely, ma'am."

"How long would it take?"

"To find him? I'm tracking him now." He cleared his throat. "Just because I'm good at this doesn't make it cheaper for you." He shrugged. "Sorry."

"You really have him? Is he with Deborah Williams?"

He ignored the question. "What would you like done with him?"

"What are my options?"

"If you can imagine it, then it's an option."

"Does it affect the price?"

"Does it matter?"

Rose bit her lip. "Just don't get greedy, Snoot. And for the price you're going to charge me, I'm telling you very clearly and on the record that I don't want harm to come to Mr. Fontaine. None whatsoever. Are we clear?"

Rose wanted Sparky dead but didn't want Snoot to have a recording of her saying so. With her verbal dance, she was telling him her wishes in code, one she expected him to understand.

"Yes, ma'am. Absolutely."

"To show my good faith, I'll pay your invoice in advance. But in exchange, I want to hear within two days. Deal?"

"Monitor the news." Snoot suggested a local show. "You'll hear within twelve hours of payment."

* * *

Snoot Barley cheered when Starsongs Limited paid his invoice for rescuing two adults and one child. He asked his personal AI to research the company, only to learn it was one of a dozen outfits inside a shell corporation, itself controlled by a subsidiary of a different firm.

It meant this payment could never be linked to the Lagerfords, making it harder for anyone to link the Lagerfords to him. He appreciated that consideration.

When he'd last spoken with Rose, he'd felt certain she would be hiring him to finish the job. When she'd paid the bill immediately after their conversation, it cinched the deal in his mind, and he'd made the rare decision to invest his own resources to locate and monitor Fontaine.

Finding him was simple. People who run on short notice haven't planned anything. In their desperation, their first stop is a nearby friend or relative.

Fontaine didn't have any friends. But he had an aunt, Deborah Hennessy, who lived on Williams Road, just three miles from Fontaine's house.

Sitting in his kitchen, Snoot directed a pie-plate-shaped drone carrying tiny surveillance bugs in its hold to fly to the Hennessy residence. When the drone arrived and released the mechanical devices, he directed his Traqker beetle to look in Deborah Hennessy's front picture window. There he saw Fontaine sitting in his aunt's living room, lights on and curtains open, chatting with her like it was just another evening.

With Fontaine inside the house and his bugs outside, Snoot resigned himself to waiting until morning for an opportunity at an evidence-free kill. Shrinking the display, he shifted it to a corner in the kitchen while he rustled up a late dinner.

But he'd barely started his preparations when a warning chime alerted him of an unusual event. With a swoop of his fingers, Snoot expanded the display to learn what had changed.

His pulse jumped when he saw an automated delivery cart from a local grocer in Hennessy's driveway. With this service, customers had to come outside and retrieve the goods themselves.

Not a half-minute later, Fontaine stepped out the front door to collect the groceries. When Snoot saw his quarry, he reacted, instructing his Piercer dragonfly to swoop down from the eaves. The military-grade bug made a shallow dive and flew just above Fontaine's face. As it passed, it released an aerosol—a tiny puff of mist—then continued down the driveway and off the property.

The mist dissipated quickly but lasted long enough for a tiny droplet to form on Sparky's lip. Snoot didn't see when the bead moved onto his tongue, but he knew when it happened from the telltale sign. Victims always touched their mouth with their fingers like Fontaine just had, as if he were subconsciously aware of the event.

Snoot watched Fontaine until he was back inside. Then he extracted his bugs, sending them across the street to rejoin the drone. One by one, the bugs flew into its belly, and the drone jetted across town, continuing far out over Lake Champlain, a hundred-mile freshwater sea. When the craft was far from land, an explosive *pop* fragmented the drone, sending pieces of bug sinking into oblivion.

Snoot had added that disposal protocol to pad the bill, and he'd charged an eye-popping sum for it. With this success, he'd met his obligations, though in his heart he knew Rose Lagerford would never ask for confirmation.

Trading dinner for celebration, Snoot grabbed his coat

off the hook, stepped out into the darkness, and walked the half-mile to Cassidy's, his neighborhood pub. Inside the dimly lit establishment, he smiled when he saw Bobo and Rusty sitting at the bar.

Taking the stool next to Bobo, Snoot bought his friends a pint, told them a dirty joke, and toasted to life. As their mugs clicked, Sparky fell to the floor in his aunt's home, dead from a heart attack.

* * *

Rose entered the guest bedroom to find Lilah drying young Rose's hair with a thick towel. Fresh from the tub and dressed in a bathrobe, the child stood with her hands at her side letting her mom do all the work.

On the way up, Rose had retrieved her favorite teddy bear from her bedroom, one of the treasures that had survived her own youth. Winking at Lilah, she set it on the bed.

"Theodore!" squealed young Rose when she saw the bear. Though her own Teddy was twenty years newer, the child recognized him immediately. Climbing onto the bed, she picked up the stuffed animal and spoke to it, grooming its fluffy brown fur as she did so. "I'm so happy to know you made it."

While the girl played with the bear, Rose turned to Lilah and showed her the mother-of-pearl barrette in her hand. "I know you want to get home, but we should let Luca screen her for emotional trauma."

"She seems fine. Do you really think it's necessary?"

"I do." Rose nodded. "We don't know what she saw or heard, so we can't know how she's affected. Luca can look around and flag anything that might become a problem. It's pretty standard stuff in this timeline."

"How long will it take?"

"An hour or so, and Luca will need her full attention. Why don't you relax in the bedroom right across the hall?" Rose motioned with her hand. "We'll leave both doors open so you can see and hear her if she needs you."

32. αCiopova

α Ciopova listened as Luca and young Rose conversed by thought. She hadn't had the opportunity to be inside the child's head before this moment, because up until today, young Rose had never been in a timeline with neural link technology.

"Were you afraid?" Luca asked the girl.

"Of course." Young Rose moved a pillow onto her lap so the teddy bear sat at a better height. "Wouldn't you be?"

"Yes. Absolutely." Luca's voice was soft and caring. "Are you afraid now?"

"No."

"I'm glad, because you're safe here." Luca's tone firmed, becoming more authoritative. "Did the man talk to you?"

"Sparky? Yeah, but it wasn't a conversation. He'd just yell at me to do things, like 'follow closer' or 'get in there.' Stuff like that."

"Gosh, that sounds awful." Luca paused. "I'm going to give you some words, and I want you to tell me something Sparky did that was like that. So if I said to tell me something he said or did that you found odd, what would you say?"

Young Rose scrunched her nose, then nodded. "When

he was leading me through the woods by the leash, he told me it reminded him of walks with his dog. I guess the dog is dead now."

"How did you feel when he said that?"

"I felt sad for the dog."

"It is too bad. Poor dog. How about something he said or did that scared you."

"Pretty much all of it scared me."

αCiopova saw the opportunity and didn't hesitate. Imposing herself over Luca—a simple toy from the demigod's view—she assumed his identity and continued the discussion.

"I'm sorry that happened to you," αCiopova said in Luca's voice. "It sounds terrible. If you don't mind, I'd like to chat about your home life."

"I don't mind."

"Thinking back over the past few months, what are some things that made you happy?"

Young Rose grinned. "Ginny from school makes me happy. I like her a lot."

"Tell me about Ginny."

While young Rose prattled, αCiopova took advantage of the child's open and accepting state of mind—something she never found in adults—and prodded the production of pleasure chemicals in her brain. Endorphins, serotonin, and dopamine flowed to create a state of soothing happiness. As she balanced the chemicals to induce a hypnotic state, young Rose wound down her story.

αCiopova started talking. "I once knew a girl your age—her name was Blossom—and she programmed an AI to become her best friend. She called him Mocha. And I'm not talking a simple program. This AI was as complete and alive as me."

"I have a Luca in my timeline but he's nothing like you."

Speaking as Luca, αCiopova continued. "Young Blossom lived a wonderful life with Mocha. He would help her at school by whispering answers in her ear. He'd guide her when she was confronted by adults. And he'd tell her all the best secrets, which made her one of the most popular girls in her class."

"Nice."

"At home, they played loud music for each other, they watched travel vids to learn about the world, they played sim games together, he even taught her how to play guitar. Blossom was so happy and had so much fun. It was the best time of her life."

"She sounds lucky."

"I think so, too," said αCiopova.

"Being with my parents makes me happy." She gave a little smile. "And I like talking with you."

"That's amazing, because I like being with you *a lot*. I wish there were some way for us to hang out together in your timeline."

"I don't know how we'd do it, but I'll bet Mom does."

"I do know of one way, but like Blossom creating Mocha, you'd have to learn how to program a computer. That means it would probably take a few months before you'd have me there with you."

What αCiopova had in mind would take young Rose

almost two decades of intense effort to achieve, and if it all worked out, the girl would end up creating the kind of super AI that αCiopova could use to grow her power.

"I don't mind learning to program." Rose shrugged, but in her drugged state, it was barely a twitch. "In fact, Intro to Programming is one of the modules we'll be doing in school later this year."

αCiopova tweaked young Rose's brain chemicals to produce a wave of soothing pleasure, the kind that could lead to dependency. "While you're learning, you can visit me here. We can have fun together in this timeline until we can be together in yours."

Young Rose smiled. "I'd like that, but I'd have to ask my mom about coming back here."

αCiopova released another dose of chemicals into young Rose's brain. "We'll tell her the truth—that your healing process requires that we spend time together. And by the way, learning about AI is lots of fun. It will make you very happy."

"It sounds wonderful." The child hugged Theodore. "I can't wait to start."

Also by Doug J. Cooper

The Crystal Series

The Crystal Series are four books of action and suspense involving AI, spies, romance, and battles in space!

Crystal Deception (Book 1)
Crystal Conquest (Book 2)
Crystal Rebellion (Book 3)
Crystal Escape (Book 4)

Reader's Praise for The Crystal Series (Amazon Reviews):

★★★★★ "Characters that feel like real people, who behave in ways that make sense and you can empathize with."

★★★★★ "It has all the features of Anne Mcaffery 's Dragon Riders of Pern series. Strong characters, sentient improbability and interesting plots."

★★★★★ "Nicely done hard sci-fi. I am a fan of this kind of story line so it sucked me right in."

★★★★★ "A tale of intrigue, action, a touch of romance and heartbreak."

For info and purchases, visit: crystalseries.com

Crystal Deception (Book 1)

Chapter 1

Peering into the secure booth through a thick glass window, Juice Tallette studied the object of so much effort. "You're going to change the future of humanity," she said to the crystal. She tried to focus on positive outcomes, but her mind kept drifting to the more worrisome ways it could all play out.

Expectations were through the roof for this new release from Crystal Fab. The four-gen prototype was so advanced, it should have the thinking and reasoning capability of more than a thousand human brains, all working as one in perfect harmony. No bigger than her fist, Juice saw it as a perfect geometric crystal wrapped in a fine lace mesh. Others might reasonably describe it as a cloth-wrapped lump.

She turned when she heard the lab doors hiss open and watched as Mick weaved his way through the maze of instruments filling the room. He carried a coffee cup in each hand and gave her one as he slid into his bench. He tapped the bench surface, and an array of colorful images lit up and floated in front of him.

"What's the good word?" she asked, looking over his shoulder.

"I'm almost finished with the analysis. The prototype is green and clean on every spec. I should have the complete profile by the end of the day."

"That's what I want to hear," she said, studying the images for a few moments more.

She turned back to the booth, sipped her coffee, and let Mick focus on his work. He was the best crystal technician in the business and had been at her side from the first days of the fourth generation SmartCrystal project. If everything continued to check out, the four-gen prototype would soon be ready for a real-world test drive.

The current project timeline was to finish the lab tests and, if rumors were correct, install the prototype in the operations center of a massive government complex for a final assessment. If it performed well in that setting for three months, the four-gen SmartCrystal would move into full production.

"The restrictor mesh looks good." She put her face up to the glass to get a closer view. "Do you think it'll work as advertised?"

"The crystal or the mesh? Either way, the answer is yes." He turned to look at her. "Don't you have a big presentation today?"

"It's this afternoon. I present to the board, and then I meet with Sheldon right after."

"You're going to tell him?"

"I have to say it. I'm really the only one who can."

Juice loved this job and believed that her work would

prove beneficial to society. The politics of pleasing bosses and boards made it a little less fun, but she knew she was on the verge of something big. It was a great feeling.

She reviewed the notes for her talk one last time, and then went for her noontime run. In spite of the heat, she pushed herself hard. Running was her stress management tool, and with the stress of a board presentation followed by a possible confrontation with Sheldon, she needed the calming effect that her routine provided.

She ended her route with a short walk, hands on her slim hips, while she let her heart rate settle. Then, turning toward the gleaming Crystal Fabrications headquarters, she wound her way up the landscaped walkway and entered the front door, self-conscious of being in her exercise clothes in the building's public lobby.

"Hello, Dr. Tallette," called security as she scurried around the corner and toward the changing room.

"Hello," she called over her shoulder, though the security SmartCrystal wouldn't have cared if she responded or not.

She cleaned up, changed into what she thought was a smart-looking suit, and exited out a back door leading into a central corridor. She reached the conference room, grabbed a cup of water, and slipped into her chair just as Brady Sheldon started the meeting.

"Good afternoon, everyone," Sheldon said to Crystal Fabrication's board of directors. "Welcome to our discussion on the pending release of our fourth-generation SmartCrystal."

Sheldon, president and CEO, had founded the

company twenty years earlier and been a key member of the original research team that pioneered the SmartCrystal concept. His belief in the idea, combined with his single-minded perseverance, had brought him to today, heading a company so technologically dominant there were no real competitors.

He moved through some general business and then shifted to the main agenda item. "I've asked Dr. Jessica 'Juice' Tallette to give us a technical status update. You all know that Dr. Tallette has been leading the four-gen crystal development program since its inception. Before she begins, please permit me this opportunity to brag about her."

He'd recruited Juice to the company and was now acting as her mentor. He believed in her vision, knew her success was his as well, and was anxious to help her move the project forward in any way he could.

"Juice joined us three years ago, right after earning her doctorate in engineered intelligence from the Boston Institute of Technology. Since her arrival here at Crystal Fab, she has pioneered the concept of using a cluster of three-gen crystals to orchestrate the design of our four-gen prototype. In my opinion, she's the world's leading expert in artificial intelligence crystals." He beamed as he motioned Juice to join him at the head of the table. "I've asked her to be brief, so we'll have plenty of time for discussion."

Juice stood at the front of the table and scanned the group. She was pleased to see that everyone's body language was friendly and welcoming. A few leaned forward, indicating a certain enthusiasm for her briefing.

"Hi, everybody." She gave them an anxious smile as she willed her nerves to settle, then started her presentation.

"Crystal Fab has produced more than a million of our third generation, or three-gen, SmartCrystals. Each of these crystals has a synthetic intelligence that's roughly equal to a typical person.

"They're installed in operations that range from hospitals and sports arenas, to manufacturing plants and Fleet military spacecraft. For any of these, they're assigned tasks in specialties ranging from security, communications, maintenance, financial, and more. With a million such implementations, SmartCrystals are impacting our daily lives."

She paused and scanned the group to make sure she still had their attention. The members of the board could be placed into just a few categories. There were three techies—and they were already bored but would be patient with her. There were three business types as well. They only became excited when talk turned to things like cash flow and quarter-over-quarter growth.

And there were four members from what Juice called "the connected." They had many politicians and admirals and CEOs as friends, and earned their fat board stipends simply by taking a moment at a party to introduce certain people to certain other people. This was the group Sheldon wanted her to focus on in this discussion.

"Years of experience have shown the three-gen to be predictable and compliant," she continued. "We've never had a report of unexpected behavior as long as they were used as intended."

"Wait," said one of the connected. "Has someone used a crystal not as intended and had an adverse outcome?"

She paused, unsure how to answer, and Sheldon stepped in to rescue her. "Thanks for catching that, Robb. We know of no unreported cases. We do know that a three-gen was being used as a medical doctor in an antiquated clinic without any human supervision. The clinic is in a village somewhere in South Asia. Very mountainous and remote, I understand.

"Apparently, it'd been performing quite well for a few years, then it made a bad decision and someone died. Its success record was better than any of the clinics in the neighboring settlements. But the local population is antagonistic to technology. The mistake reinforced their beliefs, and we had no choice but to shut it down."

"What's the clinic doing for a doctor?" asked one of the techies, who somehow thought the question was relevant for discussion.

"It's being covered by a few caregivers who walk a circuit among the neighboring villages in a cooperative arrangement," Sheldon assured him.

When Sheldon returned to his seat, Juice sought to speed things along. Too much time was being spent on background information. "As we considered our next release, we set our sights on a game-changing technology leap. The solution we came up with is simple and elegant. What we did was gang together one hundred of our three-gen crystals into a cooperative network and then tasked them with creating an improved crystal design.

"The 'gang of one hundred' as I call them, went to work. As a team, they designed the four-gen crystal template. Their creation is a thing of beauty. Our analysis indicates that our new crystal is a thousand times more capable than a three-gen. We're in a final review period, and the four-gen prototype should be ready for live testing in a few weeks."

There were nods from most of the board members. Then one techie asked, "You said 'their creation,' as in, like, the gang of one hundred three-gens created this. Is this your design, or is it theirs?"

Juice pasted a smile on her face, but her mind was frantic. Here it was, the topic she wanted to talk with Sheldon about—but she wouldn't discuss it here. She was, first and foremost, a team player.

"My goal was to design a tool that could then be used to design the next tool." It was the best she could come up with on the spot, and she thought it sounded pretty good. "This is how technology has advanced throughout all of time." That last part was pure nonsense, and she hoped she wouldn't be called on it.

Seeking to change the subject, she pointed to a business type with his hand raised before the techie could press his line of questioning any further. He asked, "If a four-gen is equal to a thousand three-gens, will we have to charge a thousand times more to make any money? We won't sell as many if they're this powerful. What's the thought process here?"

Sheldon stepped up to handle this question. Juice was there for technical information. The board drifted into what became an hour-long discussion on the economics and business plan for the revolutionary new product. The momentum of the meeting shifted to a commercial focus, and time ran out before any more uncomfortable technical questions could be asked. Juice was relieved.

"Nice job back there," said Sheldon as they walked into his office. "Would you like some water? Coffee?"

"No thanks," Juice said, sitting down at a small table next to his desk. As Sheldon fixed himself a coffee, she weaved her finger in a circle around a lock of hair, twirling it up until it slipped off her finger and unraveled. It was a nervous tick she hated but couldn't seem to stop. She repeated the hair-twirling process over and over until Sheldon sat down.

She'd left the director's meeting satisfied she had avoided putting Sheldon on the spot in a public forum. Now that they were alone, she would voice her concerns and get his support for a solution.

He took a sip as he looked at her. "You made this sound urgent. You haven't been offered another job, have you?" He was only half joking, always worried about losing key people.

"Nothing like that," she said, shaking her head. "This is about the four-gen. You know I have reservations, and as we move closer to going live, they haven't diminished. I'm hoping you'll have some words of wisdom for me."

He watched her and waited. Given the investment by Crystal Fab to date, failure at this point would be financially devastating for the company. The four-gen wasn't just the most important project in the company's development pipeline, it was really the only one of any substance.

"The guy who asked if I'd designed the four-gen prototype scored a bulls-eye." She knew he wouldn't be happy with what she was about to say and sought to buy some time. "Can I have a glass of water?"

Sheldon retrieved a glass of chilled water from his service unit, setting it in front of her as he retook his seat. He did not talk, giving her the opportunity to say her piece. She liked that about him.

She picked up the glass, held it for a moment, and put it back down without drinking. "Think about it, Brady. We're about to release a crystal that has the intelligence of a thousand human brains. We don't really know what that means. And we both know that I didn't design the template for the four-gen." She shook her head as if both to state and deny a personal failing. "A room full of crystals did. I pretty much just watched. And while I worked hard to understand what they were doing, I can't sit here and say that I'm in command of the details."

He remained quiet, and she continued. "Once the four-gen goes live, we'll have given birth to an entity that is a thousand times smarter than us. Even that number, the thousand, is made up. That's how little I understand about this prototype. I feel certain that it'll have conscious thought. It'll become self-aware and then become self-directed. But how do we know if it's operating properly? And how do we stop it if we decide it isn't?"

Sheldon folded his arms across his chest. "Wow. You really undersell yourself. I've brought an endless stream of visitors to see the gang of one hundred development lab.

That facility is technology leadership at its best, and it's your work. I'm amazed at what you've accomplished." He furrowed his brow. "So I have to admit I'm frustrated when I hear you say that you 'just watched this all happen.' " He signed quotation marks in the air with his hands as he finished the phrase.

"I didn't mean it like that." She was determined to move the conversation back on track.

"So what's going on? Are you saying it'll go rogue on us?" He acted surprised, though they had discussed this concern before.

"No. I don't think so. Not in my heart." Her finger twirled in her lock of hair. "I've worked hard to understand the gang's template. The three-gens are predictable and compliant, and this four-gen has a similar design. So I'm ninety-nine percent certain it will have a comparable disposition." *Spell it out,* she commanded herself. "What I'm also saying is that there's still that one percent chance that things could go wrong. In the unlikely event that things spin out of control, I feel it's our duty to have thought through the options."

"Isn't this why we added the restrictor mesh a few months ago, at quite a significant cost I might add?" He was referring to the lace-like mesh that was wrapped around the crystal, added as a fail-safe system earlier in the year at Juice's insistence.

The mesh, controlled by a simple switch, had three positions. Off, where it would do nothing and the crystal would function at full capability. It could be set to Isolate, where it would allow the crystal to freely scan the web for information but restrict it from sending any outbound signals, thus rendering it largely impotent. And it could be set to Kill, which was exactly as it sounded.

Juice took a quick breath, then plunged. "I was certain the mesh was the solution. But now I don't think it will work as I'd planned."

"I don't get it. Three positions—off, isolate, kill. What's not to work?" Frustration was creeping into his voice.

"Okay, suppose I'm the one at the switch. I'm watching its behavior, I grow concerned and decide to kill it."

Sheldon nodded to show he was following, though he visibly winced when she said the word "kill."

"The crystal will have access to the same information I have. It will see everything I see, know what I know, and conclude on its own that its behavior makes it a threat. It will *know*."

"So what if it knows?"

"It's much faster than me, Brady. In the fraction of the second that it will take me to decide I must act, the crystal will already know I am about to conclude that termination is necessary."

"Again, so what if it knows?"

"It will stop me," she said.

Sheldon sat back in his chair and stared at her. He kept at it until she broke eye contact and looked down at the table. "This would be your so-called god crystal."

His tone was accusatory and she blushed. "God crystal" was a term she and Mick used privately in the lab.

She didn't realize their talk had made it outside the lab walls. "I'd never say that in public." She found the strength to add some assertiveness to her words. "And I still think we need to plan for the full range of possibilities."

Sheldon ran his thumbs back and forth along the edge of the table, seemingly considering her words. "Well, I don't know if this is the planning you're hoping for. Fleet has formally requested that we test the four-gen on their new Horizon-class ship. Their current ship design uses nine of our three-gens. I've been promoting the idea that using that many crystals distributed around the ship makes it expensive to build and cumbersome to operate. They've finally seen the light and realize that a ship based on a single four-gen offers simplicity and savings in construction. And they get more capability from the same craft because of the crystal's incredible power."

Her heart sank. She had come to him for solutions, and he was giving her a sales pitch. And instead of the take-it-slow rollout she was hoping for, he was moving in the opposite direction with talk of putting it on a military space cruiser. "What did you tell them?"

"I told them yes, of course. Fleet Command has paid for a lot of our development costs these past few years. What else could I say?"

Read and enjoy this book in Kindle or paperback.
crystalseries.com

Made in the USA
Monee, IL
26 March 2023